Jobs are temporary. Murder is permanent...

Meet Bonnie Indermill—a single, thirtysomething
Manhattanite with a wide range of skills—and
a surprising knack for solving crimes...

Praise for Carole Berry's Bonnie Indermill Mysteries...

"A SPUNKY YET VULNERABLE HEROINE...
witty, upbeat."

—*Publishers Weekly*

"BERRY HAS MANAGED to make the mundane world
of office work a marvelously inventive setting for
a mystery series... Brava!"

—*Alfred Hitchcock Mystery Magazine*

"BERRY HAS GIVEN THE WOMAN'S PLACE IN
CRIME A BOOST... [a] funny and human look
at life in the big city."

—Mike Kiley, *Chicago Tribune*

"FAST-MOVING, WRY AND FEISTY."

—*Kirkus Reviews*

"BERRY HAS A GIFT for creating good characters.
deft and humorous touch."

—*Booklist*

THE DEATH OF A DIFFICULT WOMAN

CAROLE BERRY

BERKLEY PRIME CRIME, NEW YORK

THE DEATH OF A DIFFICULT WOMAN

A Berkley Prime Crime Book / published by arrangement with the author

PRINTING HISTORY
Berkley Prime Crime hardcover edition / December 1994
Berkley Prime Crime paperback edition / October 1995

All rights reserved.
Copyright © 1994 by Carole Summerlin Berry.
This book may not be reproduced in whole or in part,
by mimeograph or any other means, without permission.
For information address: The Berkley Publishing Group,
200 Madison Avenue, New York, NY 10016.

ISBN: 0-425-15008-9

Berkley Prime Crime Books are published by
The Berkley Publishing Group,
200 Madison Avenue, New York, NY 10016.
The name BERKLEY PRIME CRIME and the BERKLEY PRIME CRIME
design are trademarks belonging to Berkley Publishing
Corporation.

PRINTED IN THE UNITED STATES OF AMERICA

10 9 8 7 6 5 4 3 2 1

1

I FELL IN LOVE WITH THE FIVE FINKEL-
stein Boys during the elevator ride to my
2:30 interview. Sure, that's a whole lot of
love, but my interview was on a high
floor, the building was old, and the elevator awfully slow. Besides, you should
have seen those Finkelsteins. FIVE FIN-
KELSTEIN BOYS MOVING was stenciled in
white letters across the broad backs of
their green T-shirts. You don't often find
that much visible muscle on an elevator
in the Wall Street area. The Five Finkel-
stein Boys appeared to range in age from callow but ador-
able youth to that fuzzy area that I inhabit. (I won't get too
specific here, but when filling out questionnaires, I check
the box that says 35 to 44.)

It was a couple of days before I narrowed things down
to one Finkelstein—but more about that later. First I must
tell you about this job.

If I hadn't been broke, I wouldn't have gone on the interview. I once promised myself I would never work for
another law firm. No more compulsive, stodgy, irritable
overachievers who expect me to get as excited about
twelve-hour workdays as they do, I had sworn. I'm sure
you've heard the joke names: Dewey, Cheetum, and Howe;
Hump, Dump, Frump, and Slump. Well, here I was, waiting
to be interviewed at Nutley, Eggers, Rivens, and Davis,
known among the temp community by its acronym, NERD.

As I took a seat in the reception area, I experienced not

just my usual preinterview anxiety, but a deep gloom. Here I go again, I was thinking. How many go agains do you get on your career path, anyway?

The condition of the place didn't help. Boxes were stacked almost ceiling-high against every available wall. In some places the carpet had been ripped up, exposing taped-down electrical wires and enough dust to give New York City's huge, ever-complaining population a collective sneezing fit. You see, after fifty years the venerable firm of Nutley et al. was about to move, all six stodgy, irritable floors of it.

My old friend and former coworker, Harriet Peterson, was the one who got me the interview. She had told me that the job required almost no dealings with the attorneys. I believed her. Harriet, after all, was secretary to E. Bertram Davis himself, a name partner, head of the Litigation Department, and by all reports a raving maniac. The job I was applying for was one of those assistant-to-the-coordinator things, in this case assistant to the coordinator of Relocation Operations. The coordinator, I was told, reported to the manager of Firm Support Services, who reported to a director of something blurry, who reported to an aging partner most of the employees thought was long dead.

I agreed to the interview because Harriet had convinced me that, if I was hired, this thick layer of bureaucratic fat would cushion me from the legal staff. I also agreed to it because I was broke. Working as an office temp has its advantages, but a big paycheck isn't one of them. To put it simply, if I didn't make some decent money, fast, I was going to have to move in with my parents, back into the pink bedroom of my youth.

"Ms. Blake can see you now." A tall, lank-haired young woman had stepped from around a stack of boxes. She pointed in the direction she had come from, then turned back that way herself. By the time I caught up with her, she was behind a desk, her face buried in a magazine. She made no attempt to point out Ms. Blake's office, much less introduce me to the woman who might be able to save my financial hide. I read the nameplates on a couple of doors until I found the right room.

The door stood half-open. I could see Ms. Blake's desk, but no Ms. Blake. When I tapped on the door, there was resistance on its other side.

"Ms. Blake?"

"Come in," a muffled voice responded.

She was behind the door facing into the corner. She stayed that way as I entered the office. It was an odd start for an interview, but then, I've had odder. When I sat down in one of the chairs that faced the desk, she remained immobile.

From what I could see, Ms. Blake was a woman of about my height—five-feet-four—and weight, and her hair, though shorter than mine, was reddish blond like mine. I mention this superficial resemblance because it was responsible for the first of the many nasty tongue-lashings I later received.

Through no choice of my own, I've become quite the interview expert. I was getting a bad feeling about this one.

"I believe Harriet Peterson gave you my résumé," I said to Ms. Blake's back.

She nodded into the corner. The phone on her desk rang a few times. She ignored it. When it stopped I said, "I'm Bonnie Indermill."

That elicited a soft grunt from the corner. Ms. Blake and I were off to a great start. The phone rang again. Again she ignored it. I stared absently at the top of her desk: papers, pens, a World's Best Aunt mug, a photo of Ms. Blake with an attractive man. I was about to say something about coming back later when she sniffed. Turning, I saw that her shoulders were shaking. Within seconds she was sobbing.

For a moment I wasn't sure how to react. It's not often I'm in a power position with interviewers. But crying is something I understand. If you ask me, where most jobs are concerned tears make more sense than anything else. I pulled a tissue from my handbag and pushed it into my interviewer's hand. She blew her nose, then kicked the door shut.

"I don't want them to see me like this," she wept.

Them? Oh, God! The only thing that kept me from bolting from the place was sympathy for my interviewer.

When she had turned the lock on her door and tested it, Ms. Blake moved away from the corner and sat behind her desk. She drew in a few deep, shuddering breaths. Taking a tissue from her top drawer, she blew her nose again, then removed her glasses and wiped her eyes. After she had finished with all that, Ms. Blake proceeded to tell me what a terrific place Nutley et al. was and what a great temp job I was applying for.

Ms. Blake—Lorraine, she told me to call her—was not much of a liar. She flinched as if she'd been slapped every time her phone rang. I thought she was going to dive under her desk when her door rattled and a woman snapped: "Where the hell is she?" Lorraine's eyes, which were rimmed by damp brown mascara smudges, grew shiny as a man bellowed from the area of the secretary's desk: "Tell that Blake woman to see me immediately!" When he shouted an obscenity about a cabinetmaker—"f——ing a——," to be precise—Lorraine's tears poured once more.

After she had again taken a few minutes to compose herself, Lorraine placed her glasses back on her nose and said, "I expect that we'll need extra help here for three or four weeks, starting immediately. It will be a seven-day-a-week job. Harriet Peterson tells me you pick up things very quickly."

I knew what she meant, but I had this nutty urge to giggle. Already, I'd almost picked up a couple of the Finkelstein Boys on the elevator.

I made a noncommittal sound. When you're a temp, and the country's in a recession, you better pick things up quickly if you want to keep eating.

She glanced at my résumé. Very briefly. I don't claim that my résumé—a masterpiece of fudged dates—deserves much serious attention, but from the amount of time Lorraine gave the thing it might as well have been my laundry list. Once she verified that I had worked at other law firms, and that I was more or less sane, she offered me the job.

I'm not sure the former would have mattered to her. The latter either, for that matter.

I'm no genius, but I'm not a complete fool. This was the temp spot straight from hell. Broke as I was, I was still ready to turn it down. The tip of my tongue was poised at the back of my upper teeth, ready to form an unequivocal no.

"The hourly rate we're offering is . . ."

The figure Lorraine gave me was, by my standards, astronomical.

". . . and there will be a lot of overtime," she added.

"At time and a half?" I asked, more breathlessly than I intended.

She nodded so eagerly that her glasses slipped down her nose. "It won't be bad at all," she assured me. "We have very good professional movers. The Five Finkelstein Boys. You'll be working closely with their foreman." She pushed her glasses back into place, and then said, "We pay double time on Sundays."

That did it! I had turned into a pulsating pile of greed, topped with a little pinch of lust.

"I'll take it."

I don't know which of us was more excited. I was already multiplying hours times rates in my head. As for Lorraine Blake, I'm surprised the nasty people who lurked beyond her locked door didn't hear her relieved sigh.

"You can start right away?"

"Of course. I can be in early if you want."

Her red-rimmed eyes flickered desperately. "By right away, I meant right away, right now. If it's all right with you, we'll spend a couple hours together this afternoon. Then, on your way home—you live uptown, don't you?"

I nodded.

"Maybe you can stop and take a look at the new offices. You're going to have to know your way around there. I'll give you a set of blueprints. Take a cab there. Take one home, too. The firm has accounts with a couple private cab companies."

This was wonderful! She was doing everything but

throwing cash at me. Maybe I *had* stepped into temp job hell, but I was in money heaven.

The moment I gave a slightly giddy, "Okay," Lorraine extended her hand over the desk. I thought she wanted to shake on it, but she shoved a pen at me.

"I've got a lot to show you." She got out of her chair and headed toward the door. "You'll want to take notes. We start moving attorneys and staff Thursday afternoon. The library and file room are already being moved." As she unlocked her door she seemed to notice, for the first time, my houndstooth-checked suit and black patent shoes. "By the way," she said as she glanced at her watch, "you don't have to dress for success around here for the next couple weeks. Jeans are fine."

Lorraine herself was wearing a navy blue suit and a white silk blouse. Her earrings were tasteful pearls; her shoes, dress-for-success navy pumps. At the time I was so worked up about my hourly rate that I didn't give her outfit a thought.

My interview, such as it was, ended before 3 P.M. I spent the next hour and forty-five minutes with Lorraine, cramming. That's the best word for it. I felt like a hooky-playing kid with a semester's worth of material to absorb immediately.

As I mentioned, Nutley now occupied six cramped, old-fashioned floors in the Wall Street area. Actually, I sort of liked the little I saw of those offices during the quick tour Lorraine gave me before we got down to business. The paneling in the reception areas was a rich, dark wood. There were windows that could be raised and lowered, and the ladies' room had marble sinks. But time marches on, and so do clients, I suppose, if a firm doesn't keep up with technology. I could see that the firm had space problems. Two associates were jammed into offices that should have held one. The partners, of course, had managed to hang on to their own offices, but partners' secretaries suffered right along with everyone else. Many of the secretaries used out-moded electronic typewriters, not because the firm couldn't afford computers but because their desks had no room for them. Copiers were pushed into closets, and fax machines sat atop file cabinets.

Lorraine explained that the wiring in this old building was a problem, too. In between peeks at her watch, she told me that the computer networks and electronic phone systems needed to bring a dinosaur like Nutley—*dinosaur* is my word, not Lorraine's—into the 1990s required extensive rewiring that the old building couldn't handle.

The firm had leased nine high, spacious floors, plus some basement space, on Park Avenue. Not just on Park Avenue, but to quote my new boss, "Into a brand-new, award-winning building with a street-level atrium . . . written up in *Architectural Digest* . . . just one block north of the Waldorf-Astoria. . . ."

"And two blocks from Saks," the young secretary, who had been introduced as Hillary, added.

Lorraine ignored that. Now that I'd taken the job, she was all business. No time for tears or any other distractions. She told Hillary to take her calls, ushered me back into her office, locked the door again, and handed me a copy of *Architectural Digest*. "Take a look at this when you have some free time." She immediately started pulling files from a cabinet.

I am a quick learner, but I was overwhelmed by the amount of information my new boss tried to cram into me in less than two hours. I took page after page of notes before giving up on it. As the afternoon flew by, Lorraine talked faster and faster. It wasn't my imagination. By the time we had gone through half a dozen file folders, she was babbling as fast as an auctioneer. Whenever I asked her to repeat something, she did it, but as she spoke she thumped her fingertips impatiently on her desktop, as if that might help hammer the information into my thick head. It didn't.

Think for a moment about moving. Most of us have done it. Of all the disgusting things you can do in the name of homemaking, I suspect that getting yourself into a new home is the worst. You begin by packing cartons you've lugged from the liquor store. If you're organized, you label

them. If you're like me, you don't. Once packed, you live
on Chinese takeout. On moving day it rains. Your movers—two thugs with a truck—show up late. They're bel-
ligerent when you mention it. They drop a carton. Not the
carton of linens. The carton of dishes. They say they'll
make good on it. Fat chance. Your sofa won't fit through
the doorway. How did it ever get through in the first place?
It's maneuvered through finally, but one of the arms is now
loose. You're left with an apartment to clean if you want
your security deposit back.

Now we go to the other end. Your new apartment—your
step up in the world—has shrunken since you rented it.
The neighborhood looks even seedier than the one you've
left. Are there only three closets? Could you have counted
wrong? The electricity hasn't been turned on. The bathtub
has brown stuff in it. Please let it be mud. Something smells
funny in the kitchen. You look in the refrigerator and curse.
The last tenant clearly wasn't out to earn brownie points
from the landlord.

You start to clean while you wait for the person from
the phone company, and for your movers. They're both
late. You call your movers from a booth on the street. Their
phone has been disconnected. You're so relieved when they
arrive—after the sun has set—that you apologize when
they complain about moving you in by candlelight. The
sofa won't fit through the doorway, even with the arm
loose. It's hauled through a window. In the process, three
feet of shrubbery and a window frame are destroyed. Your
new landlord says he'll bill you. Your movers say they'll
make good on it. Again, fat chance!

Now, multiply that scenario by eight hundred, the number of employees and partners at Nutley.

The longer Lorraine talked, the more finger tapping she
did, the more lost I became. I would have been happy to
stay late with her that afternoon, especially at time-and-a-
half, but at exactly 4:50 she took a final look at her watch.

"I have to be running." She grabbed her handbag from
under her desk. "You've got the blueprints," she said as
she pulled a comb through her hair. "Hillary will type up

a building pass for you. Take a look around the new space. Get the lay of the land.'' She ushered me out of her office. ''You'll be in early. About eight.'' She called to Hillary over her shoulder, ''Take messages for me. And call the new building and tell Cornelia that Bonnie's on her way.''

Before I could say a word, Lorraine was gone.

I sank into a chair beside an empty desk, put my elbow on the notes I'd taken, and rested my chin in my hand.

''Who's Cornelia?''

''She's in charge of security for Nutley.''

''Ah.'' Extending one of my legs, I rotated my ankle.

Hillary stuck her foot out from under her desk. She was wearing sandals, no nylons. ''I don't know how you can stand wearing heels and panty hose when it's this hot. I'd die if I had to go through that.''

Slipping off my shoes, I wriggled my toes. ''Sometimes you have to almost die to get a job.''

''Not me,'' she said. ''I can hardly type and I got this one.''

Hillary was as laid-back as my boss had been tense. She had an accent. I don't mean a foreign accent, or a Brooklyn or southern accent. I mean a nasal tonal quality that I associate with young women who go to expensive private schools. A honk, I've heard it called, though I can't remember where. Hillary didn't look the private-school part, though. Her shoulder-length brown hair could have used a good trim. She was wearing a white cotton shirt and black pants. Both looked as if they'd been slept in.

''How nice for you,'' I said to her. Somebody's relative, I said to myself.

''I don't think it's so nice. It was my dad's idea. Give me a taste of the real world by making me work for the summer before I start college. He's Davis.'' Reaching into her desk drawer, she pulled out a portable tape player and a set of headphones. ''As in Nutley, Eggers, Rivens, and Davis. Wait until you have to deal with him,'' she added laconically as she inserted a tape in the player. ''He's a real pain in the rear.''

With any luck I wouldn't have to deal with him. That
was Lorraine's job.

The phone in Lorraine's office rang. Hillary watched the
light flashing on her extension. For a second it looked as
if she might spring into action and answer the thing, but
then she shrugged. "I've had it. If it's important they'll call
back tomorrow. Lorraine's not going to fire me."

I didn't know what to make of Hillary, but didn't think
I'd *have* to make much of her, either. I was even more
temporary than she was. I would blunder my way through
the next few weeks, make as much money as I could, and
wave a grateful good-bye to all of them.

It was a few minutes after five. Hillary didn't look as if
she could keep up her frantic pace much longer. "Could I
get that building pass?"

"Huh?"

"To get into the new building. I'm going there now."

Hillary took a pad from a drawer and tossed it to the
desk where I was sitting. It was to be typed, the instructions
said, but I had no typewriter.

"You want to type this for me? Lorraine said—"

"Write it out. It's no big deal."

When I had written the building pass, I jammed my feet
back into my shoes and gathered my notes, the blueprints,
and the pass and put them into my briefcase. Hillary
stretched and yawned. She was slumping deeper into her
chair and getting ready to slip those headphones over her
ears when I said, "Don't forget to call Cornelia and tell
her I'm coming."

"Sure," she said absently.

I took a long look at Hillary. Okay. So she meant nothing
to me. She was nothing more than a tiny part of a job that
soon would be history. She still managed to annoy me. It's
not that I have anything against lazy rich kids. If I was rich,
I'd probably be lazy, too, at least until I got bored with it.
It was the combination of lazy and snotty that got to me.
Hell! Hillary was the secretary. I was the assistant to the
coordinator of Relocation Operations!

"It's rush hour. I'll never get a yellow cab. Would you please call a car service for me?" I added, "Tell them to be downstairs in five minutes," before she had a chance to say, "Huh?" again.

2

THERE'S NOT MUCH GOOD THAT CAN BE said about Manhattan rush-hour traffic, but the ride uptown did give me a chance to read over my notes. Given time to think things over, I felt more confident than I had. I almost managed to convince myself that I could handle this job.

To begin with, much of the furniture in the new building was already there, built-in. As Lorraine explained it, secretaries and associates were getting built-in desks and shelves. Partners, though they either brought or bought most of their own furniture, would have built-in wall units. They could have these units in white lacquer or walnut veneer, but they couldn't *not* have the units. All these built-ins—secretaries', associates', and partners'—were being constructed by the same cabinetmaker: Pagano Woodworking. No problems there, I foolishly told myself.

All associates' and secretaries' chairs came from the same manufacturer. So did the conference room furniture. All partners had the same cream-colored silk shantung wallpaper, like it or not. Secretaries and associates got off-white paint and mottled brown carpeting. No choice. Partners could have either the mottled brown carpeting or an off-white that might as well have sported little signs reading SPILL YOUR COFFEE HERE, but that didn't matter to me. I'd be long gone before anyone started screaming about carpet cleaning.

By the time my cab hit a traffic jam near Grand Central, my confidence level was way up. This move was nothing. A snap!

The moving of offices was to begin Thursday afternoon. The old building's freight elevator had been reserved. There was no problem with elevators in the new building: so far, Nutley was the building's first and only tenant.

As we crawled through traffic the last few blocks up Park Avenue, I turned to my last few pages of notes. I had only skimmed a couple lines when the driver pulled out of traffic.

"This okay, miss?" he asked. "I can't get any closer. Too much going on there."

I looked up. Beyond two huge Finkelstein Boys vans, an unpaved stretch of sidewalk, and four stories of iron scaffolding stood the towering building that was to be Nutley's new home. I'm afraid that the first words out of my mouth when I saw the monster were: "Is it finished?"

My driver snorted. "You're askin' me? Ask me, it looks like a pile of garbage."

Architectural Digest meet John Q. Public.

Three Hundred Ten Park Avenue was a pale, steely pink. I have no idea what the exterior was made of, but it was some shiny material. On that summer afternoon, glowing under the sun's rays, it looked hot as a furnace.

I made my way between the moving vans, past a few more Finkelstein Boys—there were a lot more than five of them—and over a wood plank that was laid where the sidewalk should have been. A push at a revolving door got me nowhere, so I started through a pair of open doors the movers were using. I stepped aside as the youngest of the movers I'd ridden the elevator with earlier that day tried to maneuver an empty dolly from the building. He was a cute kid, with longish auburn hair and freckles. Under his pug nose was the fuzz of a struggling mustache.

The boy was scowling, either at the dolly or at the world in general, but I was happy to see a familiar face anyway.

"Hi," I said.

When he recognized me a smile lit his face. "Guess you

got the job, ma'am. I'm Billy.''

Ma'am!

He shouldn't have looked away from his task, not even for those few seconds it took for him to make me feel like his grandmother. The corner of the dolly he was pushing swung a little wide. Before I had a chance to answer him, it hit the open door's bottom panel. There was a nasty little pop. We both glanced down in time to see a hairline crack worm its way across one of the door's panels.

The kid slapped his palm to his forehead. "Oh, hell!" he groaned. "This is all I need. My old man's going to bust an artery." He looked back at me. For a moment he seemed on the verge of saying something, but then he gave the dolly an angry yank and wrestled it on through the door.

The lobby—*atrium* is what it was called—was gigantic. I hardly recognized it as the one I'd seen in the architect's renderings. The drawings had shown a lively space where stick-figure people sat on benches nestled among large plants. There had been shops and shoppers, fountains, pieces of sculpture. I guess that during the short time I'd known about Nutley's move, I'd formed certain expectations about the building at 310 Park Avenue. The reality of it was rather disappointing.

This lobby was empty of everything but me, an occasional mover, and a pink marble desk, if something that big could be called a desk. It stood a few feet from one of the walls and must have been forty feet long. It was where visitors to the building would stop and get information and, I assume, where I was supposed to display my building pass.

It was warm in the lobby and my feet, tired to begin with, had started feeling a size too big for my shoes. I strolled across the floor, heels ringing a lonely echo on the pink marble tile, and waited. And waited.

Behind the desk was a row of monitors, like very small television sets. Most of them were dark, but a couple showed bright areas with dark shapes moving across them. I'm nearsighted and still hanging tough on the issue of bi-focals, so my glasses are on and off all day. I dug them from my briefcase and put them on my nose. That cleared things up considerably. On one screen I saw men carrying boxes; on another, two men papered a wall.

As I stood there, a deep sound rumbled above the noise of the Park Avenue traffic. Through the open door I saw one of the big moving vans pulling away. It was almost 6 P.M. The movers would be working late moving the file room and library, but I didn't know about the other work crews. One thing I didn't want to do was look around on empty floors for someone to show my building pass to.

Feeling the heat, I slipped off my jacket, folded it, and pushed it into my briefcase. After a minute or so a bell rang from the area of the elevator banks. Two men in jeans and construction boots walked around a corner and headed for the door.

I called to them: "Have you seen the building guard?"

One of them shook his head. The other one said, "He's probably on break. Should be back soon."

Much more of this and my feet would give out. I slipped one foot from its shoe and curled my toes. That felt wonderful, but when it came time to get the shoe back on— well, it was going to take some doing. Giving up, I slipped off the other shoe. A few more minutes passed, a few more workers left, a couple of men entered and headed for the elevators. No guard. Great security this building had. Floor monitors, but nobody to watch them. The screens showed that there was still activity on the two floors. Peering more closely, I saw the floors' numbers indicated in the lower left corner of the screens. The moving men were on the twenty-eighth floor—Nutley's top floor. The men applying wallpaper were a couple of floors down.

I stuffed my feet back into my pumps. It was a real battle now.

Enough of this! Picking up my briefcase, I strode on aching feet toward the elevator bank that served the fifteenth to thirtieth floors.

One elevator, lined with thick quilted fabric and obviously set aside for moving, stood open. I would have gladly ridden up with some of the Finkelstein Boys, but none of them came along. I pushed a button on the wall, and a second later a pinging sound announced a second elevator's arrival. Stepping on, I pressed the button for the twenty-eighth floor. Above the buttons a little green arrow clicked on, pointing up. The doors slid shut. And nothing happened.

My heart thumped. My slight elevator phobia is generally limited to the dim coffinlike elevators in old buildings, but it kicked in then. This elevator may have had a high ceiling and bright lights, but it was in an unoccupied building. I didn't trust Hillary to have made that call to Nutley's security person. If she hadn't, nobody knew I was here. I could be trapped for hours. Days! I'd be dying of thirst at the same time Lorraine was cursing me for not showing up.

Beneath the panel of floor buttons was a second, smaller panel with only three buttons—Open, Close, and Alarm— and a small, built-in speaker. I was reaching for the Open button when suddenly the elevator began rising.

"Thank goodness," I said out loud.

The ride was very fast, nothing like the one in the Wall Street building. In no time at all numbers were flashing by on a indicator above the buttons. "15 . . . 20 . . . 25 . . ." I moved to the center of the elevator. ". . . 26 . . . 27 . . ."

I stepped out as soon as the door opened, then gasped with surprise. There seemed to be a white mist everywhere, almost as if as light snow was falling on a sunny day. It took me a second to realize that the mist was caused by the glare of afternoon sunlight filtering through plaster dust.

Stepping back into the elevator, I looked at the floor indicator. *Twenty-nine*, it read.

The elevator had passed twenty-eight and had stopped on an unleased, unfinished floor!

"Damn."

The little green arrow no longer glowed on the elevator's inside panel. I pushed the button for the twenty-eighth floor again. When nothing happened, I pressed L, hoping that would get me back to the building's lobby. Again, nothing. Growing increasingly nervous, I tried the red Alarm button.

A bell jangled somewhere below. After it stopped, I stood quietly, waiting for a reassuring voice to come through the speaker. A few seconds passed. I tried the alarm again. Again there was that faraway ring. Again, there was no response.

Suddenly there was a different noise. A clanking. It was in the distance, too, but nearer than the ring. It seemed to come from somewhere on the floor where I was stuck.

Nothing to be frightened about, Bonnie. It's an empty floor. Eventually someone's going to answer the alarm. But how long might "eventually" be? What if the second moving van left? What if the guard decided to take a longer-than-usual break? My God! What if the guard had gotten sick? He could have had a heart attack. Or—oh, no!— worse. What if there was a killer loose in the building?

I don't know what got me going in that direction, but once started, every psycho-on-the-loose story I'd ever heard raced through my mind. At that very moment, a crazed murderer could be watching me on one of those lobby monitors. The first taste of blood—the guard's—had only sharpened his appetite. Now he was smacking his lips at the sight of my quaking knees.

No. No. I forced air into my lungs. There was no murderer watching me. That was nuts. But what if the guard never turned on the monitors on unoccupied floors? An old suspense movie flashed through my mind: A husband locks his unwanted wife in their penthouse apartment and leaves her to starve. She tries every possible exit. Nothing works. She goes mad, slowly.

The elevator was warm, but I felt ice cold. Madness was creeping up on me. Creeping? It was racing. At this rate I wouldn't hold out nearly as long as that unwanted wife had.

I pushed the Alarm button again. No answer.

The floor's elevator-call buttons were mounted on an unfinished wall diagonally across from me. I laid my briefcase in the elevator doorway so that, should the door start to close, I'd have a chance to get back on. Then, leaping off, I dashed across the area and pushed the Down button. It didn't light.

I took a few more breaths, trying to get a grip on myself. There were people just one floor below. I'd seen them on the lobby monitor. The building had two interior stairwells. All I had to do was get down one flight of steps. If the door leading onto the twenty-eighth floor was locked, I could pound and scream loud enough to be heard. If the door leading off this floor was locked—well, I'd worry about that if it happened.

Back at the elevator door, I opened my briefcase, unfolded one of the blueprints Lorraine had given me and pushed my glasses into my hair so I could study it. Okay. This wasn't so bad. Go left at the elevators, make a second left, and there should be a door on the right. I carefully placed the briefcase back in the elevator door, then walked left.

The sun, low on the western horizon, burned unchecked through a vast wall of windows. Dust particles hung in the air so thickly that my eyes began to water. There were no interior walls, just huge concrete pilings. Tangles of wire hung from the unfinished ceiling. Beyond the elevator area, sections of the floor were incomplete, exposing massive pipes and cables.

I had made it to the place where I would turn away from the elevators when a sound came from near the west wall.

At first I was only aware of a shape, backlit by the sun and half-hidden by a pillar. I adjusted my glasses and the shape became a man, crouched low beside the pillar. As he straightened he stared right at me. Something glowed red in his hand. A burning cigarette. He was tall and thin. The sun beat through his short, curly blond hair.

I raised my hand in a greeting and said, ''Oh, hello.'' The man, rather than responding, moved closer to the pillar until finally he disappeared behind it. The notion that he was one of the construction workers, that he would help me, fled. He had been watching me. He had to know I was nervous, but he hadn't said a word.

Could there really be a psycho on the loose? I was unable to take my eyes off the pillar, and as I stared, the man moved into the open again. I cannot swear to this, but it seemed that one of his hands moved toward his crotch.

Panic seized me. My heart was crashing in my chest. I had one thought: run for the door. But where was the door? The absolute strangeness of the area joined with my fear until the clear blueprint directions vanished from my mind.

A pinging sound had started nearby. For a nightmare moment I was so frightened that it hardly registered. Then there was the sound of the elevator door sliding, opening, and sliding again.

Turning, I ran toward the elevator bank. The arrow above my elevator was bright green, pointing down. My briefcase was jamming the door. I jumped over it. As I pulled it free, a loud, high-pitched sound filled the air. The man was laughing, the most hideous laugh I've ever heard.

The elevator's doors were closing when I pushed the buttons for the twenty-eighth floor and for the lobby. I didn't care where I went as long it was off that floor.

The car descended briefly, and then the doors opened again.

There was carpeting covered with wide sheets of protective paper. There was wallpaper, and a finished ceiling, and cartons. There were . . . people! Three of them.

I stepped off the elevator and then came close to falling apart. If there hadn't been a carton handy, I might have landed on the floor. As it was, my knees gave out and I plopped onto the carton. Three people rushed to my side: a black woman of about forty whose plump thighs strained at her blue slacks, an older man in paint-smeared coveralls, and a man in a green Finkelstein Boys T-shirt. It was the Finkelstein Boy who made the greatest impression. Like the kid with the dolly, he'd been one of my elevator companions on Wall Street. He was no boy, though. He had thick, gray-flecked black hair, dark eyebrows, wide shoulders, and muscular arms I would have thrown myself into in a microsecond if he'd encouraged me in the least. He didn't, so I controlled myself.

The woman introduced herself as Cornelia Gibson, head of Security.

"Bonnie Indermill." I rummaged through my briefcase

for my building pass. "Hillary should have called to tell you I was coming. I started working for Nutley today. I have this."

"Hillary," she said, and her tone left no doubt about what she thought of the girl. She gave the pass a quick look. "You were supposed to give that to the guard at the desk downstairs."

"He wasn't there. I waited, and finally . . ."

I told her what had happened. The two men listened, too. When I got to the part about the stranger, the man in the coveralls shook his head. "The construction crew's gone for the day. They're not working up there anyhow. No one is, far as I know."

"Well, someone's up there," I said. "At first he tried to hide from me. Even when he knew I saw him, he didn't say anything. He's got to be crazy. When he saw how scared I was, he started laughing."

Cornelia glanced at the two men. "I'm going to take a look. Either of you interested in joining me?"

They both said yes.

I looked around the reception area. "Is there anyone else on this floor?"

"No."

"Then I'm coming with you."

We took the interior stairwell, the one I had been looking for. Cornelia took the lead with a two-way radio in her hand. I followed her, and the two men were behind me. I felt safe surrounded by this bodyguard, but when Cornelia turned the doorknob on the twenty-ninth floor and the door swung open, I gripped the handrail. For a moment I couldn't move forward.

The Finkelstein Boy—Cornelia had called him Sam—was behind me. "It's all right. If you want, one of us will go back down with you."

"No." I lifted my fingers from the rail. "I can show you where he was standing."

I led the others to the pillar near the southwest corner where the man had been. The butts of two unfiltered cigarettes were crushed on the floor, and the faint smell of burning tobacco lingered.

We circled the rest of the floor slowly, searching every possible hiding place. There were many small openings— in the floors, walls, and ceiling—but there were few places an adult could have hidden. The strange man had disappeared.

We found the second stairwell door standing open.

"He could have ducked down here," Cornelia said, frowning.

"Or," said the man in coveralls, "he could have climbed up a couple flights and taken a different elevator bank."

Cornelia had started to close the door. She stopped midway, and her eyes widened. Scrawled roughly across the door's surface, in thick black pen, was one chilling word: *Kill.* When Cornelia ran her finger through the ink, it smeared.

"Still wet," she said. "He left his calling card."

We took the elevator back to the twenty-eighth floor. It was the same elevator I'd battled with earlier, but it was behaving now. Once we got there, Cornelia telephoned the building's lobby. The guard at the desk answered right away, efficient as anything. No, he told Cornelia, he had not noticed a strange man entering or leaving the building, but then, with all the people going in and out, how was he supposed to keep track?

When Cornelia hung up, she said she'd contact the building's management and tell them to tighten up things in the lobby. "Let's hope the guy was just a New York City nut who happened to pass through," she added.

A high floor in a skyscraper is not a place your average nut just happens to pass through, but I didn't press it.

Cornelia gave me a temporary master key, and I spent the next hour with blueprints in hand, wandering through Nutley's new offices. Maybe a normal reaction to the sweeping views, the big, bright employee cafeteria; to the centralized fax and duplicating departments and all the other goodies would have been a lot of *ooh*ing and *aah*ing. My perspective, however, wasn't normal. Every closed door shielded that strange man. He was behind every stack of cartons, every bookshelf.

I went only to occupied floors, but the floors were huge and the handful of people working on them did not make a crowd. Occasionally, rounding a corner, I was hit by silence and emptiness. Whenever that happened I hurried back to occupied territory. This job paid well, but not so well that I'd fight off maniacs to do it.

I left Nutley's new offices after eight. My head throbbed from a combination of stress and information overflow. My feet throbbed from shoe overflow. I'd had enough of Nutley's move for my first day. It was time to go home, take off my shoes, feed my cat, Moses, feed myself, and collapse.

I was on the sidewalk across Park Avenue, flagging an uptown-bound cab, when I witnessed a brief skirmish between Sam and the young mover Billy. Maybe *skirmish* is too strong a word. No punches were exchanged; only angry words and gestures. The roar of the traffic on Park Avenue drowned out the words, but it didn't matter. Until a cab pulled over and blocked my view, I watched the pair. My glasses were firmly on my nose, and I knew by their gestures what was happening. Sam grabbed the younger man's shoulder and pointed at the cracked panel of glass in the door; the younger man jerked away and raised his hands, palms up, in either defense or defiance.

Billy and Sam didn't look alike, but there was something familial about the scene. Maybe father and son. And that reminded me. I owed my mother a call. I also owed her money, and where low finance is concerned, Mom has total recall. Sliding into the cab's mushy seat, I began making a mental schedule of payments. That was a short-lived exercise. The cab's sway seemed almost hypnotic, and soon I dozed.

A hideous high-pitched laugh jerked me awake as we moved onto the Harlem River Drive. It was a few seconds before I realized the sound came from a car's tires and not from the creepy stranger who had scribbled *Kill* on a stairwell door.

3

I WAS ON THE SUBWAY BY TWENTY minutes after seven the following morning, dressed in blue jeans and a T-shirt. I found a purse snatcher–proof seat between a wall and two elderly women and tried to doze during the long ride to Wall Street. It's amazing what the promise of an hour's overtime had done to my energy level. It worked like a shot of adrenaline. I couldn't keep my eyes shut.

I'd thrown my leather briefcase back onto the closet shelf where it lives between interviews. The blueprints and my notes were in the purple nylon tote I prefer to carry. Pulling out the notes, I went over the pages I hadn't gotten to last night. They explained the marking and tagging process.

Five Finkelstein Boys had assigned each floor in the new building a specific color, and the blueprints had been marked accordingly. Room and secretarial bay numbers were also written on the blueprints. Once the blueprints had been marked by the mover, the items being moved would be tagged. "Tags" amounted to circular labels about two inches in diameter. The outer rim of these circles was brightly colored so that the mover would know at a glance the correct floor. On the center, white portion of the label, the person doing the packing would write the correct room or bay number with a fat black pen. For instance, a partner's chair destined for room 45 on the twenty-fifth floor would get an orange tag (the twenty-fifth floor was orange) with 45 written on it. It sounded simple enough for a child, or even a temp, to handle.

I got to Nutley's offices a few minutes after 8 A.M. The receptionist, who was packing a carton with one hand and taking a phone message with the other, paid me no attention as I walked by.

This was the day we were supposed to pack up Lorraine's office, all the move-related material in the cabinets behind Hillary's desk, and the contents of Hillary's desk. What Hillary's desk contained I couldn't imagine. Fashion magazines? Paperbacks?

The corridor lights hadn't been turned on, which surprised me. I didn't expect Hillary to be in yet, but Lorraine had talked as if she got there at 6 A.M. The area was quiet and dark, lit only by the morning light creeping in under closed doors. My experience with the laughing man the evening before had me spooked and I was nervous until I located the light switch. Once the area was bathed in bright blue-gray fluorescence, I relaxed. It took me a few more minutes to find an electric coffee machine and make a pot of coffee.

I expected Lorraine to supervise our packing and was unsure where to start. After a few minutes, though, when she still hadn't shown up, I sat down at Hillary's desk and started looking through the cabinets behind it. Lorraine's phone rang almost immediately.

"Lorraine Blake's office," I said

"Is she in?"

The voice was that of a very upset woman. Probably an important woman, too. It had that kind of force to it.

"Not yet. I expect her in a few minutes."

"This is Kate Hamilton. Tell Lorraine I want to see her the moment she gets here."

Slam!

I was jotting the message on a pad when the phone rang again.

"Bonnie? It's Lorraine. I'm going to be a little late. I went back to the office and worked half the night."

"Oh," I said. "Then I'll start packing up some of these

file drawers. Kate Hamilton called. She wants to see you right away.''

"I'll bet she does, the witch!''

"Who is she?''

"A senior litigation partner. A very difficult woman. She's unhappy because someone with more clout grabbed the corner office she was supposed to get. That's Nutley for you,'' Lorraine added caustically. "The phone directory for the new building's already out of date and they haven't even moved yet. Anyway, Kate's decided to make my life miserable. If she calls again, find out what she wants. Maybe you can handle it. I've got a lot of personal errands to run. I'll be in around noon.''

Noon is not a "little late,'' especially in an office on the verge of a major move.

"So you can't be reached?''

"I'll be at home for at least another hour. My number's on Hillary's Rolodex. But Bonnie, you should try to handle anything that comes up.''

"Well, all right.'' I didn't expect I'd be very effective, not with my half a day's experience on the job.

"Start packing my office,'' Lorraine told me. "Get the key from the receptionist. I'm . . . well, I'll tell you about it when I get there.'' And then, before she hung up, Lorraine chuckled into the receiver and said, "See you shortly,'' so happily you'd have thought we'd just made a date for brunch.

What an odd call. Lorraine hadn't struck me as someone who would run personal errands when an angry partner was after her, much less as a chuckler. Maybe she was having an emotional collapse. She hadn't seemed far from it the day before.

I got the key to Lorraine's office. As I fitted it into the lock, I wondered what would happen if Lorraine did fall apart. If she was unable to work, who would handle the move? Certainly not Hillary. Lorraine's immediate boss, the manager of Firm Support Services, would probably take over. Firm Support Manager. That sounded like something you'd call some kind of no-funny-business underwear. Was this manager a no-funny-business type? Would I like him? It seemed strange that Lorraine hadn't mentioned his name the day before. And who managed this Firm Support Manager? As I've said, the chain of command was blurry.

These thoughts were bumping around in my head when I made my first attack on the packing cartons Nutley was using. They came unassembled and opened flat. Along the edges were all these wings and flaps and cuts. Fold the wings properly into the cuts and there you go! You end up with a big, sturdy box. Any moron can do it. Right?

Pulling one cardboard flat away from the others, I stared at it, baffled. On one side of the cardboard were instructions. I'm sure you've seen similar explanations. "Fold flap A over flap B and then bend both of those over flap C, which tucks into cut D, etc." I read them through. They made no sense at all, so I just jumped right in and started fighting with the cardboard. I bent it one way and another, trying to force it into a rectangle. The thing was huge and had a definite mind of its own. Within seconds flaps were going every which way. I managed to make part of a carton, but unfortunately the bottom wouldn't hold. I was trying to wedge flap C through cut D when the beast came alive and sprang in all directions, trapping my legs against the wall. I couldn't see the instructions anymore, and I felt so dopey trapped behind that half-opened box with all those flaps flapping that I started giggling. The harder I tried to fold the carton, the harder I giggled, until I was cracking up so much I couldn't hold on to it anymore. It flew from my hands.

"Excuse me. Perhaps you'd like to share the joke."

The carton had flown all right, right into the legs of a tall, slender, gray-suited woman. Either out of necessity or to put on a good show for me, she had braced herself against the door frame when the cardboard hit her. She was not, by any stretch of the imagination, interested in sharing my joke.

"Didn't you get my message, Lorraine? You were to see me as soon as you came in. Have you taken it upon yourself to ignore me?"

I recognized the voice. This was Kate Hamilton, the woman who had called earlier. She appeared to be in her midforties. Her suit was severe and her shirt buttoned to the neck. This outfit, and the way her graying brown hair was pulled into an old-fashioned French twist, seemed chosen to add to the severity. In spite of this, she had a delicate look to her features and such pale skin that blue veins showed in her eyelids. My eyes were drawn to her shoes when she kicked the carton away. Sling-back high heels. Sexy stuff for someone in law-firm battle armor.

I said, "I'm sorry," meaning that I was sorry for flinging the carton. She thought I meant I was sorry for not seeing her that morning. I opened my mouth to tell her that I wasn't Lorraine, but she didn't give me a chance.

"I'm on my way to court. You better plan to spend a few minutes with me this afternoon. The carpet in that room I've been given won't do. I understand it's already been laid. Whose idea was white, anyway?"

"It's actually ivory. I'm not Lorraine."

She narrowed her green eyes. "So you're not. Are you working with her on the move?"

Lorraine had told me to handle things, but I didn't know how to handle this angry woman. I didn't want to handle her, either.

"I'm working for Lorraine. I'm only a temp."

That phrase, "I'm only a temp," is the office worker's version of pleading insanity. Nobody who hears it wants anything to do with you, or trusts you with anything more than typing drafts. Ms. Hamilton looked like the stubborn type, though, so I added, "I don't know a thing about the move or your carpet problem. You had better wait for Lorraine."

"All right," she said. "I'll call her when I get back. She knows that I wanted the flecked sienna. The fact that that horse's ass got my corner office isn't going to change my mind about the decor. If anything, I'm more determined to get exactly what I want, and if Lorraine thinks that has something to do with spite on my part, she's exactly right!"

She stormed off, leaving me trying to sort out what she'd

been talking about. As I bent to pick up the carton, I heard her say, ''Good morning, Hillary.'' She didn't say it very pleasantly, either.

Here came Hillary, sandals slapping against the floor. She stepped around me and my carton, tossed her handbag—one of those pricey little leather ones with *G*s all over it—onto her desk, and said, ''Morning, Bonnie.''

''Good morning.''

''I guess you met Kate. She's a real terror, isn't she. Everyone's scared of her.''

''For a second she thought I was Lorraine.''

''You're sort of the same type, I guess.'' As Hillary pulled a couple magazines from a shopping bag, an animated smile spread across her face. For a brief flickering instant all traces of boredom left her.

''Do you know who the horse's ass is who got Kate's corner office?''

I shook my head.

''My father.'' She glanced at my cup of coffee, which I had yet to touch. ''Oh, good. You already made it. I hate waiting for it to brew.'' She stepped over my crumpled carton once more, and her boredom returned. ''Aren't those boxes a pain,'' she whined. ''The movers should put them together for us.''

''That would be nice, but we don't have a mover handy,'' I responded. ''As soon as you get your coffee, I need some help with them.''

Hillary glanced back over her shoulder. From her expression you'd have thought I'd ordered her to get a mop and meet me in the public toilet at Grand Central. Once she got some coffee in her and got working, though, she wasn't a complete disaster. In fact, she turned out to be a real champ at putting cartons together.

''Must be my background,'' she said.

''Oh yeah?'' Rich kid?

''I'm going to be an art major. In high school, my art class was heavy into squares. You know, perspective. Like dimensions and all. We made box kites.''

She stepped back to examine a completed carton. I admired it, too. Heavy into squares. And I wasted all that time on Gregg and touch-typing.

Two hours later we had packed up the filing cabinet in Lorraine's room and the two cabinets behind Hillary's desk that held the diagrams of partners' offices, with corresponding furniture specifications and upholstery swatches. Leaving Hillary to pack the two remaining cabinets in her area, I dragged another carton into Lorraine's office and sank into her chair.

The top of Lorraine's desk had been stripped of everything personal. The World's Best Aunt mug and the photo were gone. When I had packed Lorraine's regulation desk calendar, regulation desk blotter, pencil cup, and stapler, I opened one of her drawers, the big one on the top. In it was a lined tablet full of neat notes. There was nothing else. The day before Lorraine had taken a tissue from a box in that drawer. The tissues were gone.

In another drawer I found some blank scratch pads and a couple of taxi vouchers. The big drawer on the bottom was empty of everything but a couple of pencil stubs and a broken ruler.

I tossed the pencil stubs and the broken ruler into the trash and slumped back in Lorraine's chair. Or was it still Lorraine's chair? She wouldn't dare walk out on the eve of a major move, would she? Of course not, I told myself, but something was wrong here.

I travel light when I work as a temp. Why accumulate shoes and makeup in your desk when every day may be your last one there? Lorraine, though, she was a long-time employee at Nutley. Where was her mug? How about some hand lotion? An address book? Okay, maybe she didn't trust some of her things to the movers. Maybe she'd taken them home to move herself. Tissues, though?

I was thinking about this, and becoming more anxious by the second, when Lorraine called again. Hillary answered and buzzed me. "Lorraine wants to talk to you."

Call it intuition, call it paranoia. Whatever it was, there was a nervous flutter in the pit of my stomach.

"Bonnie?"

"Yes, Lorraine?"

"Listen. Everything's going to be all right."

Nobody ever says that unless everything is going to be absolutely awful.

"If you look in my top drawer you'll find a detailed timetable of the move. I wrote down everything, every step of the move. I went back to the office and did it last night. You wouldn't believe how long I worked on it. No matter what goes wrong now, you'll be able to handle it."

Her words were tumbling out, but not so fast that I couldn't make sense of them. I just didn't *want* to make sense of them. Ignorance is bliss.

"What are you talking about?"

"I have something to tell you."

I crumbled deeper into her chair. My bad feeling was suddenly much worse. "You're taking a vacation during the move," I said weakly.

I have no idea whether Lorraine smiled or not, but I could almost feel a smile coming through that phone. "I'm taking a vacation," she said, "and when my vacation days are used up, I'm leaving. Forever. I resigned. You should have heard Ferguson."

"Who's Ferguson?"

"That fat fool I work . . . worked for. Manager of Firm Support Services. Oh, Bonnie! You have no idea how good it feels to talk about that man in the past tense."

I was speechless while Lorraine told me about the great position she'd been offered the previous afternoon, and about how lucky she was to have gotten a flight to Colorado this afternoon so she could visit her family before starting her new job.

"But what about the move?"

She let loose such a wild yelp of a laugh that I had to hold the phone away from my ear. "What about the move? I'll tell you what I think about moving Nutley. Before I went there I would never have imagined attorneys would call me at home in the middle of the night to yell at me about wallpaper. I wouldn't have dreamed that some crazy woman would insist on ripping up brand-new carpet . . ."

She must have realized that she was shouting. There was a pause. I heard her breathe—in, out—slowly before she continued. "There's no point in my going on about it, Bonnie. Nutley made my life hell for over a year, and now I'm returning the favor. I'm out of there, and that's that."

I didn't come unhinged. I didn't start to giggle hysterically, or to cry, but I could easily have done either. I said, quite simply, "What about me?" For me, that was the bottom line. Let's be realistic. Nutley would take care of itself. Somehow—be it money or threats or sheer momentum—the firm's bloated bulk would get moved to Park Avenue. You don't stop an avalanche once it's started. Temps, on the other hand, are easily eliminated. The flick of a finger, the shake of a head, and that's the end of a temp job.

"You?"

"Yes. Me. The assistant you hired yesterday."

My now-ex-boss hesitated long enough for me to realize she felt guilty. "I had to hire someone in case I didn't get another job," she finally admitted. "The condition Nutley reduced me to, I couldn't have gotten through the move without help. Hillary's the secretary for Firm Support Services, but she's almost useless," she added. "You've probably noticed."

I could see Hillary through the open door. She was pretending to read a magazine, but she hadn't turned a page since Lorraine's call came through.

"If you haven't already seen what I mean, you will. But listen. There's no reason why you shouldn't get something out of this. Nutley will keep you on as long as the move's incomplete, but you can get more money from them. Ferguson started to panic when I resigned. He said he might try to hire a consultant to run things, so I told him you'd done corporate moves before."

"You didn't!"

"Sure I did. At this point they're not going to check your references. Listen, Bonnie"—her voice grew soft, almost as if we were co-conspirators—"that's a rich firm. They pay first year associates over eighty thousand dollars a year. Get what you can out of them. Believe me, they're going to get what they can out of you. If you hang in for the next couple weeks, you'll make a lot of money."

I could hardly believe the woman who had hired me the day before was saying this. "You really think I can fake it?"

"Why not? You're bright. You've got a detailed schedule. You've got a list of all the contractors. All the move files are in order. As for Ferguson . . . well, you'll meet him. He's not exactly . . . astute. It's . . . em . . ." Her words wandered off. She wanted to be done with this conversation, with Nutley, and with me. In her place I might have done the same thing. Still, she was leaving me in some mess.

"You're going on vacation, but can you be reached?" I asked.

"No," she said emphatically. "But listen, Bonnie, you'll probably handle the move better than I would have. You're not as close to a nervous breakdown."

At that moment I wouldn't have bet even an hour's overtime on that.

I spent the next quarter hour or so sitting in Lorraine's chair—maybe it could be my chair if I wanted it—trying to collect my wits. They were all over the place.

The sane, honest thing to do was find this Ferguson character and come clean instantly. Tell him Lorraine had misread my résumé. Tell him to call in a consultant. Offer my services as that consultant's humble, harried temp.

Before this harried temp did anything that sane and honest, though, she had to get some lunch. Nerves probably had something to do with it, but my stomach had started complaining. I'd had nothing to eat since early that morning. Through the open window I could hear the faint rhythms of a swing band playing in the public plaza across the street. The sun was high and hot. I'd probably have to fight for six inches of shade. But I was not only hungry, I was getting claustrophobic, too. Mountains of boxes, not to mention mountains of troubles, were closing in on me. I needed some space. Maybe I could find a quiet place to think.

• • •

Quiet places are rare in Manhattan. It's a city of noise. Night and day, sirens scream and horns erupt. Kids cruise the busy streets, car stereos blaring. Subways rumble beneath your feet, while an occasional helicopter, checking traffic or disasters, whips the air above. It's a city of crowds, too. So many people in such a small area, all trying to be heard above the din. People who live here will tell you that the city doesn't work very well. When you think about it, though, the amazing thing is that it works at all.

It seemed as if all of Wall Street was buying lunch at the same time I was, and from the same street vendor. The cuisine of choice that noon was Middle Eastern—steak (or some approximation thereof) and peppers on a stick, or falafel in a pita pocket. By the time I reached the front of the line I was shaky from hunger and headachy from the sun. The falafel was faster and safer. I got two of them— "Hold the hot sauce"—and a soda.

The plaza was laid out in a rectangle buttressed by two buildings and two streets. The band was at one end, in the sun, and most of the crowd was, too. I found a partially shady step to sit on at the other end. The air was hot and still and didn't smell so fresh, but at least I wasn't surrounded by cartons. I couldn't see the band, but I could hear them when the traffic wasn't too wild.

"Take the A Train," they played. I take the A train. Duke Ellington might want to rethink this homage to the IND if he took the A train these days. But then, he probably wouldn't take it, the jazz scene in Harlem not being what it was.

Ravenous, I dug into the white paper bag that held my lunch. I was finishing my first falafel and feeling a little better when Sam Finkelstein walked up, white paper bag in his hand.

"Want some company?"

"Sure." I made room for him on the step, keeping the shady spot for myself. I wasn't feeling so giving.

"You recover okay from your scare yesterday?"

"I guess so."

"Gutsy lady, but you should find some company the next time you have to go to an unoccupied floor. If I'm around I'll make time."

"Thanks."

Sam was having hot dogs. Two of them, dripping with sauerkraut, chili, onions and everything else the vendor had on his cart. I watched him bite into one. Actually, that isn't true. I watched his lips, and his straight white teeth. You can't stare at an almost stranger's face hard for long though, unless you don't mind being thought of as weird, so I shifted my eyes to the hand that held the hot dog. Wrong hand for a wedding ring, if there was one. My gaze drifted up the arm attached to the hand. Tan and muscular, with the prominent sinews of a man who does manual labor. A sexy arm.

It had been six months since I'd been around a man who appealed to me. With all my money troubles, I'd hardly thought about men in that time. But there I was, with my new job falling apart, savoring the sight of Sam Finkelstein's right arm. Isn't it strange how for a long time there can be nothing and you think you don't even care, and then suddenly there's a tan forearm hoisting a chili dog and there you go, over the deep end!

"Must be good," I said when he'd downed the first hot dog.

"Just like mother used to make." He gave me a wry look. "I just ran into Ferguson. He told me Lorraine quit. Do you okay my bills now?"

"Me? I don't know . . ." I had started say that I didn't know a thing about moving a company, but I did know something. Not a whole lot, but something. And I did have Lorraine's timetable. "I don't know much about Nutley's move," I said.

"Nutley's move isn't different than any other corporate move. The antique desks are the ones that are going to be damaged, and the expensive lamps are the ones that are going to get lost or stolen . . . or broken."

Sam had paused. I adjusted my sunglasses and followed his glance across the street. Billy was grappling with two cartons, trying to maneuver them onto the back of a van. The top carton had begun sliding. We watched Billy side-step trying to balance his load. The effort was too little, too late. The carton tumbled to the pavement.

"Whoops," I said.

Groaning, Sam looked back at me. "You have just summarized Billy's career as a mover. Whoops! I can't stand watching him. He's a disaster. He's been on the crew for three months and I can't trust him to move . . . pillows."

For obvious reasons I sympathize with anyone who's having job trouble. Billy, from the little I'd seen, was a sweet-natured kid, too. "Are you going to let him go?"

"I can't. He's my son, you know." Sam sounded pretty unhappy about that situation.

I glanced at the auburn-headed, freckled-faced, pug-nosed kid. "You don't look alike."

"He looks like his mother did when she was eighteen. Irish. One of those cheerleader types guys like me weren't supposed to take up with," he added. "Maybe Billy's an example of what happens when you don't listen to your parents. On the other hand, my daughter's in her last year of medical school, so . . ."

And the Irish cheerleader? Was she still around, aggravating her in-laws? I couldn't ask Sam, but I wondered. His manner wasn't flirtatious, but it was personal. Confiding. I don't have to tell you that by then I'd managed a surreptitious look at his left hand. There was no wedding band, but we all know that doesn't mean a thing.

"Actually, I could lay Billy off, but then I'd spend all my time worrying about what he was doing," Sam said. "He hasn't always spent his spare time . . . constructively."

Sam's eyes were focused into the distance. It took me a second to find what he was staring at. A woman. An attractive one, at that! She had snaking tendrils of dark brown hair and possibly the shortest skirt this side of Las Vegas. Sam watched her cross the plaza.

"Have you met Rhonda yet?"

I shook my head. "No." But I already hated her guts.

"She's Bertram Davis's decorator. You'll like her. Nice

gal. Anyway,'' he said, ''getting back to the move, Lorraine's job would be a step up for you. Why not go for it?''

Better yet, why don't you forget Rhonda and take me away from all this and make me your love slave? That seems like a better step up. Sam didn't seem inclined to offer, though, so I nodded as if seriously considering what he'd suggested.

''Let's face it, Bonnie,'' he continued. ''After you've done one or two corporate moves, you're an expert.''

I bit into my second falafel. ''That's the problem. I've never moved anything but households. Little households.''

''Ferguson thinks you have.''

''Lorraine may have . . . exaggerated my experience.''

Sam was working on his second hot dog more slowly than he'd wolfed down the first. When he finished he said, ''That puts an interesting spin on things. I wonder who Ferguson will try to hire when he finds out. If he finds out.''

''You're not going to tell him?''

He shook his head. ''That's not my style.''

''But he'd catch on fast enough, wouldn't he? I mean, I wouldn't know what I was doing. I could make a terrible mess.''

Sam nodded at the people around us. ''You think that's unusual? I'll bet half these people don't know what they're doing at work. Most of them probably spend most of their time patching up the messes they've made.''

I looked out into the plaza. Over by the band the crowd was especially thick. It was a happy looking bunch of people, some clapping to the rhythm, others smiling and chatting with friends. Would most of those people go back to their offices and feel barely competent, the way I generally did?

''But what if. . . .''

I stopped midsentence. A man, lingering at the edge of the crowd in the shadow of a tree, had caught my eye. It looked as if he was staring at the building Nutley was currently vacating. He was tall and thin, with light hair. Even from a distance I could make out his curls. In one of his hands a cigarette burned. Despite the heat, a chill ran up my spine when I thought of the word on the hallway door: *Kill.*

Sam was waiting for me to finish what I'd been saying. Turning to him, I nodded toward the tree, but when I looked at it again, two young women stood in its shade. I quickly glanced around the plaza but the man had disappeared.

"What is it?" Sam asked.

I shook my head. It wasn't possible. It just couldn't be the laughing man.

"Sorry. I thought there was someone I knew."

I'm not sure why I didn't tell Sam the truth. Maybe I didn't want him to think I saw scary strangers everywhere I went.

"You were saying, 'But what if . . . ?' "

I forced my gaze away from the crowd and looked back at Sam. "But what if things go wrong with the move?"

"What if?" A grin spread across his face. "You can bet on one thing with a move of this size, Bonnie: anything that can go wrong will. But the thing to keep in mind is, it will go wrong no matter who's running the show. Lorraine was a pro. She knew that. The Jock knows it, too."

"The Jock?"

"Ferguson. You'll understand when you get to know him. Anyway, what I'm telling you is, if you have common sense and you're able to follow a timetable and remember which contractor is responsible for what, you'll do as well as any consultant Ferguson could bring in."

Back to that consultant. I had a pretty good idea what it would be like if Ferguson hired someone to supervise me. The consultant, wearing a suit and a suitably harried expression, and earning roughly six times my hourly wage, would probably rush to meetings while I, lowly temp, fielded a thousand panicky phone calls, helped label hundreds of cartons, dealt with dozens of movers and construction workers, got yelled at, got sweaty, and basically did all the work. Not that business meetings are fun. They can be brutal, too, but at least you don't get sweaty.

I gave Sam a long look. "You really think I can do it?"

"Sure. It'll be hell on you for a while, but it will be hell if you're assisting someone Ferguson brings in, too."

It was as if he'd just read my mind.

"Big moves are hard," he continued, "but they end. I've been doing this over twenty-five years. Everything that needs to be done always gets done, and then you walk away from it."

He didn't have to add that a consultant walked away from it a lot richer than a temp did.

I drained my soda and accepted Sam's offer of an ice cream cone (double-dip fudge ripple and butter pecan—disgraceful!). While I finished the cone, I convinced myself that this consultant person would be a gross waste of Nutley's money. Decisions made when you're punchy from too much food, too much tension, too much sun, and a re-awakened sexual appetite are not always wise, but by the time I walked back into the building I had decided that I would do everything possible to talk Ferguson out of hiring a consultant.

4

I DIDN'T HAVE TO TALK NEARLY AS HARD as I'd thought.

When you've spent enough time in enough offices, you become familiar with certain managerial types. After a few minutes with Freddie Ferguson, I recognized that he was the type who is fired later rather than sooner because he hasn't offended anyone important and no one is quite sure what he does anyway. What this type generally does is as little as possible. That way they don't make many glaring mistakes.

Ferguson had damp palms. I know because he began our talk by shaking one of my hands in both of his. It was one of the eagerest handshakes I've ever gotten from an employer. Almost made my teeth rattle.

On Ferguson's breath floated bracing whiffs of whiskey and Italian food. His ruddy complexion was probably a testament to the former, and the greasy spot on his necktie, which when he sat down rested comfortably against his paunch, to the latter. The roughly three dozen hairs on the sides and back of his head swooped up over his otherwise bald pate in one of those intricate, gridlike arrangements. Why do they do it?

As for his office, what a wreck! Ferguson didn't have a clear space on his desk or on the credenza behind him or on the window ledge behind that. It had nothing to do with the move. His cartons were still flat against a wall.

I didn't spend long with Ferguson. No, he hadn't read my résumé. "But I know it's here," he said. He waved his hands over the papers before him as if hoping the thing would magically rise from the clutter. When it didn't, he told me it didn't matter. Lorraine had given me high scores.

"Of course, I'm disappointed with Lorraine," he said, his voice rising to the pitch of a manager who's realized that a managerial-sounding statement is called for. "She was a key player in the starting lineup. However, based on her opinion. . . ."

That's what I mean about this type. An hour earlier Lorraine had kicked him in his substantial bottom, and here he was taking her word about me because if he didn't he would have to do something on his own and make a decision that would cost Nutley big money and that he would have to answer for!

I, on the other hand, was costing Nutley only small money.

"I agreed to my hourly wage, Mr. Ferguson . . ."

"Freddie."

"—Freddie, because I was the *assistant* to the coordinator of Relocation Operations. Now that I'm handling Lorraine's . . ." I caught myself before I said, "job." When you get to this level what you do isn't a job; it's a position. The difference between a job and a position can be considerable. "Lorraine's position . . ."

How high could I have gone? I didn't want to press my luck, so the figure I suggested merely doubled my salary.

Ferguson blinked and cleared his throat. "I see no problem there. Of course, I'll have to toss that around with the Management Committee, but I'm sure it will be fine." For a second he paused, concerned. "Although if you could fix me up with a game plan I could present to them . . ."

Game plan! Now I knew where "the Jock" came from.

"That's a great idea, Freddie," I said, in a managerial tone I had forgotten lay in some unused recess of my larynx. It's probably baloney, but I've read that in conversation, the more powerful speaker leans forward aggressively, and the less powerful obligingly tilts back. I leaned forward.

"Unfortunately, the relocation of attorneys and staff commences Thursday afternoon. As much as I'd like to formulate a game plan"—my best smile went along with this ridiculousness—"the starter's pistol is about to go off." I drew in a deep breath. My next words had to hit him hard. "It's time for me to get my players on the field and get the ball rolling so that Nutley can score a touchdown."

Wow! Deep breath or not, I was drained when I finished that lunacy. I felt sort of like that kid in *The Exorcist*, spewing nasty green stuff out of my mouth. I don't know where my sports speak came from, but it scored a knockout on Ferguson. By the time I caught my breath, he had flopped back in his chair and his head was bobbing like the head on one of those toy dachshunds in the back windows of big old Buicks.

"Yes. Of course," he said. "You know best. You play the game the way you know how. I'm sure you'll play to win."

I was so surprised that I almost started bobbing along with him. I was on a roll. It felt great. And why quit when you're ahead? I tried dumping two of my more pressing problems in Ferguson's lap.

"I don't know if you've heard about this, Freddie, but last night I had a scare in the new building."

I explained about the errant elevator and the laughing stranger and scary graffiti. That elicited much outrage, visible in the quick frown and the deepening crimson of Ferguson's complexion. He was going to have words with the elevator people, I could be sure of that! And he would see that the building beefed up security, too! Several harrumphs went along with these statements. He even made a note on a lined tablet, and said in a manly fashion, "Don't you worry. I'm not going to allow anyone on the field who doesn't play on our team."

I actually had hopes, until Ferguson tore the note from the tablet, folded it, and dropped it into the chaos on his desk. Ferguson was no more capable of taking care of the laughing stranger than he was of taking care of the national debt.

"And there's the matter of Kate Hamilton's carpeting," I said. "She ended up with the ivory. She'd like it changed, but I don't know if we have time. Or whether the firm would pay. Is that your decision?"

It was a mistake to use that word. *Decision.* The second it was past my lips, Ferguson's head stopped bobbing. The blood drained from his face. I'd asked too much of him. He went into such a dexterous little dance of "ums" and "wells" that I was forced to revise my initial impression of him. This was no second-rate bureaucrat I was dealing with, at least when it come to the fine art of evasion. At that Ferguson was first-rate.

"Well, yes." He looked down at his hands. "Kate is being . . . well . . . em . . ." He lowered his voice. "She has a reputation . . . you understand . . . difficult. A difficult woman. At times. Brilliant, though," he added loudly, covering himself in case Kate Hamilton had planted a bugging device in his lamp. "She had been slated for . . . em . . . a corner office, but . . . well . . . you know the M-COM— that's what we call the Management Committee—had the final say about who went where. I had very little to do with decisions about that. Nothing. However, circumstances might dictate . . ."

I waited to hear what the circumstances might dictate.

The phone on Ferguson's desk rang. He grabbed it like a drowning man grabbing a life preserver. "Let's be sure to touch base often," he mouthed at me before he began a conversation that was sure to last until I was out of his sight.

Slick.

Okay, Ferguson might not do much about security, and he would do nothing about Kate Hamilton's carpeting. I still left his office feeling good. I'd gotten my salary doubled and had demonstrated a fluency in a major area of business babble: sports speak. Business babble is a quagmire, thick with nuance. The wrong word and you're dead.

I felt forceful, a power in the business world. It was an unusual and heady sensation.

The conversation Billy and Hillary were having, which from the little I heard consisted of "All right! Yeah! Totally!" ended when I rounded the corner from the hall. Billy sat slumped on the corner of Hillary's desk. Hillary slumped in her chair. The pair of them looked so relaxed that I almost gave in to my impulse to snap, "Get busy!"

My big news that had me so excited—"I'm taking over as move coordinator"—elicited a truly apathetic shrug from Hillary and a "That's cool" from Billy. When I asked Hillary if she was able to do overtime for the next few days, she got a little more worked up. She shifted her gaze to Billy. A signal of some sort passed between them before she looked back at me and managed a lethargic nod. "I suppose so."

There were half-packed boxes all over the place, and bags half-filled with trash. The circular labels that would mark the boxes' destination in the new building—they were green, indicating that they went to the twentieth floor—had fallen from Hillary's desk onto the floor. From what I could see, none had yet been affixed to a carton. Our small department, the move's so-called nerve center, was in desperate need of a shake-up.

Being an old poop isn't second nature for me, but Hillary and Billy got my mostly dormant work ethic in a lather. Lorraine had tiptoed around Hillary. A permanent employee who wants to stay permanent can't bully a senior partner's daughter. But a consultant . . . At the least, I could toss out some hints.

I eyed Billy, he being the more vulnerable to my new power. Resisting the urge to use that horrible line that's been irritating me since grade school—"Don't you have any work to do?"—I instead asked, "What are you doing right now, Billy?"

It was perfectly clear what Billy was doing right then. He was talking to Hillary. "Hanging out," in the language both of them probably preferred. But I was still using the subtleties of business speak. It was a language Billy hadn't mastered. He tilted his head quizzically.

I gave him a hint. "Were you helping Hillary put the files from these cabinets into cartons?"

He caught on and grinned guiltily. "Oh. Well, I'm tagging boxes over in Accounting."

"Oh. Then we'll let you get back to that."

He was good-natured about this. "Okay. Later, Hillary." He slumped off. What a ball of fire!

"Billy's not just a mover, you know," Hillary said as she slid open a cabinet drawer. "Not really."

"No? What is he really?" Picking the green tags from the floor, I marked them with the office number and handed them to Hillary. In case Hillary had problems working and talking at the same time, I added, "Tell me while we tag the cartons."

The tagging was easy; Hillary had only packed four cartons. Four hours, four cartons.

"He's in Crisis," Hillary said, fixing a round tag to the end of a carton.

"Aren't we all." I had pulled an unassembled carton away from the wall. As I expected, it flopped in a dozen directions. "I don't seem to have a knack for this."

Hillary took the deranged cardboard from me. In seconds, it was a box. The kid had talent. "Crisis is the name of his rock group. They've had some club dates on Long Island. You probably haven't heard of them."

"No," I admitted, suddenly a couple of decades older than I had been seconds before.

"Billy's lead guitar. He sings, too."

Lead guitar. Oh my! That one brought back memories.

Every woman should have a lead guitar—or something similar—once in her life. I don't believe I've told you about mine, but, a long time ago, I almost married the lead guitarist in a rock band.

We were in Nogales. That's a patch of adobe in the dust on the Arizona-Mexico border. My lead guitar and his band were playing in a club on the Arizona side. They were godawful, sure, but they didn't bite the heads off rats or anything like that. Considering the times, that was a plus. I met him while I was recuperating from my first husband. I was weak. What else can I say?

It wasn't common sense that saved me from my lead guitarist. It was an attack of turista contracted, perhaps, on the Mexican side of the border. Wherever I got it, it left me too worn out to march down to the local justice of the peace. Every now and then I think about that and say to myself, "Thank heavens I drank the water."

I'll admit something, though: Hillary's relationship with Billy, whatever it was, gave me a twinge of jealousy. It wasn't because I had any interest in Billy myself, or that I wished—God forbid!—that I'd beaten the turista and married my lead guitarist. My jealousy was strictly an age thing. Or better put, a time thing. My past stretches back farther and farther. Some of my most memorable escapades—Nogales, for one—occurred while Hillary and Billy were in diapers.

Seen through time's rosy filter, I don't regret most of the things I've done. After a while even the glaring mistakes take on a nice nostalgic patina. The big problem I have with my past is this: as my past grows longer, my future grows shorter. In life there comes a time when you're simply too old to rely on an intestinal parasite to save you from yourself. I was fast approaching the first of the filthy "F-word" birthdays, and I don't mean fourteen, either.

"Are you and Billy dating?" I asked my secretary.

"Sort of, but my dad doesn't like him. He thinks he's a loser. I don't think Billy's own dad likes him, either. Did you meet Sam?"

"Yes."

"Sam won't even let Billy practice with Crisis, or audition or go out on gigs or anything while he's working with Finkelstein Boys. Sam says it interferes with Billy's real job. He's trying to turn Billy into a moving man."

I shrugged. "It pays the rent."

"It stinks," she said adamantly. "I mean, it's okay to be a moving man. I'm not a snob or anything like that. But Billy's got real talent. Sam's trying to keep him down."

"Does Billy live at home?"

I could have kicked myself the minute that was out of my mouth. Dumb dumb dumb. If I'd been thinking, I would have asked if Billy lived with his dad and his mom, that auburn-haired cheerleader. I got the answer I deserved.

"Yes, but he wants to get his own place so he can do what he wants."

I made sure Hillary was doing what I wanted, packing and tagging, before retreating to my desk. I spent a little while looking over the timetable Lorraine had prepared the night before. As she had promised, the schedule was laid out clearly. In fact, with the help of her notes I was able to take care of about half of the zillion phone calls I got during the next fifteen minutes: "Which department is moving first?" "Litigation, to the twenty-eighth floor." Attorneys from other departments asked, "Why does *Litigation* get to go first?" Litigation attorneys asked, "Why do *we* have to go first?" Everybody asked about valuables, plants, confidential papers. While answering these questions, I kept an eye on Hillary and got her moving twice when she paused over the magazine that lay open on her desk.

I must tell you, when I was able to overlook my two någging fears—that a laughing lunatic was stalking me and that I would ultimately be exposed as incompetent—I felt pretty good about things. In less than one workday I'd been promoted from temp to consultant. I'd doubled my salary, established a working rapport with my secretary and entertained some fun libidinous thoughts about a moving man. Every workday should be that good.

And then Kate Hamilton got hold of me.

Hillary took the call first. I heard her saying into the phone: "No. Lorraine quit. That's right. Bonnie's in charge of the move now. Indermill. Right. She's a temp. Sure. Hold on, Kate."

I picked up my phone. Everything about the woman I'd met that morning made me want to call her Ms. Hamilton, but taking my clue from Hillary, I said, "Hello, Kate."

There was a moment's quiet, just long enough so that I

knew that this "Kate" business was unexpected. "Bonnie," she said finally. "I would like you in my office immediately."

That was when my new confidence began to ebb.

Freddie Ferguson, for reasons which surely included covering his you-know-what, had already spread the word that he had hired a "heavy hitter" to coordinate the firm's move. During the few minutes it took me to get to Kate's office I discovered that my reputation was spreading rapidly. I was confronted at every turn in the hall and from every secretarial bay. Questions followed me and jumped at me from doorways. Sure, my confidence was founded on quicksand, but I thought I was doing pretty well. The questions I could answer, I answered. The ones I could take a good guess at, I answered too. As for the ones I was in a fog about, I nodded thoughtfully and gave an answer right out of the business-speak handbook: "I'll look into it and get right back to you."

Kate Hamilton's secretary, a middle-aged black woman who looked as fiercely competent as her boss, was named, aptly, Margaret Brusk. She shared a cramped secretarial bay with my friend Harriet Peterson.

A couple years before, after years as a legal secretary, Harriet had found herself in the ignominious position of pounding the pavement. Nutley was the best she could do. "They gave me the worst partner there—Davis!—and an associate, too," she'd told me at the time, her well-kept being quivering with outrage. By now, she had adjusted nicely to her associate, Andy McGowan. She already had started hinting that he and I would be a "cute" couple. Unlike Margaret Brusk's associate, Jonathan "the drudge," who was "guaranteed to make partner," Andy was "lots of fun." But Harriet had said, with a turn to her mouth, that Andy's partnership wasn't a sure thing. It figures, doesn't it. In dairies, cream rises to the top. In law firms, it's the drudge that skyrockets.

Nameplates had already been removed from doors, so while Kate's secretary, Margaret Brusk, buzzed her boss, I leaned over Harriet's desk. "Which one is the drudge?"

"Jonathan's there." She nodded toward a closed door.
"He gets more work done with his door shut. Andy's office
is on the other side."

It's always interesting to see the local rascal. I took a
step toward Andy's room. "Ms. Hamilton can see you
now," Margaret announced, putting an end to my wandering.

Kate Hamilton was behind her desk banging away on an
old electric typewriter. "I'll be right with you."

I was unsure about what came next. There were a couple
of chairs, but I hadn't been invited to sit and I wasn't about
to take any chances. Quick in, quick out was the best way
to handle this. I noticed that Kate hadn't begun packing
yet. She was scheduled to move Thursday with the first
group, but her cartons leaned unassembled against a wall.

Ignoring me, she worked for another few seconds, then
read over what she had typed, pulled the paper from the
typewriter, and placed it facedown on her desk. Then she
looked at me, her lips in a tense, angry line, her eyes
frankly disapproving. In seconds my palms were as clammy
as Freddie's.

"Bonnie Indermill," she said finally. "Wonder
Woman."

"Pardon me?"

"You must be Wonder Woman." Taking a pencil from
her desktop, she twirled it absently between her fingers.
"When I met you this morning you were fighting with
cardboard boxes and twittering like a half-wit. You were,
to use your own words, 'Only a temp,' and you knew nothing about my carpet. Isn't that true? Or is it possible I
imagined our conversation?"

Those two falafels and that double-dip ice cream cone
went to war in my stomach. My belt suddenly felt like a
tourniquet. I glanced at the chair by my side, wishing I
could sink onto it but not daring to.

"That's true."

"Yet, twenty minutes ago when I called Freddie Ferguson about my carpeting, he told me to speak to you. You

are our new move coordinator. A 'heavy hitter,' according
to Freddie. Is that also true?''

I saw my newly won, big-money job sailing out the window. Judging from Kate Hamilton's expression, I could
very well go sailing out the window after it. There was
nothing to do but be truthful.

''I didn't know about your carpet this morning. I have
learned about it since then.''

''And you have also learned enough''—she glanced at
her watch—''in a little more than six hours, to go from
know-nothing temp to heavy-hitting move coordinator?''

To my relief, Kate's phone gave two short rings, indicating that she had a call from outside the firm. Looking
toward her open door, she shouted, ''Are you there, Margaret?'' When there was no response, Kate grabbed the
receiver with the same hand that held the pencil.

''Hello?''

If Kate had become involved in one of those windy
lawyer-client conversations, the awfulness of my own situation would have made me oblivious to it. Instead of
speaking, though, Kate listened quietly. Her narrowed eyes
widened and the tight line of her lips gave way as her
mouth opened. For an instant she appeared stunned, and
then, though it seemed completely out of character, I
thought she looked plain scared. The pencil dropped from
her fingers and clattered onto the desk.

Ten or fifteen seconds must have passed before Kate suddenly yanked the phone from her ear. When she hung up,
her hand was shaking noticeably.

For some reason, the word scribbled on the stairway door
ran through my head: *Kill*. ''Are you all right?''

Kate responded curtly. ''Wrong number.''

I didn't believe her, but it was clear she wasn't going to
tell me about the call. In the brief moment Kate took to
draw a shallow breath and release it, my nervousness about
my job diminished slightly. Under Kate's tough façade
there was a human being who had just heard something
that frightened her.

"As I was saying," she began, "you have gone from being a temp—"

If I was going to lose this job, I was going to lose it with dignity. I interrupted. "I'm still a temp. The difference is, now I'm getting a decent salary for my work."

It didn't take Kate long to get her fierce veneer back in place. "Assuming you can do it," she shot at me. "Time will tell. In any event, let's talk about my new office, and in particular the carpet. You understand the situation?"

"Yes."

"And you're going to get something done about it before I move in?"

I considered waffling, using another version of the business speak I'd used on Ferguson, talking about coordination and work flow and that most hideous word ever plopped into the office management lexicon—*prioritizing*. But then, on top of all the horrors of the move over the next few days, I'd have the additional horror of knowing this woman was gunning for me. This was no Ferguson I was dealing with. Business babble wouldn't do.

"No," I said firmly. "It will be several weeks before I have time to deal with anything like your request. After the physical move, when things have calmed down, I'll take care of cosmetic changes."

I braced myself, waiting for Kate Hamilton to shout, "You're fired."

To my surprise, she nodded. "Well, at least that's a straight answer. You don't get many of those around here. Please do deal with my carpet as soon as you're able, Bonnie." Looking beyond me to her open door, Kate scowled. "Oh, yes. Jonathan." The first two syllables of his name were pronounced clearly, but the last one came out like a growl. It sounded like poor Jonathan was in trouble.

The drudge wasn't bad looking. A little on the tall and stooped side, but with broad shoulders and thick blond hair and . . . well, not bad at all. He was in uniform—gray suit, white shirt, dull tie, and wingtips. And the uniform expression, too—that strange combination of eagerness, gravity, and fear that must be taught in the top law schools. If my experience with Kate Hamilton was typical, the fear was justified.

"I don't have time for you now," Kate said to him. "I've got another appointment." She glanced at her watch. "We'll talk later."

That meant I was dismissed, too. As I left Kate's office, Jonathan was just closing his door.

"Not bad, but he looks kind of dull to me," I whispered to Harriet.

"The associates are being reviewed," she whispered back. "They're all nervous."

"Why should he be nervous? I thought he was hot stuff."

"Kate's his supervising partner. She's tough."

"Do you think he'll get a bad review?"

"No, but—"

Margaret Brusk cleared her throat. Harriet looked at her and said, more loudly, "Bonnie, you know I don't gossip."

I know nothing of the kind. Over the years Harriet Peterson has shared some wonderful gossip with me. What stopped her was the withering look she got from the other secretary. Grabbing a stack of papers, Harriet stood and motioned that I should follow her. We walked down the hall into a tiny room mostly occupied by a copy machine. Harriet slapped the papers into the feeder and pressed a button. The machine started pumping out copies.

I'd always found that Harriet had a hard time saying anything bad about people flat out. She liked to sneak up by telling you what someone did and then waiting for your shocked response before going for the throat. Her stint at Nutley had cured that. She spit it right out.

"I can't endure Margaret."

"She seems rather stiff," I said.

"And she never takes a sick day or anything. Nine to five, day after day. The only time I have any fun around here is when Margaret goes on vacation. She takes her entire four weeks at once. It's wonderful—almost like a vacation for me, too. You understand, don't you Bonnie? You've worked with people you didn't like."

I nodded sympathetically.

"The last time Margaret was gone, the nicest temp worked for Kate. A young woman. Veronica. We chatted and joked all day." Harriet smiled hopefully. "Bonnie? Could you have my desk moved to another spot in the new building? I'm stuck next to Margaret again. No one to talk to."

"Oh, Harriet, I'm sorry, but I don't have any say about where people sit. Maybe you could talk to Mr. Davis."

She rolled her eyes. "Have you ever tried talking to E. Bertram Davis?"

I shook my head.

"Well, you just wait! I would have quit the first week if they weren't paying me so much. Hazardous-duty pay. Mr. Davis is a horror. I'm sure the E in his name stands for evil."

She grabbed her copies from the machine. I thought we were through, but no such luck.

"I got you this job, you know," she said.

"Well, of course. And I'm grateful."

"And now you're in a position to do a little thing for me and you won't."

"I'm sorry," I said to Harriet's back. She gave no indication that she had heard.

Great! My only friend at Nutley was mad at me.

I left Nutley about eight that evening. For the first two nights of the actual move, I'd be staying at the Waldorf along with a couple dozen other Nutley employees. I wanted to stock up on cat food for Moses and start packing.

It was still daylight, and still hot, but people no longer lingered in the plaza across the street. They hurried now, down subway entrances or toward the terminal where the Staten Island ferry docks. I headed for the subway, eager as the others. When I was midway through the plaza, I hesitated. The laughing stranger's hideous giggle came back to me.

As I walked over to the tree where I'd seen him earlier, or thought I'd seen him, I told myself this was silly. How many men in New York City smoke and have blond curly hair? Lots. Too many for me to spend my time searching for cigarette butts under a tree in a public plaza.

I found three. One had a lipstick stain on the filter end. The other two had been ground flat. Using a tissue as a glove, I examined one of them. It was unfiltered. The brand was the same one we'd found on the twenty-ninth floor on Park Avenue. The second butt was, too.

I was crouched on my heels in the fading daylight, examining these two nasty pieces of evidence, when a long shadow fell over me. It was unexpected and I spun, my heart jumping.

Margaret Brusk was watching me from a few feet away. She wore an expression of undiluted disgust.

"Oh," I said. "I was just . . ."

"Good evening." She hurried toward the ferry.

That night I lied to my mother. I'm not proud of it, but it's a fact. If you know me, you know it's also a fact that I've done it before—told variations on this same lie.

I'd been putting off calling her, waiting until I had something upbeat to say about my financial situation. Now I did. I babbled excitedly about my new job—position—never mentioning that it was temporary. I gushed about the money and about the posh new offices. I carried on about how I'd be staying at the Waldorf-Astoria for two nights, hoping that my mom would be so wowed by that she wouldn't ask any questions like, "Do you think this job will last?"

Mom said she was happy for me. She always says that. But she's grown wary about these job shifts of mine. I can't blame her. She's worried about me.

I suspect she's lonely, too. My moving back home, a bleak necessity for me, would have been a pleasure for her. As we spoke, her disappointment was obvious. She'd been envisioning our morning chats over coffee and our afternoons at the mall.

"Well, honey, you can live here and commute to New York City," she said, making a last-ditch attempt. "It's not that far. Lots of people do it. Then you don't have to worry if anything goes wrong with your new job. I've already planned how we can redecorate your bedroom," she added hopefully, as if the decor in my old bedroom were the culprit keeping me from moving to suburban New Jersey. "That old wallpaper with those silly puppies is much too young for you."

"I like the puppies. Please don't change it."

"But Bonnie Jean, I've been looking around. Did you know you can get light gray pinstripes on a charcoal background? I saw it in a sample book at Home Depot."

"It sounds like an interview suit."

"If you don't like that there's a black background with silver swirls. . . ."

Gray pinstripes? Silver swirls on black? For bedroom wallpaper in suburban New Jersey? Had my mother lost her mind? "Black, Mom? Why would I want black wallpaper in my bedroom?"

"I know how you New Yorkers wear black all the time and have black dinner plates. I've seen pictures of restaurants with black walls."

What lengths she was going to to please me! Maybe it had something to do with the day I'd had, but I had an urge to cry. I didn't. Instead, I told the one lie guaranteed to make my mom feel that somehow, someway, things were going to turn out all right for me.

"Mom, the thing is, I can't move out of New York right now. I've met a nice man. We're pretty . . . serious."

There was a moment of quiet on the line. Then she was off, bubbling with excitement.

"Oh, Bonnie. I'm so thrilled. What's his name?"

Wouldn't you know she'd want specifics! I said the first thing that came to mind. It might have been Freudian, but it might have been fatigue, too, or the simple fact that I had no other options. After all, he *was* the only man I'd spoken to on anything near a personal level in a while.

"His name's Sam. Sam Finkelstein."

She repeated the last name softly, with something close to awe. "Finkelstein." Then louder, with excitement. "Finkelstein! He's Jewish."

I'd made an awful mistake, but I couldn't very well change my boyfriend's name now. "I suppose so. Yes."

"Oh, Bonnie Jean . . ."

I know my mother. She was as close to tears as I was. Don't misunderstand. Hers were tears of happiness. For my mother, a Jewish husband is nothing short of the promised land. Mink coats, top-quality wall-to-wall carpeting, live-in help. At long last, after all my false starts and dashed hopes, all the good things in life were going to come to me via Sam Finkelstein.

"You know, Bonnie Jean, I've always said that Jewish men make the best husbands."

"Yes, Mom. You've always said that."

"I'm so pleased. What does Sam do for a living?"

Sam! She was already on a first-name basis with him. I knew what she wanted to hear. She wanted to hear that Sam was a doctor or lawyer. An accountant or a dentist would be okay, too. Full professor? Sure.

Things had gone too far. I wasn't about to confess that I'd made the whole thing up, but I couldn't tell her Sam was a moving man either. Good God! Five Finkelstein Boys was a big outfit. She might know their trucks. This horrible vision made me shudder: my mother cornering a burly guy in a green T-shirt and announcing that her daughter was dating Sam.

My day's mail lay on the table next to my phone. My cat, Moses, lay next to my feet. A veterinarian? No. There aren't that many. She could try to look up his office in the phone book. Fingering my Con Ed bill, I said, "He's a mailman."

"A mailman?"

A long pause.

"Mom? Are you still there?"

"Are you sure Sam is Jewish?"

Yes, she was still there.

"Yes," I said.

"And he's a *mailman?*"

There went my mink. I had managed to latch on to the world's only nonprofessional Jewish male.

I must tell you here that my father is not the president of a bank. He's a machinist. He works in a shop that belongs to someone else. Both my grandfathers were farmers, the kind who plowed behind mules. Where did my mother's ideas about who was good enough for me come from?

"Sam's going to medical school," I said defensively.

"At his age?"

This had gotten completely out of hand. "How do you know how old he is?"

"Bonnie Jean, if he's old enough for you he's no spring chicken. At least I hope he isn't," she added, the implication being that with me she couldn't be sure.

"He's in his forties." Way into them, I suspected, but there was no point in making things worse than they were.

"Forties! Don't *you* think Sam's too old for medical school? It will be years before he can support a wife. Oh, Bonnie Jean," she said, "I don't know about this. Sam doesn't sound like such a good catch to me."

I could picture her shaking her head in despair. "He's young for his age!" I snapped. Besides, you should see his arms.

"Why didn't he go to medical school when he was younger?"

I gritted my teeth to keep from yelling, "Because he was in jail." This was insane. I was fighting with my mother over a figment of my imagination.

"I'm too tired to argue, Mom. I'll call you next week."

Her parting shot was a beauty considering that I couldn't pay my rent.

"I hope this character's not after your money, Bonnie Jean. Don't you support him while he's in medical school. You do that and once he gets rich he'll dump you and get himself a stewardess. They always do."

When I finally got her off the line, I scooped up my fat cat and stared into his thuggish mug. "You'll never run off with a stewardess, will you?" He squirmed free and trotted into the kitchen, an action that suggested that if the stewardess opened the right kind of cans . . .

Later that night I woke abruptly from a bad soap opera

of a dream. The dream's details were muddy, but Sam Finkelstein was there. He was walking out my door. There was no stewardess in sight, but Moses was clutched in his arms. I woke muttering, "But I gave you the best years of my life," to my sleeping cat.

5

THURSDAY, THE DAY THE MOVE OFFI-
cially began, was quite a day at Nutley.
An eighteen-hour day for me. Not the
first eighteen-hour day of my life, but it
certainly was the first that involved eighteen straight hours of work. I got to Nutley on Wall Street at 6:30 A.M., toting a
suitcase. The sun was just rising. By the
time I left Nutley Park Avenue, it was
close to one o'clock Friday morning. I
felt as if I'd never see daylight again.

Actually, the early morning wasn't
bad. For the first hour I was almost alone in the office.
Without continual interruptions, I was able to cover the two
floors that were being moved that evening. I made sure each
office and secretarial bay had a good supply of cartons and
tags in the proper color, and checked the cartons that had
already been packed to be sure they had proper tags. On
every desk I placed, dead center, a memo I'd written the
previous evening. It read, in part:

> Cartons should have color-coded tags affixed at
> both ends under the handhold openings. This way the
> movers will be able to see the tags when cartons are
> stacked on dollies. Carton tops should be folded but
> not taped unless you are concerned about confidential
> documents.
>
> Five Finkelstein Boys will move your personal be-
> longings if you desire. However, neither the mover nor

*the firm takes responsibility for any loss or damage to
those items. For your own protection, you may want
to move fragile and/or valuable artwork and other
personal items yourself.*

It was a little past nine that morning before things started
going nuts. I was on my way to my office when I was
confronted by a madman. No, not the laughing stranger.
Madmen, as all office workers know, don't necessarily hide
in corners and smoke unfiltered cigarettes. It would never
have occurred to this madman to hide. He dressed in full
uniform—navy suit, white shirt, necktie with diagonal
stripes.

"You're this move-coordinator person, right? I'm E.
Bertram Davis."

This was Hillary's father, old Evil Bertram himself,
member of the M-COM, head of the Litigation Department,
Harriet's awful boss, and in Kate Hamilton's opinion "a
horse's ass" who had stolen her river-view corner office.
Nothing I saw of Davis that morning made me think that
Kate might be mistaken.

He had stepped out of a doorway into my path. He was
tall and, like his daughter, lanky. But Hillary's sharp angles
were softened by youth. Her father's were not. Frown lines
were etched deep in his forehead. His nose was long and
thin, but his nostrils flared. His bony cheekbones made his
eyes look mean and squinty. Or maybe it wasn't his cheekbones. Maybe his eyes simply revealed his character: mean
and squinty. It looked as if Davis had put many years of
meanness into developing his face. He was trouble, I'll tell
you that.

"Yes. Bonnie Indermill." I stuck out my hand. He
grabbed it quickly, shook it once—the process was surely
a waste of his time—and said, "I've just come from my
new office. I'm disgusted."

There was a flash of movement behind Davis. A door
clicked shut, momentarily distracting me. Davis glared over
his shoulder, then back at me.

"It stinks. My new office stinks."

My immediate reaction, though of course I didn't say this, was, "Well, you wanted it, Bozo."

What was I supposed to call this man? Surely not E. Bertram? Bert? I played it safe. No name.

"It stinks?"

"That's right. It stinks. And the dummies who installed my wall unit didn't realize that the people who put in the air-conditioning were morons, too. My office is so damned hot that all the drawers and doors are stuck."

He wasn't quite yelling, but he sure wasn't whispering.

"What is it that stinks?" I naively asked.

He leaned forward and put both his hands at his waist. His mean little eyes got meaner and littler. "You tell me! Aren't you supposed to be the expert? Isn't that why Ferguson hired you?"

It was at that moment that I saw the truth about my job. On the surface, Ferguson was paying for my expertise. Beneath that came my sweat. But peel away everything else, and what it came down to was this: I would stand in the line of enemy fire. E. Bertram and the rest of them would have to hack their way through me to get to my boss.

"I suppose so," I said.

"You suppose so? Then suppose you handle it!" He marched back into the office he'd come out of, slamming the door behind him.

He left me shaken. Even more than Kate had. I was standing there, still reeling from the assault, when Freddie Ferguson walked out of what I thought was an office at the end of the hall.

"Mr. Davis seems upset about his new office," he said softly.

Upset? There was an understatement. "Do you have any idea what he's talking about?"

"No, but maybe you had better—"

At that instant, Davis charged back into the hall. Pushing past us, he gave Ferguson a curt nod. Ferguson, who had been speaking at something near a whisper, raised his voice by about twenty decibels and commanded, "Make Mr. Davis's office top priority, Bonnie! Don't give the job to one of the scrub team. You do it yourself!''

Yeah. This was a job for the quarterback. Rah, rah!

Freddie hurried off in the direction opposite the one Davis had gone in. I started back to my office. As I passed the door Freddie had emerged from, I glanced at it. It was too narrow to be an office door. Grabbing the knob, I swung the door open.

The room was about two feet by four feet, and contained one dirty sink and one damp string mop.

A utility closet! My boss, head coach of the move team, had jumped into a tiny, filthy closet when he heard Davis yelling at me.

Oh, Lorraine, I said to myself, what have you done to me?

It wasn't until I got back to my office and talked to Hillary that I learned exactly what it was about E. Bertram Davis's office that stank.

The problem was, I had not taken him literally.

"It smells, you know, putrid," Hillary explained when she had detached herself from her earphones. "We stopped by there last night on our way home. It's gaggy. You know what I mean? Like something died in there."

I'd seen the fought-over corner office two nights before. The floor was covered with the flecked sienna carpet Kate Hamilton coveted. Along one wall was the built-in wall unit. Walnut finish. Other than that the room had been empty. I asked Hillary if anything had been moved in since then.

"No."

"Did it smell like the carpet was moldy?"

She shook her head. "I know what a moldy carpet smells like. Our house at the beach is real close to the water, and once in a storm all the carpets were ruined."

She just had to mention that house on the beach, didn't she? The morning sun shining through the window was bright and inviting. It was going to be one of those rare low-humidity summer days when the sky is a perfect blue. There would be a breeze at the beach. Not a big one; just enough to keep you cool between dashes into the waves.

And I was grappling with a stink in a mean, skinny lawyer's office.

"It must be in the wall unit, then."

Hillary shook her head again. "They're all empty. At least they should be. Some of them are stuck. The stink, though, it's like"—she raised her arms dramatically—"in the atmosphere."

"Like, in the atmosphere." I thought that over for a second, then picked up the phone. I was about to dial the maintenance people in the new building and ask them to take a look when Jonathan, the drudge, rounded the corner. Ignoring me, he made a beeline for my secretary.

"Good morning, Hillary. How are you?"

As I've said, he wasn't at all bad-looking. His features were regular and his blond hair fell appealingly over his forehead. I've always had a weak spot for blond men, but Hillary's reaction was anything but cordial. She began pulling files from a cabinet and packing them into a carton. "I'm really busy, Jonathan," said this sudden paragon of efficiency as brusquely as Margaret Brusk herself.

"Oh. I hear there's someone new in charge. Some relocation 'heavy hitter'?" There was a sneering edge to his words.

Hillary nodded in my direction without looking at him. "Bonnie."

"Bonnie? I'm Jonathan Nash. I visited my new office this morning. I'm very disturbed."

Oh, no. More stink? What if some hideous pervasive smell had taken over the entire building, like in a horror movie?

"It's the grommets," he said.

Grommets? What's a grommet? Sounds like a small, fuzzy animal that you'd like to cuddle. But maybe they weren't so cuddly. Maybe they were rats. Maybe the building was haunted by smelly little rodents. Would I have to man the have-a-heart traps?

"I think they were there last weekend, but I can't swear to it. In any event, they're not there now."

Ah! What a relief. He didn't want me to exterminate his

grommets. He wanted his grommets back.

"Do you think someone took them?"

"Why would they?" he responded, scowling.

Why, indeed. The person in charge, if she wants to pre-
serve her reputation as a relocation "heavy hitter," cannot
say, "What's a grommet?" Nothing I'd seen mentioned
grommets. Hoping for a hint, I gave Hillary a quick look.
Her face was hidden in a carton. Glancing down at Lorraine's timetable, I ran my finger through the various items.
There wasn't a word about grommets.

"Grommets. I saw that somewhere. Ah. Here we are.
Grommets." I smiled up at him. "You're on which floor?"

"Twenty-eight."

"Do you need them badly?"

"Well," he said sarcastically, "how badly can one need
grommets?"

I shrugged. For all I knew, one's need for grommets
could be desperate. If grommets weren't important, why
was he nagging me about them? His next words cleared
that up.

"Most of the other associates on twenty-eight have their
grommets," he said accusingly.

That's 'cause the grommet man likes them better than he
like you. "Some have grommets, some don't." I looked
back at the timetable. "Friday. Not tomorrow," I cau-
tioned, least this paranoid idiot expect his grommets before
I found out what they were. "Next Friday."

At that he sniffed, mumbled, "I might have known I'd
have to wait. And, by the way, one of the arms on my new
chair is loose. See you later, Hillary."

"Uh-huh," she responded. Her face didn't emerge from
the carton until Jonathan had disappeared.

"Not if I see you first, dork," she muttered.

"Don't like Jonathan?" I certainly didn't. I made myself
a mental note: if and when I got a supply of grommets,
Jonathan would be the last to get his.

"He's a jerk," Hillary said, confirming what I already
suspected. "Nobody likes him."

I grinned. "Actually, from what you've told me, nobody

likes anybody around here. Except for us, of course. Everybody likes us.''

Hillary thought about this for a second. "It's not what you'd call a 'fun' place." She brightened. "A lot of people like Andy McGowan. Have you met Andy?''

"No, but Harriet Peterson adores him.''

"He's great. Not like Jonathan. Jonathan's always sucking up to the partners. He treats everyone else like garbage. Except for me. Jonathan adores me. Because of my dad, naturally. That's really why he stopped by.''

"He's not bad looking,'' I said.

"Until he opens his mouth,'' she countered. "He's asked me out. A couple times. I had lunch with him once. It was gross!''

"What did he do? Slobber? Pick his teeth?''

"No. He's just . . . you know. Nerdy. Not to mention that he's about thirty-two!''

Groan. "Let's not forget that. What's a grommet, anyway?''

She shook her head. "I dunno.''

Oh well, I had a week to find out. In the meantime I had to get hundreds of people moved four miles uptown. In the face of that, grommets, whatever they were, paled.

Five-thirty that afternoon. Countdown was over. Lift-off had begun. I was in the hall near Kate Hamilton's office. This was the first group to move and I had become an obsessive wreck about their cartons. I felt that if I could get this maiden voyage launched, then the journey that followed would work out fine. Ridiculous? Of course. Think about the Titanic. That was a maiden voyage, too. The launch went great; it was on the journey that they ran into trouble.

The excitement and confusion had put Harriet into such a flutter that she didn't know what to pack first or where to pack it. Into a carton went her tape dispenser. "But I may need that,'' she said. Out came the dispenser. In its place went the electric pencil sharpener, which promptly spilled its lead-and-wood-shavings guts onto everything else in the carton. And on and on. Margaret Brusk, on the other hand, was a model of efficiency, packing her belongings with such care she might have been packing her parachute. Since catching me picking up butts in the plaza, she had ignored me.

Billy Finkelstein leaned on a dolly half-loaded with cartons. Billy was neither fluttering nor efficient. He was Billy: friendly, relaxed, willing in the spirit but not so hot in the flesh. At least not in the flesh that had to load the dollys. I think it was Billy's misfortune to always look as if he was loitering, even when he wasn't. In this case, he was.

I had finally gotten a look at Harriet's associate, Andy. A cute guy, as she had promised. A little short, with brown hair getting a little thin, but appealing. He had a wide smile. And he probably wasn't young enough to be my son. Why, an eighth-year associate might be no more than five or six years my junior. There's nothing wrong with that in theory. In practice, either. Ask Elizabeth Taylor. Except that after getting a look at Andy throwing his belongings into a carton with one hand, bouncing a tennis ball off a wall with the other, talking into a speaker phone, and at the same time keeping Harriet, myself, Billy, and perhaps even Margaret entertained by making faces at the telephone, I turned to Harriet and shook my head. She lifted her shoulders, playing dumb.

"He's a baby," I whispered. Thinking of my mother, I added, "Find me a nice divorced partner."

Margaret caught that and gave me an eyebrows-up glance that told me what she thought my chances of getting myself a nice divorced partner were. *Nada.*

In deference to the occasion, Margaret had worn a pair of loose pants. I glanced into Kate's office and saw that she hadn't deferred to the occasion by so much as a thread, even though she was packing her own belongings. She was blue suited that afternoon and starchy as my sister-in-law's Sunday tablecloth.

A thick red folder was balanced on her lap. Seeing me, Kate said, "I suppose I can survive without this for a day.

If it gets lost, though, I'm dead. And so are you," she added, smiling.

It was nice that something made Kate smile, but what a sense of humor! The thing both our lives hinged on was an accordion-type file with thirty-one separate slots, one for each day of the month. I've heard these things called "tickler" files. If, on the tenth of the month, you get a letter from Hump, Dump, Frump, and Slump that requires an answer by the twentieth, you file it in a slot for a day falling before the twentieth—say, the eighteenth. Then, if you're like most of us, you forget to check the slots for days at a time, and Hump, Dump ends up bellowing at you over the phone. If you're a superefficient type, though, you religiously check the slot for the eighteenth on the morning of the eighteenth. And Hump et al. is happy.

If I hadn't been sure that Kate was in this second, superefficient category, the way she carefully tucked that tickler into the carton would have convinced me. Closing the carton, she said, "Tape, please."

"Did you read my memo?" I asked, handing her the tape. "You aren't supposed to tape cartons unless they contain confidential or valuable material."

"I can read." Kate stretched the tape across the top of the carton and pressed it down. "You can have someone take this now."

As I stuck my head out the door and motioned to Billy, Kate was jotting RIGHT DESK DRAWER across the top of the carton with a black felt-tip marker. She double-checked the color-coded tags on the carton's end and then double-checked the tape sealing the carton. "This had better end up where it's supposed to. There are important confidential documents in here."

"It won't get lost," I told her. "The tagging system is foolproof."

"Nothing is foolproof."

Maybe it was coincidence, but Billy had just walked into the room. We watched him slide the carton out the office door. That part was easy. When he tried loading it on top of the other cartons, though, he ran into trouble. The entire pyramid began wobbling.

"Whoa," Andy yelled from down the hall. "I'll help you."

A second later the two had stacked Kate's carton of desk contents on the pile.

Kate joined me at her office door. "A system is only as good as its weakest link." She was looking right at Billy, and spoke loud enough for him to overhear. There was no doubt about who Kate thought this weakest link was.

"Kate," I said, "the carton is clearly tagged. It will be delivered to your new office tonight."

She looked at Margaret. "You will be there, I hope."

"Of course." With a tilt of her chin, Margaret added, "I'll be staying at the Waldorf for two nights." She said this as though she were a guest of the Queen Mother. In reality, Margaret was one of the staff members who had agreed to work past midnight—at time-and-a-half, of course—and then stay at the hotel.

"Do *not* unpack that carton," Kate ordered her secretary. "Just make sure it's in my office. And be sure to lock my office door before you leave." Kate glanced down the hall. "Now where has that kid gone?"

The top-heavy dolly sat deserted at the end of the hall. Andy poked his head from his office.

"Billy went to get some help. The thing is too much for him."

"I suspect that most things are too much for Billy." With that, Kate went back into her office, grabbed another carton, and tackled her bookcase.

By my estimate, Kate had two more cartons to pack. Margaret had one, and Harriet, who had made almost no progress, had three. Andy's slaphappy method had worked for him. He was packed, tagged, and ready to go on the dolly.

The loaded dolly was just outside Jonathan's door. Stepping past it, I looked into Jonathan's office. He was scowling and writing furiously on a yellow lined pad.

"I don't have time for this," he said when he saw me.

"I don't understand why we have to be the first to go."

Andy called, "We're first 'cause we're best."

"I'm afraid you're going to have to make time," I said. "They're going to want your cartons on the next dolly."

"You mean everyone else is packed? I'm the one holding up the works?"

"Andy's finished, Kate and Margaret are almost done . . ."

The charmer sniffed, shoved his yellow pad aside, grabbed a stack of purple tags, and began scrawling his room number on them. "Never let it be said that I held up the works. You just be sure you don't forget about my grommets. Or my chair arm."

It was going to be a long night.

6

TEN O'CLOCK. PARK AVENUE. IN NEW York, the temperature had reached a record high that afternoon. Since about 4 P.M., the city had been plagued by a series of brownouts. Con Ed swore that they had everything under control, but at Nutley Park Avenue, lights dimmed and elevators inched their way up the shafts. As for the air-conditioning, forget it.

Nevertheless, two floors, consisting of the belongings—books, computers, files, plants, photos, the odd shoe, all the detritus of office life—of forty attorneys, thirty secretaries and a dozen legal assistants had been moved. Or sort of moved. Or, I'm sorry to say, were missing in the wilds of Manhattan somewhere between Wall Street and Park Avenue.

I won't bother you with descriptions of all that had gotten lost, misdelivered, scratched, or broken. But I'll tell you this: you can forget foolproof. There's no such thing.

There was also no such thing as my boss. Freddie's new office was next to mine, but I had yet to catch him in it. On and off during the evening I'd looked for him, paged him, asked about him. There were occasional rumors of Freddie—he'd been seen on an elevator, spotted darting across the lobby—but Freddie in the flesh? No. Now I knew what Lorraine had hated about him. It wasn't that he hovered, or yelled, or any of those other awful boss things. Freddie just . . . wasn't.

As for Hillary, she was keeping a low profile, too. So, I

was it—boss, slave, target. I don't believe I've ever had so many people furious at me at the same time. My mantra, repeated until it pounded in my head, was "Put it on your punch list." That's what lists of complaints in a move or construction project are called. The response to this, generally delivered at a bellow, was also pounding in my head: "You had better believe I will!"

These big-firm lawyers! At first glance they seem to be among the least physical people on earth. Real desk potatoes, they have two body types: paunchy and scrawny. But let little things go wrong. Let them lose control of their stuff, and—wham! You've got a building full of Rambos on your hands.

There was the tiny, apple-cheeked Napoleon who delivered two swift kicks to the wall outside his office when the carton containing his baseball memorabilia, including a ball autographed by Reggie Jackson, didn't arrive. And how about the partner with the berserk white hair who discovered that a carton containing four full bottles of Chivas Regal and some other happy liquids hadn't turned up. That cutie actually made a fist at me. Thinking better of it, he managed to divert its route from its first target, my solar plexus, and let his leather desk chair have it instead. You should have seen the chair jump on its springs.

Even those without power, but with powerful connections, went nuts. Davis's decorator, Rhonda, stormed up to me while I was on the phone in the twenty-eighth floor reception area and asked—demanded—that the door to Davis's coat closet be unstuck, then and there, and threatened me with the wrath of Davis himself.

"Am I going to have to call Bertram at home? Is that what you want?"

Rhonda's madwoman tendrils hung limp around her pinched face. I was glad to see that a big red hive had developed on one side of her nose, giving it a comic lopsided look. She had her hands on her hips. Those—her hips—were encased in a beige skirt so tight that I can't imagine how she got it over her thighs without screaming in pain. She topped that with a lime green jacket with foot-ball-player shoulders. On her feet were platform-soled high heels. Comfort clearly was not an issue with this woman.

I'd figured Rhonda for about my age, but seeing her close up and frazzled, I realized she was older. That realization cheered me, as much as I could be cheered under the circumstances.

"Do you really want me to call Bertram?" she repeated.

"No," I said. "What I really want is a shower and a bed." It was eighty degrees outside and felt about one hundred inside. I was trying to reach someone from building maintenance and make some demands of my own about the faltering air-conditioning system. And Rhonda needed a coat closet opened up.

I had no intention of obliging her that night. I was about to repeat my mantra and, perhaps, add a "please" to it, when the elevator arrived. A delivery man from a Chinese restaurant was partway through the door—the big bag he carried was all the way through—when the door began to close. The man made a valiant leap into the reception area. Unfortunately, in the process he and the bag parted company. One container tumbled from it and did a flip. As it turned in the air, the lid came off. The contents—it looked like moo-shoo pork—ended up christening the carpet.

I snapped at Rhonda, "If you think calling Bertram Davis at home will get his closet opened, call him!"

"Forget it," she grumbled. "I'll put it on his punch list."

"Anybody around here named Billy?" the delivery man called.

"Here."

Billy, his hand full of cash, hurried from what should have been an unoccupied office. Suspicious, I walked to the door and looked in. The room contained exactly two chairs, one little table, and my secretary.

"Hillary! I've been paging you for half an hour."

"I didn't hear you."

"And you didn't hear me just now, standing twenty feet away from this room?"

"Sorry," she whimpered, "but I've got to eat, haven't I?"

I controlled an urge to do a Rambo bit of my own. "I want you to get hold of the building engineer and find out what's with this air-conditioning. I'm making that your responsibility." As if this kid craved responsibility.

"After I eat. Okay?"

"Eat fast!"

I left before I said anything that would get me fired.

Billy was looking at the mess on the carpet and shaking his head. "I'll get blamed for that, too, I bet."

I was past all sympathy.

It was an hour later when I received the worst blow of the night. No missing liquor or baseballs, no broken chair legs quite equaled this. It was Margaret Brusk who delivered the hideous news.

I remember coming out of the stairwell on the twenty-eighth floor's southwest corner feeling light-headed. I'd been awake and working hard for too long. My last real meal had been a hot dog grabbed from a street vendor at noon. Since then two candy bars had been it. I leaned my back against a secretarial station divider. Hot air poured from every ceiling vent and the temperature in the building was killing.

Did the Waldorf offer room service at 1 A.M.? If they did, could I stay awake long enough to enjoy it?

"It never got here."

The voice seemed to come from all around me—over, under, on all sides. The words were a variation on the theme I'd been hearing all night, and in my loopy condition I thought, for a moment, that I'd imagined them. No such luck.

Margaret was standing on a step stool, placing supplies into a built-in cabinet behind her desk with the precision of a Marine Corps sergeant. I stared up at her.

"Is there an echo?"

She glanced toward the ceiling. "Probably. This is a dreadful building they've moved us into. But that's not your problem." Scowling back at me, Margaret said,

"Your problem is going to be with Ms. Hamilton."

My stomach, which was in no shape for bad news, clenched. "Why is that?"

"The contents of her lower right desk drawer have not arrived. You gave your word that the carton would be here. It is not. The evaluations for the associates Kate supervises are in that carton."

"It will show up. She must have copies, anyway."

"No," Margaret replied. "Ms. Hamilton typed them in draft herself. She hasn't given them to me to be put in final yet."

"I thought she'd already met with her associates about their evaluations."

Margaret raised an eyebrow. Such nerve I had, questioning Kate Hamilton's evaluation process. "She talks informally with her associates before the evaluations are finalized. Ms. Hamilton feels they should have a chance to defend themselves."

"Isn't she a sweetie," I said sarcastically. "How many evaluations were there?"

"Two. Jonathan's and Andy's."

Two! I'd expected to hear that a dozen evaluations were missing. What was such a big deal about two of them?

Something in the way I was raised tells me to make people in authority happy. And, in that particular corridor on that particular night, Margaret, by way of her boss, was authority. But there's something else in me—I can't imagine my parents instilling this, it must be some rogue gene, the legacy of a crazed Celt—that makes me want to stick out my tongue at them.

I rubbed my forehead. Uck. My skin was oily and disgusting. "The carton will turn up. Put it on her punch list."

Margaret's eyes rolled upward, presumably to the heavens, where the likes of Margaret look for the patience to deal with the likes of me. She then showed me a face that would stop a buffalo stampede.

"Punch list? Oh, that will make Ms. Hamilton happy. You don't seem to understand that the contents of her right desk drawer are very important."

I straightened and glared back, just as fiercely, I hope. I had nothing to gain, and a lot to lose, by telling this woman where she could shove the contents of Kate Hamilton's right drawer when they turned up, but I wasn't far from doing just that.

"Let me see the boxes that arrived."

She made a sweeping motion with her hand. "I've unpacked most of them. Tomorrow evening I'll get to the rest."

I quickly looked through the empty cartons that were stacked against the corridor wall. None of them had RIGHT DESK DRAWER scrawled on them, nor did any of the four unpacked cartons that were inside Kate's office.

I walked to Andy's new office. His door was open wide. He was sitting on the floor, his back propped against his desk, arms deep into the bottom drawer of his built-in credenza. Torn cartons surrounded him. Apparently he'd gone at them like a three-year-old going at the boxes under a Christmas tree. He had taken off his shoes, and in his T-shirt and jeans and socks, he looked like a kid.

"Find any extra cartons? One of Kate's is missing."

"Oh, please," he groaned. "I've got enough trouble. Unfortunately, this is all mine."

I tried Jonathan's office next. His door was shut, but light showed from under it.

"Jonathan?" I tapped lightly.

"Yes."

The drudge was bent over a yellow legal pad, pen in hand. No necktie, but I would have bet that under that desk his wingtips were tied tight.

"You didn't end up with any extra cartons, did you?"

"No. Why?"

"One of Kate's hasn't arrived. Yet," I added.

He glanced at a couple of still-packed cartons on the floor beside his desk. "You're welcome to look."

The stickers on the cartons' sides indicated that they had been destined for Jonathan's office.

"Any word on my grommets?" he asked. "It looks like hell without them."

"No word yet." Jonathan's grommets were hardly a burning issue with me, but I scanned his office quickly, trying to see what looked like hell.

"Please close my door. On top of everything else, I've got to get this finished," the long-suffering drone said. I pulled the knob extra hard, so that the door slammed nice and loud behind me.

Margaret had stepped off the stool. "Kate's going to be very unhappy with you."

"She's got a lot of company."

"I'll be going to the Waldorf now."

"Sleep tight."

Okay, so the carton wasn't there yet. Surely it would turn up. While I was on that part of the floor, I could at least deal with another one of my problems. Using my master key, I unlocked Bertram Davis's corner office.

I had hardly cracked the door when the smell hit me. It was the smell of rotting food, of garbage, of unwashed people on the subway. The heat wasn't helping, either. Opening the door wide, I took a quick tour of the room.

It was impressive, no doubt about it. Bigger than the other partner offices, its two walls of windows showed a stunning panorama of lights to both the south and the east. Whether it was worth fighting over I can't say. In its present state it sure wasn't. With the door open, the smell wasn't quite unbearable. It was one of those awful smells that you can briefly accustom yourself to. Still, on a long-term basis I would rather set up shop in the janitor's closet.

I didn't want to spend any more time in the room than necessary. Moving quickly, I tried the doors and drawers in the wall unit. Several were stuck, but the ones that opened were empty. Davis's desk, a couple of chairs, a small sofa, and a table were in the room. Cartons—all of them labeled for Davis's office—were stacked in a corner. Folded curtain panels lay on the sofa waiting to be hung. All of this had been moved in that evening, long after Davis reported the smell.

Walking to one of the windows, I stared into the distance. The river view had been exaggerated. By pressing the right side of my face against the window, I was able to see a fragment of the East River. Sitting that way, I caught a glimpse of a boat moving through the water. It looked like one of those dinner boats that circle Manhattan in the summer. A trickle of sweat ran down my back. I had pulled my hair into a desperate, tight ponytail to keep it off my neck. My shirt was damp, my bra wringing. It would be cool down there on that boat. I'd have some sort of cold drink in my hand, and maybe some attractive man would be trying to make an honest woman of me. Attractive? Hell, right then I wouldn't have cared if he looked like a toad. I like toads.

As I stood there, drifting into a fantasy world, the faltering air-conditioning briefly came to life. The vent on the ceiling above me spewed out a short blast of cool air. At the same time, it spewed out a megaton dose of the awful smell. No sooner had I backed away and looked up at the vent than the air-conditioning stopped again. The powerful stench clung, as Hillary would say, "like, in the atmosphere."

I was reaching for the phone when it surprised me by ringing, two short rings for an outside call. Ordinarily I wouldn't have answered Davis's calls. Put it down to being in the wrong place at the wrong time.

"Hello," I said.

"You dirty whore! I know everything about you. Everywhere you go, bitch, I'm watching. Remember that."

It was a man, his voice low but intense. The noise of traffic traveled through the receiver before the phone went dead.

I sat down on the edge of Davis's desk. The call had happened so quickly that I hadn't had time to be frightened. Now, though, the sweat on my back turned icy. I flashed back to the call Kate had gotten in her Wall Street office, the so-called wrong number that had shaken her. And then I flashed back farther, to the horrible sound of the strange man's laugh when he had frightened me and to the word on the stairway door: *Kill*

What was going on? Was this man targeting women at

Nutley? How had he even known that I'd answered Davis's phone. No one—and certainly no one outside the building—could have known I was in Davis's office. No one but Margaret.

Margaret Brusk? No way. I dialed Security.

"Cornelia," I said. "Two things. First, I've just answered an obscene call on Bertram Davis's phone."

I told her what the caller had said and asked if any other women at Nutley had reported similar calls.

"No. But if it came from outside, it couldn't have been meant for you."

I knew that she was right, but she hadn't gotten the call.

"Let's hope it wasn't. The second thing is, the smell in Davis's office seems to be coming out of an air-conditioning duct. When the air-conditioning switches on, it's vile."

Cornelia promised to check that out. I'd be around for another hour or so, and I asked her to page me if she found anything.

Cornelia found something. I was in my office going over the next day's "game plan" when she stopped by.

"You got a few minutes? I've got a surprise for you."

"Is it a nice surprise?"

"Well . . . you'll see."

We took the elevator to the twenty-eighth floor, then went up one flight of stairs to the twenty-ninth. As Cornelia pushed open the door, I caught my breath.

Exposed bulbs had bathed the floor in a warm yellow light so that the eerie white dust, so visible in the daytime, wasn't apparent. The million lights of a Manhattan night shone through the windows, making the vast expanse of concrete look almost beautiful. The empty floor seemed to have assumed a different character from the one I associated with it. It was an improvement.

Of course, I immediately looked at the corner where I'd seen the laughing stranger. There were two men there now, both crouching over something, neither attempting to hide. Both wore dust masks over their noses.

"They found the smell?"

She nodded. "You were right. Just wait until you see this. Be careful where you step."

We made our way across the floor, dodging pipes and exposed wires. As we approached the two men, the smell grew stronger. By the time we reached the corner where they crouched, it was downright awful, much worse than in Davis's office.

In addition to their masks, the two men wore thick, elbow-length rubber gloves. They huddled around a big gray conveyor tube that was constructed of sections of metal bolted together. One of the sections had been re-moved, leaving an opening of about eighteen inches. And to one side of that opening, on a sheet of plastic, lay just about the most repulsive pile of garbage I've ever seen.

It was a horrible stew of everything nasty you can imag-ine—fish heads, broken eggs, greenish hunks of meat, and slimy unidentifiable things I don't want to think about. A muck-covered broom rested on top of the mess.

One of the men had stretched out until he lay flat on the floor. He was shining a flashlight into the opening, rotating it around for a better look.

"A little more and we'll have it all."

Withdrawing the flashlight, he grabbed the broom. A sec-ond later several hunks of something awful had been added to the pile on the plastic sheet.

By then Cornelia and I both had our hands over our noses. She motioned me to step away, then nodded at the mess on the plastic.

"There's Davis's stink."

"It sure is," I said. "How did it get in there?"

"Someone—probably your friend with the sense of hu-mor—removed a section of the duct and shoved all that mess in there. When he replaced the section, he didn't put all the screws back. That's how I found it so quickly once you called."

"Weird," I said. "Why would he do that?"

"Guess he doesn't like Bertram Davis. I can understand that," she added. "Personally, I can't stand the sucker."

We left the two unhappy maintenance men washing out the conveyor tube.

I was done in, physically and mentally, by the time I left that night. Night? It was morning, if you want to get technical. My brain was mush, my body was punchy. I'd eaten nothing.

All in all, I thought the move was going well. In addition, I'd located and taken care of the smell in Davis's office and had even managed to write my elusive boss a note about this and leave it in his office. Yet, despite these victories, the specter of Kate's reaction the next morning loomed large and scary, possibly out of all proportion.

An idiotic second wind, fueled by this anxiety, took hold of me as I stood at the elevator bank. Before I headed for the Waldorf I'd make one last try for Kate's carton and take a look at the holding area near the loading dock on the main floor. Maybe . . .

I punched the elevator call button. It lit dutifully, but . . . no elevator. I was alone in the area. The doors to the reception area were open wide, though, and from a radio somewhere I could hear a song. It was from an old Fred Astaire/Ginger Rogers movie.

Someone had put a big sheet of plywood on top of the carpet. As I walked across the wood, it gave just slightly, like the sprung floor of a theater. The feel of it woke an old memory. It was a floor for dancing, an activity a good part of my life had been devoted to.

I must have lost my bearings for a moment, lost contact with where I was and what I was doing there. I bent my knees, then straightened them. Rose to my toes, then down again. Almost unconsciously, I extended my right foot. *Shuffle, ball, change. Shuffle, ball, change.* A basic step. The floor felt good, but it was hard to make any sound with my sneakers. I stepped harder.

A couple loud claps broke my concentration. Stopping instantly, I planted both feet firmly on the plywood.

Sam Finkelstein was just inside the reception doors.

"Very good," he said with a nod of approval.

I smiled sheepishly. "For a second I forgot where I was."

"I wish I could. You getting out of here?"

"In a few minutes. I want to check the loading dock for a carton. How about you?"

"I've had it. Got to get some sleep." He glanced down the bank of elevators. "Are any of these things running?"

"A couple," I said. "They're tied up with moving."

Overhead the lights dimmed. Sam looked up at them. "Or brownouts."

"I just hope we don't have a blackout," I said, though, if I had to be stuck on an elevator, Sam wasn't a bad person to be stuck with.

Probably, without too much of a stretch, I could have said something that brought the words *your wife* into the conversation. Does *your wife* wait up for you? I was too tired to make the effort.

"Where do you live?" I asked.

"Out on Long Island. I'm not going that far, though. We have a couple beds fixed up at the warehouse in Queens."

"Oh. That's nice." And how does your wife feel about that? Does she miss you? Does she not give a damn?

He lifted an eyebrow. In my woozy condition, I had a fleeting thought that I'd said those things out loud.

As I stood there, dumb as a stone, Jonathan Nash hurried through the doors. Like Sam, Jonathan glanced at the six sets of firmly shut elevator doors. Unlike Sam, he jabbed impatiently at the call button.

"I already did that."

As if I'd lied, a pair of elevator doors slid open. The three of us stepped onto the elevator.

Sam smiled at me when the doors had shut. "It isn't really nice."

"What?"

"Staying at the warehouse. It's not really that nice."

"Oh." Ooooh. He had said *staying* at the warehouse, not *sleeping*. Just the same, was he flirting? Maybe even angling for an invitation to the Waldorf? Within inches of Jonathan? Not that Jonathan would notice. Yes, he was flirting, and I couldn't think of a thing to do about it.

"You going to check the loading dock now?" he asked, all business again.

"Yes." I told him about the liquor, about the baseball souvenirs, and a signed Steinberg print a corporate partner had reported missing. "And," I added, "one of Kate Hamilton's cartons didn't get to her office tonight."

Sam's expression grew stony, but he didn't say anything until the elevator had arrived on the ground floor and Jonathan was gone.

"If Kate Hamilton keeps making cracks about my kid the way she did when he loaded her cartons, she's going to have to deal with me."

"Billy told you about that?"

Sam shook his head. "No. Billy doesn't tell me much these days. He told one of the other guys. Told him he'd like to 'punch her lights out.' It got back to me."

One of the big vans started up out on Park Avenue. "I'm going to check what's going on out there," Sam said. "I'll meet you on the loading dock in a minute."

I hadn't asked him to, but I wasn't going to argue.

The holding area—a big windowless rectangle lit by fluorescent lights—seemed to contain nothing but furniture. I wanted to be certain, though. I wandered between desks, glancing into the spaces under them. Along one wall was a tangle of new chairs—big executive-type chairs, armless typists' chairs. There was a narrow aisle between that and a collection of bookcases.

I was pushing through the chairs, shoving them aside, when the fluorescent lights dimmed. They flared then, brighter than normal. Suddenly, from the corner of my eye, I glimpsed something. Or someone. I couldn't have identified it as male or female. Not even as human. It was a shape, a shadow, movement among the bookcases.

"Is anyone there?"

Dead quiet.

The lights faded again. I peered through the gray space, sure the lights would brighten. They dimmed further, then further still until I could barely see.

I wasn't going to be caught in there in the dark. At the far end of the space were double doors that opened onto the loading dock. They had been open when I'd been there earlier that day, but now they were closed. I started toward them.

The room went completely black. My shin cracked into a metal chair leg. "Oh," I cried out.

There was the sound of furniture being pushed around. Then I heard footsteps coming down the narrow aisle. Backing away, I stumbled into another chair. As it rolled across the floor I fell into it. The chair's arm gave, and I lost my balance and tumbled onto the floor.

The footsteps were closer. Someone brushed past me and stumbled over my extended leg. A second later the loading dock door opened and moonlight streamed in. The person passed through the door and was gone.

As I rubbed my shin, the door at the lobby end of the area opened. A flashlight's beam swept the space as Sam hurried down the aisle. "Are you okay?"

"I'll live. There was someone in here," I told him as I untangled myself from the chair. "He ran out when it got dark."

"Probably one of my crew loafing. My son, most likely. Come on." Pulling me to my feet, he led me out the door.

The night air hit me like a tonic. It was hot, sure, and it was the middle of Manhattan, which probably has some of the crummiest air around, but it still felt better than inside 310 Park Avenue. Though we couldn't see the moon from the dock, the night sky was light.

Two trucks were backed up to the platform. Both of them had been emptied. Near the freight elevator about a dozen cartons sat on an unattended dolly. Sam moved them around and, with the help of his flashlight, I checked the labels.

When I realized that Kate's box wasn't there, I felt the last of my energy leave. "Do the tags ever fall off?"

"Not that I know of." He demonstrated by scraping his fingernail at the edge of a tag. It held fast.

I stared glumly at the little tag. "There were a lot of

cartons on that dolly. What if someone was in a big rush, not paying attention, and stuck on a second tag over Kate's. The carton would be directed to the wrong room.''

Sam looked doubtful. "There should have been two tags on every carton. It's hard to imagine someone being so distracted that they would cover up *both* of Kate's tags."

He was right. I was desperate and my reasoning showed it. "Damn. Kate is going to be so mad." My shoulders sagged. I slumped my elbows onto a carton and rested my face in my hands.

When the overhead lights flickered on, Sam clicked off the flashlight and stared at me from the other side of the gurney. "What was in that carton, Bonnie? Gold bullion?"

"Paperwork." When my second wind left me, my common sense did, too. Moisture was building up behind my eyelids.

"Paperwork! Then it will turn up." He tilted his head. "Are those tears? Are you going to cry over paperwork?"

I shook my head but a lone tear escaped and slid down my cheek. Sam reached across the dolly and wiped it away with a fingertip.

"Bonnie, let me tell you the facts of life when it comes to moving: You'll never see the autographed baseball or the Steinberg print or the Chivas Regal again. The best the owners can hope for from us is insurance money. That's the way it is. But nobody steals paperwork."

"I know, but—"

A noise from the cab of one of the trucks stopped me. "Who's that?"

"It's me, Dad." Billy stuck his head through the window. "I was resting."

"Was that you in the holding room a minute ago?" I asked.

"No. I've been in here for a while."

Billy had positioned himself so that we couldn't see into the cab. When Sam started toward the edge of the dock, I put my hand on his arm, stopping him.

"Would you mind walking me to the Waldorf? In case I fall down in front of a speeding taxi?"

He looked at me, and at Billy, and at me again. A hint of a smile crossed his face. "Of course. I'll be back in about five minutes, Billy," he said. "We'll leave then."

"That will give him a chance to say good night to that Davis girl if she's in there with him," Sam said the minute we had left the loading dock.

"I'm sure she is. She was supposed to work a double shift, but I haven't seen her in hours. They had dinner together," I added.

"Hum," he said. "And that's okay with you? That she's being paid overtime to hang out with my son?"

"No, but . . . I understand it."

"You've got a romantic soul, haven't you," he said as we crossed the lobby. "Just the same, I want to keep Billy busy. If you need help with anything, feel free to ask him."

We didn't speak again until we left the building. The full force of Park Avenue at night hit me. Even though it's never very quiet, it's beautiful—wide and clean, with a landscaped median strip. That night an almost-full moon hung over the southern horizon.

"Wow! Look at that," I said.

"You're a romantic all right."

Am I? During the past few months I'd been so preoccupied with paying my rent that romance, a gossamer notion if there ever was one, hadn't been much in my thoughts. When you're broke, you hardly have time to think about the fundamentals. Something as elusive as romance was impossible.

Sam took a light hold of my arm as we crossed Park. I was in no real danger of falling in front of a speeding taxi, but I liked the feeling that someone was there to catch me if I did. I was tired and punchy, but as he walked me past the taxi stand and into the lobby, I felt . . . taken care of.

I don't know what got into me. I'll blame it on fatigue, or those two candy bars. Or maybe it was the moon. Before I dashed up the few steps just inside the Waldorf's entrance, I rose to my toes and kissed Sam Finkelstein, square on the mouth.

I was at the top of the stairs before he reacted.

"Wait, Bonnie."

He looked astonished, but he didn't look unhappy.

"What was that about?"

I shrugged. "An impulse, I guess."

"Oh." Tilting his head quizzically, he asked, "Do you have any other impulses?"

"Not right now."

"Just checking."

"See you in the morning." I had walked a couple of feet when he called me again.

"Bonnie? You were a cheerleader, right?"

I nodded.

"Figures."

My room, a blue chintz extravaganza, was on a low floor on Park Avenue. Tired as I was, I took complete advantage: in the marble shower I lathered myself with the Waldorf's almond-scented soap and my hair with their strawberry shampoo. When I'd finished, I wrapped myself in thick white towels and unlocked the room's little refrigerator. What a selection! Sodas, beer, wine, hard liquor, potato chips, candy bars, salted nuts—a nutritionist's worst nightmare.

I added a bag of Fritos, some cashews, and a little bottle of white wine to the other atrocities I'd committed against my digestive system that day. I didn't need room service. Elvis lived on junk food for years. A day or two of it wasn't going to kill me.

As I ate at the table in front of the window, I looked out over Park Avenue at Nutley's new home. Lights still shone on the upper floors. In one window I could see someone at a desk. Through another, I saw a man in a green T-shirt wrestling with a carton.

It was time for Hillary to be leaving. I had bolted the Fritos and the cashews. Now I sipped my wine. I was curious enough about my secretary's work habits to glance down at the street. Within seconds, Hillary walked out of the building. She had managed to last the full double shift, though she'd probably spent the last hour in the truck with Billy. I watched her climb into a cab.

Tilting my glass, I finished my wine and thought about that kiss. I shouldn't have done it. I was going to hate myself in the morning when I had to face Sam.

My eyes slid shut. I forced them open. Time to crawl into that king-sized bed between those cool clean sheets. Standing, I glanced sleepily down at the lobby of 310 Park Avenue. Something jerked me awake!

There was a man on the sidewalk, standing in the shadows at the side of the building. I might not have noticed him except that as my eyes swept the area, he was caught, briefly, by the headlights of a car speeding through the intersection.

I reached into my bag for my glasses, but by the time I had them on one of the moving vans had pulled up at the traffic light, blocking my view. I waited, but when the van moved away, the man was gone. Was it the laughing stranger? Had he made the obscene call? Had he been in the holding room with me?

Or was my mind finally going? It sure seemed to be. I was kissing men I hardly knew and seeing laughing strangers in the shadows. It was time to get some sleep.

7

I SPENT—WASTED—A GOOD BIT OF THE next morning looking for Kate Hamilton's carton. I visited the downtown building and made several trips to the Park Avenue loading dock. Enlisting Billy Finkelstein, I had him search every nook and cranny in the new building.

The bad news that Kate was gunning for me reached me while I was in the big conference room on the twenty-eighth floor where unclaimed items were being held. There were a few untagged cartons there, and I'd worked up a good sweat moving them around. None of them was Kate's.

An old wood coatrack, arms waving like a hysterical baby's, had been propped in a corner. If Davis's closet still wouldn't open, could I fob that off on him as a temporary fix? Other than that, nothing in the room seemed worth salvaging. There were hideous tables and rump-sprung old chairs with torn upholstery that ran the stylistic gauntlet from lion's claw feet to motel modern. There were no autographed baseballs, no valuable art. If there had been any Chivas Regal, I might have taken it myself.

Against one wall a barrel of wastepaper threatened to overflow. I was absentmindedly pressing the paper deeper into the barrel with my fist when a yellow legal pad tumbled from it and fell to the floor. The top pages were blank, but as I picked the pad up, a page flipped open, revealing something wonderful.

Using nothing but a pencil, some genius, some kindred spirit had made a fantastic caricature. There was skinny-necked E. Bertram Davis himself, sitting behind a desk, incisors bared, sharp and glittery as stilettos. The best part was the nose. It was Davis's nose, no cute button to begin with, grown gigantic! And, even more outrageous, his eyes, those little, glinting hideous things, appeared to be peering cross-eyed down the nose, focusing on its inflamed glaring tip.

That nose. Those eyes. What a sight! It temporarily took my mind off Kate's carton. Hoping to find some more of the artist's work, I flipped through the pad. There was only that one drawing. Enthralled, I sank into a chair. Who had done it? Was the artist someone like me, just passing through Nutley, or was it someone who had known and hated Davis for aeons?

The crackle of the speaker on the ceiling overhead broke into my thoughts. The paging system operated by Nutley's operators was still far from perfect. A long squeal of static came next. Then the awful message:

"Freddie Ferguson and Bonnie Indermill. Please report to room twenty-eight sixty-two right away. Ms. Hamilton would like to see you."

The operator had a teary my-love's-gone-and-left-me delivery. Figures, doesn't it?

My stomach flipped. Why did I care so much? Fear played a part. Kate's temper could be scary, and I surely hadn't seen her at her worst. But when you really break down what I was feeling, it wasn't all fear. I mean, what could Kate actually do to me? She wasn't allowed to hit me. This isn't one of those countries where servants get slapped in the face.

Kate could fire me, I suppose, but would she? In the middle of the move? Okay, so I wasn't exactly the relocation heavy hitter I'd led them to believe. I still knew more than anybody else there.

No. I think that my anxiety came down to this: I'd given my word, one woman professional to another. The other professional woman had accepted my word. And I'd flat out failed. Technically the failure wasn't mine. I hadn't touched the damned carton. But . . .

A shroud of job memories possessed me then. A series of upbeat interviews rolled through my mind, followed by half a dozen enthusiastic first days when the bloom was still on my professional rose. Office manager, data-base manager, fund-raiser . . .

And now, after less than a week at Nutley, my relocation heavy hitter hash was about to be settled.

My thoughts strayed back to the house my parents live in, the house that waited for me. I pictured myself sprawled across my bed with the pink chenille spread. Okay, so the wallpaper was childish. That was easily rectified. I had more closet space in that one room than I had in my entire Manhattan apartment. And now I wouldn't have to share the second bathroom with my brother Raymond.

Hell! Suburban New Jersey isn't so bad. Mall walking, done at a good clip, can be invigorating.

The speaker crackled again. "The new cafeteria is opening tonight," the operator announced. "The special will be Caesar salad, turkey turnovers, and for dessert, a chocolate surprise." A pause, some static, and then she started tormenting me again: "Will Freddie Ferguson and Bonnie . . ."

She'd sounded spunky enough about the turkey turnovers, but she delivered this second announcement slow and somber, the way the warden in an old prison movie says, "Do you have any last requests, son?" My heart sank at the sound. Shouldn't have killed that cheatin' woman, son. Shouldn't have shot that convenience-store clerk, boy. Shouldn't have lost that carton of paperwork, Bonnie Jean Indermill.

Carton of paperwork!

Snap out of it, Bonnie Jean!

Sinking back in the chair, I gave the speaker on the ceiling a dirty look and said out loud, "Lighten up, lady. The cure for cancer wasn't in Kate's carton."

"You can bet she's going to act like it was."

It was Cornelia from Security, looking guilty.

"Ms. Hamilton sent me to find you. She's looking for Freddie and that Finkelstein kid, too. The one with the red hair. You seen him?"

"No, but if I had I wouldn't tell. What's her problem, anyway? It's nothing but a box of papers."

The other woman lifted her shoulders and let them drop. "I don't know. Something's been bothering Kate. A personal matter, I think. I was supposed to meet with her earlier today, but she canceled. Too busy."

I got up slowly. "Do I get a last supper or anything?"

"I could go find the kid and tell her I couldn't find you. Maybe she'll take it all out on him."

"No. I'll be a man about this." As I stood, I held the drawing of Davis so Cornelia could see it.

She laughed. "Isn't he a sight! You do that?"

"Goodness no. I'm in enough trouble. I found it in the trash." Tearing the page from the pad, I rolled it into a tube. "I think I'll keep it."

"Yeah," she said. "Around here you need all the laughs you can get."

I ran into Freddie on the way to Kate's office. When he greeted me with a smile, I realized he didn't know what was coming. I wasn't surprised. He'd done a good a job of staying out of sight the day before.

"I understand Kate wants to get into a huddle with us," he said.

Huddle! Kate probably wanted to do a number of things with me and Freddie, but I suspected we were in for more of a scrimmage than a huddle.

When we walked into Kate's office, she nodded at the chairs in front of her desk. "Have a seat, both of you."

I felt like I was lowering myself into the electric chair. As I might have expected, Kate's office was already in pretty good shape. Her bookcases were full, her desktop organized. Empty cartons were stacked against a wall, waiting to be disposed of.

"I understand you have no idea what's become of one of my cartons, Bonnie," she began. "True?"

I nodded.

"I've got Cornelia looking for that boy," she said. "You know the one?"

"Billy Finkelstein."

"Yes. Billy Finkelstein. Since you have no explanation for what happened, and"—Freddie got an especially nasty look here—"I'm sure you won't, perhaps that boy—"

From the corner of my eye I saw Freddie turn toward me. "Bonnie! Don't tell me one of our shots missed the basket."

I almost felt sorry for him. Wait until he found out that several dozen of our shots were rolling all over the court and under the bleachers. "Yes, Freddie. One of our shots—"

"Speak English, for heaven's sake," Kate snapped. "Important confidential papers of mine have been lost!"

Freddie let out a gasp. The man was sincerely and utterly baffled. "I don't understand how that happened, Bonnie."

"Neither do I, but it happened."

"That's all you've got to say? That's a nitwit answer." That was Kate, of course.

"It's an honest answer. I can also say that I've spent most of the morning looking for that carton, that I've searched the other building and every holding room—"

"You assured me the system was foolproof."

"When I told you that, I thought it was foolproof. Pretty much."

" 'Pretty much foolproof'? I see. Now come the disclaimers." Kate glanced toward her doorway. "I believe, Bonnie, that you underestimated the caliber of fools currently working at Nutley. Come in," she barked.

Billy took a few steps into the room. Unlike my boss, the poor kid knew he was in for a hard time. Never what I'd call a prepossessing specimen, Billy positively drooped. His shoulders sagged. His focus was glued to the carpet.

"Yesterday I watched you put one of my cartons on a dolly. RIGHT DESK DRAWER was written on it. Do you remember that?"

"Yes, ma'am."

"And you're aware that that carton didn't get here."

His lifted his gaze and his eyes searched mine. I recognized a desperate plea for help.

"Billy's been helping me look for it," I said.

"Billy's helping you look?" Kate's voice rose dangerously. "I doubt if Billy could find an elephant if it was lost in this room."

Kate looked from Billy to Freddie and finally to me. "Now, what is going to be done about my missing carton?"

Freddie made the mistake of opening his mouth. "As manager of Firm Support Services, I suggest that a team—"

Kate drummed her fingertips on her blotter. "Oh please, Freddie. The only thing you support with any success around here is your drinking habit."

Freddie grunted as if he'd been punched. I was afraid to look at him. On my other side, Billy's fingers twitched against the fabric of his pants.

"Did you put anything with a monetary value in the carton?" I asked. "Otherwise, a couple of associate evaluations will have to be redone, but . . ."

Kate's eyebrows shot up. "What difference does it make what was in the carton?"

"It makes a big difference. If it's just papers that are missing, the carton is sure to turn up."

Kate sat quietly for a moment. "It's just papers," she admitted, "but there were confidential documents. And my monthly tickler file. I depend on it." She waved her hands helplessly, a gesture that surprised me. "I'm lost without it—"

A knock at the door interrupted her. Sam walked in and stood beside his son.

"I hear one of your cartons is missing. I'm the one you should be talking to. Billy doesn't know anything."

He sounded firm but not angry. Not yet.

"I'm inclined to agree that Billy doesn't know anything," Kate responded. "Nevertheless, it was Billy who loaded the carton on the dolly and took it away."

Maybe the presence of his father gave Billy courage, or

maybe he didn't want to seem like a wimp in front of Sam. Whatever, Billy spoke up.

"Yeah," he said, omitting the 'ma'am' this time. "And the minute I was out of your sight I ripped it open so I could read all your confidential documents and go through your tickler file. Like I give a flying f—"

Sam said, "That's enough."

It wasn't enough for Billy. "Sometimes shit happens." After he'd said this to Kate, he gave a bored shrug and added, "So shoot me."

Kate went ballistic. "Don't tempt me," she shrieked. She leaped from her chair, darted around her desk, and shouted into Billy's face; " 'Sometimes shit happens'? That's all you've got to say for yourself?"

Sam stepped between the two of them, shoving his son back as he did. "Billy doesn't have to say anything for himself, but what he means is, things occasionally get lost. They almost always turn up." He bent and stared into Kate's eyes. "When it's paperwork that's lost, it always turns up. People do not steal paperwork."

"Oh," Kate said. "First I had Bonnie's guarantee of 'foolproof.' Now I have your guarantee that it's going to turn up? Why don't I believe you?"

Billy, his courage now running wild, tried stepping around his father. Sam gave him a quick look. "You've got work to do."

"Yeah, but—"

"So go do it."

Billy stalked from the room. A second later he poked his head back through the door. His eyes glistened. The poor kid was on the verge of tears. He wiped his hand across his face to pull himself together, then glared at his father. "I could've handled it fine. You didn't have to butt in." He turned his attention to Kate. "I'm not as stupid as you think, and you better not keep saying that about me."

On that cheerful note, he left.

Freddie cleared his throat. He'd been so quiet through all of this that I'd almost forgotten he was there. We all looked at him, each in our own way. I couldn't tell what

Sam was thinking. I was hoping, against all evidence to the contrary, that my boss would say something intelligent to cool everybody down and get me out of that office. Kate stared at Freddie contemptuously, tapping a toe. Once again I noticed her shoes—those sexy sling-backs. Does she get them at a big discount? I wondered. They sure didn't seem to fit her personality.

Freddie rubbed his hands together and stood. "I had better climb back into the ring." He hurried—slithered—from Kate's office. The snake.

That left me and Sam. Not for long.

Kate had circled her desk. When she sat down, I was surprised to see that she looked more sad than angry.

"If my carton doesn't turn up . . ."

Here it came, the "You're fired." My body tensed in the chair. My fist closed tight around the caricature of Davis I'd torn from the yellow pad.

Kate put both elbows on her desk and rested her forehead in her palms. Shaking her head slowly, she mumbled, "Both of you please get out of my office. And shut the door behind you."

I followed Sam into the hall. My kiss, that nutty impulse from the night before, was the last thing on either of our minds.

"What a bitch," he said. "What's her problem, anyway?"

"She's . . ." Freddie's words came back to me. "A difficult woman."

"Difficult? She's a flaming lunatic. Somebody ought to put her out of her misery." He rubbed his temples with his fingers. "I am wrung out. I'm going to the warehouse. Maybe a shower and a nap will help."

I nodded. "See you later."

"How late are you going to be here?"

"I don't know. Not as late as last night."

"Me neither. There's no point in killing ourselves for people like that woman." Sam studied me intently for a moment. "Billy's not bad, you know."

I nodded. "I like him."

We started down the hall.

"He got in trouble when he was fifteen. Stolen car, joy-riding. The usual," Sam said. "He straightened out, though. Graduated high school. Then his mom died around Christmas. He's been hell to live with ever since. I probably haven't been much fun for him, either," he added.

Well, if nothing else had come out of this, I knew about the wife. Dead. How awful. It sure put Kate's missing carton in perspective. Billy was right: sometimes shit happens.

Friday night around nine-thirty.

"Party time!"

The words boomed from the ceiling speakers. I didn't believe them. It was a male voice. Men didn't speak over the loudspeaker system. I'd worked too hard, and was having aural hallucinations. There were no parties at Nutley. There was nothing at Nutley but work. Work and heat. It was 150 degrees in the building. Okay, I exaggerate. But it was hot!

"All litigators, staff, and consultants report to the big conference room on twenty-eight immediately. And that goes for the movers and anybody else who's crazy enough to hang around here on a Friday night."

By then I had recognized Andy's voice. There was a burst of giggles, and the sound of a microphone being grappled over.

"We've got a couple cases of beer, a few sacks of chips . . ."

The speaker went dead.

I was on the twenty-fifth floor. I took the interior stairs two at a time, and the conference room was already crowded by the time I got there. Andy waved when he saw me.

The junk furniture had been compressed into a pile at one end of the big room. Someone had put a plastic sheet over a section of the rosewood conference table. And on that plastic sheet sat sacks of potato chips and pretzels and two buckets of ice filled with sodas and beer.

Margaret walked into the conference room behind me.

Her eyes followed my hand into the ice bucket and watched disapprovingly as I extracted a beer. First cigarette butts, now liquor. What was next? I was on a fast slide into the gutter.

I popped the top on the can, took a long swallow, and grinned at her. "There is a god," I said.

Whatever Andy was talking about with Harriet Peterson and Rhonda had him so worked up that his arms were slicing the air. He laughed when he heard my comment.

"That's me. The God of Parties." His eyebrows shot up as Margaret reached into a bucket. "Don't tell me *you're* going to worship at my altar."

Margaret smiled stiffly. "I'll have a Diet Coke, thank you."

Andy whispered to Harriet, and she let loose a high-pitched giggle. That ended abruptly—mid-tee-hee—when her boss, E. Bertram, walked in.

The God of Bad Times put a stop to the God of Parties, fast. "You ready for me to take a look at that summation?"

Andy's smile disappeared. Draining his beer, he lifted the can and executed an overhand toss across the table and into the trash basket. "Just need to put on a few finishing touches," he said to Davis on his way from the room.

I took a handful of chips and washed them down with another slug of beer. I'd passed on the cafeteria's opening that evening and given myself over to the God of Fat and Pimples.

From across the room, Davis's eyes locked on mine. I tensed. One corner of his upper lip lifted. I braced for a verbal assault.

"Freddie Ferguson tells me he found the source of the odor. An air duct. My office smells much better already."

It was a smile Davis was showing me. The man had a smile that looked like a sneer. I tried to return it, but I was overcome with anger at Freddie.

My boss was one of the last to get to the conference room. He poked a cautious head through the door, and his eyes darted around the crowd. I sidled up to him.

"Kate's not here."

"Oh. Well, maybe I'll stop in for a second." Glancing at me, he whispered, "It's correct, isn't it, that the odor in Davis's office has been eliminated?"

"Yes."

Freddie mopped his brow with a handkerchief and made a beeline for the beer. With that security blanket in hand, he headed for Davis. I smoldered as Davis thanked Freddie for getting rid of the smell. I'm surprised smoke didn't come out of my ears when I heard Freddie take the credit and claim that he had "played hardball" with the smell.

"But I'm still having trouble with those cabinet doors sticking," Davis told him. "I got the closet open, but that's about it."

"I'll tackle that one first thing in the morning," Freddie responded.

Talk about a sneer. I can imagine what my expression was like when Hillary walked in.

"What's wrong?"

"Nothing."

Like me, Hillary had pulled her hair back. Without the hair hanging down its sides, her face was prettier than I'd realized. As I've said, she had inherited her father's sharp features. She had the advantage of youth, though, and if her disposition didn't go completely to hell, she might not end up looking like him. She was wearing a Five Finkelstein Boys T-shirt. It hung almost to her knees, but the color was good on her.

"You look nice in green," I said. "You should wear it more."

The girl grinned. "Instead of basic black, you mean? That's what my mother always says. She says that my friends and I look like vampires."

Hillary stuffed a handful of chips in her mouth, then studied her watch. "I haven't seen Billy in a while. Have you?"

I shook my head.

"He told me Kate was rotten to him."

"She was rotten to all of us."

"She was rottenest to Billy," the girl said bitterly. A bit

of E. Bertram appeared in her frown.

"Kate will get over it," I countered, but I wasn't actually sure of that. Kate was so obsessed with her stupid carton that she could carry its loss to her grave.

Hillary's eyes flickered across the room. Her father was thundering away about some ghastly legal brief he'd filed. Freddie, the toady, was trying to look as if he really cared about the filthy thing. Rhonda, showing an intelligence I hadn't credited her with, had escaped from Davis's group and cornered one of the men from Pagano Woodworkers.

Hillary leaned in closer. "Look how Rhonda's neck sags. She's not aging well. That's what my mother would say."

A wave of affection for Hillary's mother, a woman I'd never even seen, rushed over me.

"Grommets."

That was Jonathan. He was wearing jeans—with a neat crease, of course—and a polo shirt. In his hand was a soda; in his eye, a demented gleam.

"Grommets," he repeated.

How could a man who looked so good be such a stiff. Pretending I didn't hear him, I turned away. Hillary, the stinker, had disappeared.

"No word yet?" asked the persistent devil.

"None."

His business with me finished, Jonathan said to another associate who was unfortunate enough to be standing close by, "You hear about that new insurance case? Tomorrow I'm deposing a witness . . ."

I'm sure my eyes glazed over. I stood, sipping my beer and enjoying my potato chip dinner, as Jonathan went on and on. It took Sam Finkelstein's arrival to wake me up.

Sam had put his time out of the building to good use. He looked rested, he'd shaved, he'd traded his green tee for a short-sleeved striped shirt. I couldn't look at him without remembering that kiss. My face grew warm. What had gotten into me? Sure, he'd liked it, once he adjusted to it. But talk about making a fool of yourself!

Sam took a beer and then joined our group. "I have a

copy of our bill," he said to me. "Are you the one I should talk to about that?"

The associate Jonathan had been droning on to grabbed this interruption like a drowning man grabbing a life preserver and slipped away. Jonathan was left with his mouth open and nobody to talk to. He had no interest in Sam or Sam's bill, and only a grommet interest in me. Looking past us, he scanned the room.

On the other side of the conference table, Davis was now holding court with a deadly account of a motion for summary judgment. Jonathan charged around the conference table. "You have a minute for me, Bert? I'm deposing a witnesses in that product liability . . ."

Oh, spare me.

So I was left with Sam. And Sam's bill. And I was close to tongue-tied. When he had finished his beer, Sam cleared his throat.

"About our bill. Maybe you'd like to go over it."

He sounded strangely formal, almost as if he'd rehearsed his words. Had the scene with Kate turned him against the whole bunch of us, me included? Or was it that kiss?

"Now?"

"If you have a few minutes."

Oh, my. Here he was, standing not two feet away from a kissing fool, and he wanted to talk about his bill.

"You're not planning to quit now, in the middle of the job, are you?"

"Of course not."

Bursts of a conversation about expert witnesses assaulted us from the other side of the conference table. "Bring in our own expert . . . ," Davis trumpeted.

"Let's get out of here," Sam said.

I followed him from the room and started toward the elevators, but Sam stopped me. "No. Let's go this way."

We walked around the corner, down the corridor, and, eventually, to the western end of the twenty-eighth floor. It was quiet there. Most of the office lights were out and some doors were shut. I was surprised when Sam tried the door to Davis's corner office.

"What are you doing?"

He shrugged, distracted. Kate's door stood open, but her office lights were out.

"This will do. We can see it in here."

"You're nuts," I said. "I don't want to look at your bill in there. I don't want to do anything in there, ever again."

"Come in for a second," he pleaded. "She's probably gone."

Giving in, I stepped into the room and reached for the light switch. Sam put his hand over it.

"No lights. Come over here." He ushered me ahead of him until I stood at the window facing southeast.

The moon was full and gigantic—a bright ornament, a silver filigree ball in the sky.

"Wow."

Sam put one of his hands on my waist. "Do you like it? It would be better out Davis's window, but this isn't bad."

"It's wonderful." A delightful thought danced through my head. "You don't really have your bill with you."

"Of course not."

It was inevitable. I turned in Sam's arms. This time it was his lips that found mine. His hand moved up my side, slipped beneath my shirt onto my bare skin. My knees felt as if they would give out.

There was a noise outside the office. A scrape, like a chair rubbing against a desk drawer.

We jumped apart, sinners caught in the act.

The hall outside the office was quiet now. At the door, I looked both ways.

"Nobody's there," I whispered. "This makes me nervous."

"We can go to my place."

"The warehouse?"

"God, no. Huntington."

Sam and I looked at each other through the dim light. There wasn't any doubt about what we both had in mind.

"The Waldorf's closer," I said.

•   •   •

It was 11:00 P.M. Sam had given me a fifteen-minute head start so that we wouldn't be seen going into the hotel together. You've never seen anyone take a shower as quickly as I did. I'd just knotted my robe's tie—thank God I'd brought my slinky red one instead of my fuzzy pink number—when there was a knock on my door.

I took a quick peek through the peephole to make sure I wasn't letting just any maniac in, and then opened the door.

A lock clicked across the hall. As I moved aside to let Sam in, the door opposite mine swung wide. Margaret Brusk lowered a room-service tray onto the floor. When she straightened, she blinked her dark, don't-miss-a-trick eyes right at us. The corners of her mouth plunged in disapproval. Her forehead folded like a deflated accordion.

As I closed the door, Sam and I heard Margaret's opinion about what was going on: "Unbelievable!"

Sam raised his hand to my throat and ran his fingers beneath the collar of my robe. "Looks like your reputation in this neighborhood is shot."

"I'm moving tomorrow."

"Good idea." His fingers were under the silky fabric. His hand slipped down, caressing my bare skin, until it reached the loose knot at my waist. So much for Margaret.

8

MONDAY MORNING I WAS IN A TERRIFIC mood, and it didn't have a thing to do with corporate relocation. I'm sure there was a goofy smile on my face when Davis caught up to me.

I had just pried the lid off my coffee. Davis roared into my office and jutted his bony head over my desk. I studied his face, easily done since it was inches from mine. For a second I thought that his murderous expression was actually another smile, but no such luck. This time it was a real, world-class sneer.

"The damned thing smells worse than ever! I've had to move out. I'm working in an associate-sized office!"

God forbid! My response to that was as brilliant as one his daughter might have given him. Maybe it's part of the language of love.

"Huh?"

"And my built-in cabinets the firm paid a fortune for still stick whenever the air-conditioning isn't working. Which, if you haven't noticed, IS MOST OF THE TIME. AND MY MARBLE AND BRASS SCALES OF JUSTICE, PRESENTED TO ME BY THE BAR ASSOCIATION, HAVE BEEN STOLEN, AND SOMETHING HAS BEEN SPILLED ON THE CARPET . . ."

He was speaking in GREAT BIG LETTERS this time, just short of a shout.

". . . AND RHONDA TELLS ME TWO OF MY CUR-

TAIN PANELS ARE MISSING!''

I opened my mouth.

''AND I WON'T PUT IT ON MY DAMNED PUNCH LIST! AND FURTHERMORE, I BELIEVE YOU ARE RESPONSIBLE FOR THE CONDUCT OF THE MOVERS. WHAT DO YOU KNOW ABOUT MY DAUGHTER'S LATEST FIASCO?''

I shook my head.

''THAT'S WHAT I FIGURED!''

His departure was even faster than his arrival.

I felt lazy and happy, and not particularly upset. I had met the man of my dreams. For a laugh, I rummaged into my top drawer and dug out the caricature of Davis. Who was the artist? Davis's own daughter? I'd never seen Hillary's artwork, but if this was an example, the kid was brilliant.

After putting the picture safely away, I drank my coffee and played back my phone messages. There was the usual litany of scratches and breaks, but not a word from Kate Hamilton or her secretary. Life was okay. No. Life was great.

I wandered next door to the office Freddie was supposedly occupying. There wasn't even a pencil on the desk. His still-packed cartons were stacked against a wall. I was beginning to have serious doubts about whether Freddie had spent any time at all there. He knew where it was. He'd gotten my first note. I left him another, terse, one: ''The smell is back.'' He'd know what it meant. I also left him a preliminary list of things that had been lost in the move. Let him worry about them.

Somewhere along the line Hillary had decided I was all right. When she showed up—late, as always—she plopped herself in my guest chair, a cup of coffee in her hand, her headset around her neck, her portable tape player clipped to her belt.

''Bonnie?''

Until that moment, I hadn't really focused on her face. I did then, but I couldn't quite believe what I was seeing.

''What's that?''

She touched the glittering gold spot on her nostril and said casually, "I had it pierced. Billy had his ear pierced. My ears are already pierced, so I decided to have my nose done."

"Jesus."

"It's no big deal. Can I ask you something?"

"Sure." I couldn't take my eyes off her nose.

"Do you think eighteen's too young to get married?"

Hillary was just full of surprises this morning. I chewed my bagel slowly, as if giving her question a lot of serious thought. I wasn't. Having traipsed down the aisle in a loopy teenage daze myself, my feelings on the subject are pretty strong. "Yes," I said finally.

"Harriet told me you're divorced. How old were you when you got married?"

"Eighteen. It was a disaster. Are you and Billy talking about getting married?"

"No," she answered, shaking her head. "He hasn't said anything about it. I was just wondering. What about living with someone?"

"I thought you were going to college."

"I'm supposed to, but I'll really miss Billy. When Crisis goes on the road, I'll never see him. They're going to make it big," she went on dreamily. "They're so cool. You and Sam could come hear us some night if Sam wasn't such a jerk about Crisis. Billy has to sneak out whenever he's got a gig."

So she already knew about me and Sam. I let it pass.

"And what would you do if you traveled with Crisis?"

"Oh, I could be . . . well . . . I could do lots of things." A huge smile spread across her face. "I've already got one job with them. I'm going to design their first album cover."

"Crisis is doing an album?"

"Not yet, but they're so fantastic it has to happen."

Crisis was "so cool," "so fantastic." I loved Hillary's enthusiasm. It made me a little sad, too. One day, I thought cynically, she's going to realize she was "so naive."

I changed the subject. "I understand the smell is back in your father's office."

"Oh, yeah." Pulling her headset over her ears, Hillary turned on her tape player, left my office, and began unpacking a carton. The smell in her father's office was even less important to her than it was to me.

I managed to find enough to do to keep me away from Davis all morning. There were, after all, eight other floors full of griping lawyers and staff. It was noon when I got to the twenty-eighth floor's south side.

Someone had put two fans in Davis's office. They spun furiously, churning the sweltering air. The view that he had fought for was a mixed blessing, at least with the air-conditioning out. It was probably ten degrees hotter on that side of the building.

Rhonda stood in Davis's open door. As always, she looked as if she'd stepped straight out of a Seventh Avenue showroom. Everything was oversized except for the minuscule skirt. When she saw me she started up right away.

"Did Bertram tell you that some things have been stolen? I counted the curtain panels Friday and there were eight. Now there are six. That fabric is imported from France."

"Good afternoon, Rhonda," I said.

"And the carpet already has to be cleaned. Some workman must have spilled something. Maybe that's where the smell is coming from. I can't tell."

Curiously, this time the smell was strongest just inside Davis's door. As I moved farther into the room, it faded. Back at room's entrance, I took a deep breath. I was right. The smell was coming from the built-in coat closet just inside Davis's door. Could the strange laughing man have gotten onto the floor and into the office? It seemed impossible with the warnings we'd given the lobby guards. I yanked on the closet door, but it wouldn't budge.

Harriet wasn't at her desk. Using her phone, I called Cornelia. "The smell is back."

"That can't be. Even if the sucker got by the lobby guard, the elevator service to twenty-nine has been turned off since your first encounter with him, and you need a key for the stairs."

"I don't think it's in the duct this time," I said. "It seems to be coming from Davis's closet. The door's stuck, though."

"I'll come check it out."

"You better bring someone with tools."

At the desk next to Harriet's, Margaret's fingers were moving quickly over her keyboard.

"Good afternoon, Margaret. How are you today?"

She answered by crinkling her face into a prune and asking the question that wouldn't go away: "Have you located Ms. Hamilton's carton?"

"I've been busy with other things."

With an eyebrow cocked, Margaret said, "Yes, I know."

"Is Kate still upset?"

"I haven't seen Kate today. She must have had a meeting that isn't on her calendar."

"Maybe she's with her lost carton," I said.

Margaret didn't think that was funny. Pushing back her chair, she said, "I'll be back." She was at the other side of her partition when, as an afterthought, she returned and took her handbag from a drawer.

I stuck my tongue out at her stiff retreating back. The woman actually thought that in addition to scrounging for butts, drinking beer, and sneaking men into my hotel room, I might be a thief.

"Did you say one of Kate Hamilton's boxes is missing?" asked Rhonda. "There's something with Kate's name on it under Harriet's desk. I was down there looking for an extension cord so I could plug in these fans and . . ."

I got to my hands and knees. There was a fair amount of space under the secretarial desks. One glance, though, and I knew there was no lost carton there. There was a trash can, a coil of wires for the computer, the inevitable pair of shoes, and a big red accordion-type folder.

"It's not here."

"It was there a couple hours ago. A big red folder."

I dragged the folder from under the desk. Sure enough, the label on it read "Kate Hamilton."

It was a tickler file, with slots numbered one to thirty-one for each day of the month, exactly like the one Kate had put in the missing carton. This couldn't be the same tickler, though, could it? Maybe she had more than one of them, or maybe Margaret kept one for her boss.

It was August 16. I dug my hand into the slot numbered sixteen and withdrew a handful of papers. The first couple were letters to be answered. They were dated earlier in the month, so what I was looking at was current.

I was shoving the papers back into the slot when one of them caught my eye. Protruding from an envelope was the top third of a drawing done with colored pencils.

In offices you often see artwork done by children, grandchildren, nephews, and nieces. Curious about whether Kate had a soft spot for some child, I peeked at the drawing.

"Oh!"

"What's the matter?" Harriet had come from the supply room, her arms loaded.

The air-conditioning duct over Harriet's desk spit out a short gust of cold air, and the sheet of paper fluttered before my eyes.

"Harriet? Tell me what this looks like to you."

Craning her neck, Harriet focused on the drawing. After a second she reacted by dropping her entire armload of pencils, scratch pads, and paper clips.

"Eeeew! Where did you get that filthy thing, Bonnie?"

Rhonda's attention was diverted from Davis's problems. "What's filthy? Can I see?"

I laid the drawing faceup on the desk, and the three of us gaped. It was well-done, with realistic perspectives and skillfully handled colors. The people in the drawing weren't perfect—the artist didn't seem to have a knack for faces, or much interest in them, for that matter—but the details he had caught were . . . astonishing.

A man and a woman were depicted on a bright yellow bed. Sun poured through a window with yellow curtains. At one side of the bed, a blue lamp was perched on a table. The man on the bed boasted a friar's ring of white hair, a slight roll of fat at his waist, and his birthday suit. What appeared to be his discarded clothing—a red-and-white-striped polo shirt and khaki slacks—lay on the floor. On the third finger of his left hand a big gold ring shone. His right hand was lost between the woman's legs.

The woman, also nude, was slender, with small breasts. Her brown-gray hair fell straight to her shoulders. One of her hands fondled the man's genitals.

"That's Kate," Harriet said softly.

I pointed at the words typed along the drawing's bottom. Rhonda read them out loud, and Rhonda, out loud, was very loud indeed: " 'I see you all the time, you whore.' "

"Kindly watch that kind of talk around me." Margaret, handbag clenched firmly under her arm, was back. None of us paid any attention to her command.

"I have never seen anything so shocking," Rhonda said. An almost breathless squeak in her voice announced that she was enjoying this immensely. "Let's see if there are any other pictures here. Who do you suppose this fellow is, anyway? He's kind of cute."

"He's a little overweight, if you ask me," said Harriet, who is something of a health nut.

Rhonda tilted her head. "Oh, I kind of like them with meat on their bones." She started digging through the red folder.

The envelope the picture had come in was plain white and inexpensive. Kate's name and address were typed. There was no return address. The postmark was "10001—GPO." That's Manhattan's big General Post Office on Eighth Avenue.

"Here's another one," Rhonda squealed, holding up a second drawing.

The same couple was shown in different positions. There was different text, too. " 'You can't ever hide from me, you slutty bitch,' " Rhonda read.

"Kill," I whispered. The word on the stairway door hadn't been meant for me at all. The laughing stranger wasn't harassing random women at Nutley. He was harassing Kate Hamilton. Things began falling into place. Kate was getting not only obscene drawings, but obscene calls, too. The one I'd answered in Davis's office had been meant for her. The phone directory for the new office building hadn't been updated to indicate Kate's last-minute office switch with Davis. And the garbage in the duct. That had been intended for Kate, not Davis.

Margaret was glaring over the divider. "Do you mind! I'm trying to work. This is an office, you know, not a brothel."

With Margaret around, we weren't likely to forget that. Gripping Rhonda's wrist, I lowered it so that the drawing was out of Margaret's sight. Both my companions glanced at Margaret. It must have struck all three of us at the same time that we were snooping where we shouldn't be. I certainly didn't want to get Kate any more riled up than she already was.

Harriet was suddenly 110 pounds of efficiency. "You'd better put them back where you found them," she ordered me. "And get that tickler file away from my desk."

"It was under your desk. I wonder why?"

I didn't intend to accuse my friend of being the creative genius behind the drawings, but Harriet reacted as if I'd done just that. Hands on her hips, she snapped, "Well, it certainly doesn't belong there. I've never seen anything so disgusting in my life."

When we had put the drawings back, Harriet shoved the tickler across the counter between her desk and Margaret's.

"I believe this is yours."

"It's Kate's. Just leave it there."

"Does Kate use more than one of these tickler files?" I asked Margaret.

"Of course not. Why would she?"

"I don't know, but she packed one like this in the carton that's lost."

Margaret looked at Harriet. "Then what was it doing under your desk?"

"I'm sure I don't know," Harriet responded, "and I'll thank you to keep your things on your side of the partition."

The air-conditioning sputtered again. A cool wind from the vent fluttered across my damp neck. Davis rounded the corner and came at me like a bull coming at a red flag. A second later Cornelia arrived from the other direction, a Pagano man in tow.

I wanted to talk to Cornelia about the drawings, but first I had to get Davis out of my hair.

"The garbage isn't in the air-conditioning this time," I told him. "I think it's in your closet."

Cornelia, the Pagano man, and I followed Davis into his office. "In my closet," he was saying. "Now that's dandy. If you can get the door open without tearing the overpriced piece of junk apart . . ."

The man from Pagano—the same man Rhonda had latched onto during the party—set his toolbox down and took a deep breath. His nose crinkled.

"Man, this building is rotten."

"Save the commentary," grumbled Davis. "Open the damned door!"

The workman gave the knob a hard yank. The thing didn't budge. He tried raising the door on its hinges. No luck. Finally he took what looked like a plasterer's tool from his box.

"This might scratch the finish."

"Do it!" Davis barked. "I'm ready to have the whole unit ripped out."

While the Pagano man worked, Davis ranted. He went at me first, blasting me about the wall unit and the air-conditioning. I'd had nothing to do with either of them, but that didn't stop him for a second. Then he struck out at Cornelia. "Where the hell is Security while some nut is sabotaging my office?" Just on general principal, he screamed at Harriet through his open door. Spotting Rhonda cowering in his doorway, he brayed about his missing curtain panels.

"They didn't walk away. You must have miscounted." Slapping his forehead with the heel of his hand, Davis growled, "Why oh why am I surrounded by idiots?"

Rhonda's face crumpled as Davis paced the floor raving. Everybody involved with the move was a fool, everything in the new building was trash.

It didn't take long once the tool had been forced into the space between the door and the cabinet. A little wrenching, a little splintering of wood, a little cringing by the Pagano man. Standing back, he clenched the knob and gave another yank.

As the door burst open, Rhonda, whose view into the closet was obstructed by the door, clapped her hands. Possibly trying to lighten the general mood in the room, she squealed, "Voila!" Then she peeked around the door, gasped, and grew as quiet as the rest of us.

I don't know what the others were thinking as we stared into the closet. The whirring of the two fans was the only sound in the room. My mind went blank for a moment before I was rocked by a terrible understanding.

The upright body in the coat closet, no longer restrained by the door, shifted a few inches. One of us, maybe several of us, whispered, "Oh."

The body slid farther. At the door's protruding frame, its progress was stopped. There was another shift of weight before the body toppled from the closet. It tilted to one side as it fell. The blood-splattered silk curtain panels that covered its head and neck remained in place, but a patent slingback shoe had fallen free. Lying on the dark rug beside the bloated foot, it looked incredibly delicate.

Despite my shock, I knew that I was looking at Kate Hamilton's corpse.

9

FOR TWO DAYS THE NEWSPAPER HEAD-lines and television news shrieked. "Stalker Strikes in Park Avenue Sky-scraper." "Closet Is Counselor's Cof-fin." I liked the one that read: "Law Firm Employees Work in Terror." Think about it.

There were vague mentions of black-mail schemes, compromising materials—a nice way of saying dirty drawings—and a "cooperative eyewitness."

That was me, and the statement was mostly correct. I was cooperative as all get out, and I had witnessed "the Stalker," but I'd never really gotten close enough to the man to see his face clearly. I could tell the police only this: he was tall and thin, had frizzy light hair, and smoked like a locomotive.

Of all the headlines, my favorite was one in a morning tabloid that read, "Senior Partner Tried to Cover up Mur-der."

Again, the statement was mostly correct. The senior part-ner was Davis, that font of legal expertise, that pin-striped corner-office paragon. That blowhard.

I remember that we all stood, staring at the body, for what seemed an eternity. Davis, the Pagano man, and I were on the side of the body near the office's door. Cornelia and Rhonda were on the other side of it. Cornelia had made a guttural sound, and for a moment I thought I would be sick. Rhonda was making a high-pitched noise—less than a wail, more than a squeak—that careened off the room's bare surfaces. She had backed to a window and seemed unable to take her eyes off the body. Davis's mouth was opening and shutting but he was, for once, speechless. Only the Pagano man had anything sensible to say.

"I'm outta here!"

He dropped his tools and turned toward the door. Without a second thought, I started after him.

"Where do you two think you're going?"

Jumping in front of the man, Davis slammed the door, locked it, and braced his back against it.

"Nobody's leaving this room until I say so."

I guess it's a given that in any group, the person who carries the biggest stick is obeyed, at least for a while. Cornelia and I exchanged glances, but neither of us moved.

"We're all staying here until the M-COM decides how this should be handled," Davis said in what I must describe as a muffled roar. "And you," he growled at Rhonda. "Shut up! I can't think with that howling."

"But someone's killed Ms. Hamilton."

Davis's eyes flickered over the body lying a few inches from his wingtips. He bunched his shoulders and breathed hard a couple times.

"Killed her?" Lifting his hands, palms up, in one of those "Who knows?" gestures, Davis then said something incredible: "We don't know for certain that someone killed her."

Faced with that profound reasoning, Rhonda caught her breath, whimpered once or twice, and shut up.

At this point, Davis must have thought he had whipped his troops into line. He stood quietly, thinking things out, before speaking again.

"It may not be in the partnership's best interests if that"—another glance at the body—"is found in my office. The chairman retires next year. I'm a candidate for his spot." He looked at Rhonda, the only person in the room who might conceivably be sympathetic. "Something like this could ruin things."

The Pagano man shook his head as if he were hearing voices.

There was a knock on the door. "Is everything all right, Mr. Davis? I heard screaming."

"Everything's fine, Harriet. Rhonda saw a mouse. See if you can get the chairman on the phone."

"The chairman? For a mouse?"

Harriet's words made sense under the circumstances, but hearing them, Davis, this voice of calm reason who was blocking our exit from his office, went wild.

"JUST GET ME THE CHAIRMAN!"

The chairman of the firm, an ancient from the Tax Department, still had not moved into his new office. While Harriet called downtown, Davis shut his eyes tight. You could almost hear him thrashing his brain cells. Think. Think.

Another knock on the door. "The chairman's at lunch, Mr. Davis. I left word. Shall I try someone else?"

"NO!" Davis yelled over his shoulder. "GET BACK TO YOUR DAMNED DESK AND STAY THERE!"

With the shock of seeing the body on the floor, I had forgotten about the smell. It came back to me suddenly. My stomach churned. If I stayed in that room much longer, it was going to become even less inhabitable than it already was.

Cornelia moved toward the phone on Davis's desk.

"What do you think you're doing?"

"Calling the cops."

"I'll decide when it's time to do that."

"I'm the head of Security," she countered.

"And if you were any good at your job, this wouldn't have happened. We call the cops when I've spoken to the chairman." Wrinkling his forehead, he added, "Maybe we'll conference in the other members of the M-COM."

This lunatic actually intended to keep us trapped in that office with Kate Hamilton's body until he had a conference call? I've had some desperate moments in my life, but even during those I never thought up anything so outrageous.

"I don't think that's a good idea," I said.

"You don't think? What you think isn't important. The M-COM will decide how this should be handled!"

Cornelia's pent-up dislike of Davis burst free of its bonds. "You're out of your mind," she said angrily. "I'm not handling anything but that phone. And you can stop this M-COM bullshit. You going to make me a partner, a member of your fancy M-COM, pay me a million dollars a year if I go along with this trash you're talking?"

"Don't push your luck, lady. You touch my phone I'll make you unemployed. That's what I'll make you." His lips tightened into a mean wad.

"I'm going to be sick," I said.

Taking his eyes off Cornelia, Davis shot me an ugly glare. "Try to control yourself, woman!" He turned to Rhonda again. "The best approach might be to wait until the staff goes to lunch at one o'clock. Then we can call the M-COM in—"

"In?" asked Rhonda. "You mean we have to stay here with . . . it . . . until one?"

"I'm not staying," said the woodworker.

"Keep your voices down."

Rhonda let out a squeak. "I'm going to faint."

Cornelia had both hands on her hips. "That's the stupidest thing I've ever heard. Your clients find out you locked your staff up with a corpse for a half hour, you'll be the one who's unemployed."

As Cornelia and Davis continued their battle, I crept between Davis and Kate's body and made my way to the far side of his desk. I had the phone in my hand before Davis noticed me.

"Put it down!"

"No." I pressed the intercom button.

"No? You're standing in my office, being paid by me, and you're telling me no? If you value your job, you'll put that phone down."

He moved toward me, but another knock on the door diverted him.

"I told my moron secretary to stay at her desk," he complained.

"If there's a moron around here," said Cornelia, "it's you."

"Bertram?" The door knob jiggled. "I understand the odor has returned."

Freddie Ferguson, riding to the rescue.

"Harriet," I said into the phone. "Get the police here right away. Ms. Hamilton is dead."

"Dead? How do you know?" Harriet asked. "She's not even in the office yet."

"Trust me, Harriet. She's in the office, and she's dead. Someone murdered her. See if Tony LaMarca's on duty."

Davis showed me most of his teeth, a scary sight. " 'Murdered,' " he said from deep in his throat. "You had to say that, didn't you. Don't you ever come to me for a reference."

The Seventeenth Precinct is on Fifty-first Street between Park and Lexington avenues, so there was no fighting traffic. Five minutes after Harriet called, two detectives and three patrolmen had arrived.

My friend Tony LaMarca, an NYPD detective who was assigned to the Seventeenth Precinct, wasn't on duty that afternoon. Detective Kevin Connor was in charge of the team that showed up. Connor looked about sixty, though I knew he was younger. His suit looked about sixty, too. With the afternoon sun beaming through all eight of Davis's windows, the thing glowed.

I'd never met Connor, but I knew a little about him through comments Tony had made. A bachelor in his early fifties, Connor lived with his aging parents. He was, according to Tony, a careful, even fussy, policeman. He'd made detective not by being an aggressive cop, but by being a restrained one. Tony didn't actively dislike the other detective, but he didn't like working with him. He thought Connor was overly cautious and too quick to take the easy way out. Connor, according to Tony, wanted the job to be "neat," even when it couldn't be.

When this rumpled cop introduced himself and showed his shield, Davis tried to reclaim the control he'd lost.

Clasping the other man's hand, he did everything but gen-
uflect.

"Thank you for getting here quickly," the two-faced
bastard said. "I'm glad to see you, Lieutenant. I've been
. . . I've been . . ."

I cleared my throat. Cornelia muttered something unin-
telligible. Once again, words failed Davis. He couldn't very
well tell this cop that what he'd been doing was trying to
force his employees to sit around with the body until he
could gather the M-COM. His eyes darted from one of us
to the next. When his beady gaze met mine, I think there
was something new there—fear. Fear was an emotion Davis hadn't had much experience with, and a hint of confusion seemed to mingle with it. This was a man
accustomed to having absolute power, the captain of a well-
behaved crew. But this time the crew was out of control.
Mutinous. And they were going to get him in trouble.

Connor was eyeing Kate Hamilton's body sadly. "It's
not Lieutenant. It's Sergeant." He glanced at a pad he was
carrying. "We got this call a few minutes ago. Twelve-
forty. I take it that's when you found the body?"

It was like Hoover Dam let go. Everyone in the room
started talking.

The detective held up his hand. "Please! We have to do
this one at a time." He turned to me. "Is there a room we
can use, miss?"

How Connor knew that I was the room person I'll never
know. Maybe I just look like that type.

"You *have* to question us separately?" Davis croaked.

"Yes, Mr. Davis, I do."

They say a drowning man sees his life flash before him.
I hope that during those few moments, every tongue-lashing
he had ever delivered to a cowering employee, every sneer
he'd ever flashed across a desk at a stenographer, every
typo he'd ever raged over flashed through Davis's mind.

The office door was open now. I stepped into the hall
and breathed the relatively cooler air, decidedly fresher air.
Two of the patrolmen were cordoning off the hallway from
the far side of Margaret's desk to the far side of Harriet's.

Beyond their yellow crime-scene tape stood a knot of Nutley employees—Freddie and some others who hadn't gone to lunch.

Margaret sat weeping softly at her desk. Harriet Peterson stood next to her archenemy, urging a cup of hot tea on the distraught woman.

I waited my turn, and was finally questioned after four that afternoon. I gave Connor my version of finding the body. I also told him about the laughing stranger and the graffiti, and that I'd definitely seen the strange man once and possibly several other times.

When I talked about the obscene phone call I'd gotten, and about the obscene drawings in Kate's tickler file, Connor averted his eyes from mine and his cheeks flamed red. What a modest man for a cop. And what a pallid one, too. Once the blood left his face, the ashen tone of his skin was obvious.

"I saw the two drawings," he said, staring down at his notepad. "We've got them in evidence. As far as you know, that tickler file was in the missing carton?"

"That file, or one that looked exactly like it."

"And you saw Miss Hamilton put it in the carton and tape it shut?"

"Yes."

Connor yawned behind his hand. "Ugh. The air-conditioning in this building is terrible."

I was tired of explaining about the air-conditioning, and I sure didn't have to explain to Connor. He didn't even have a punch list. "Yeah," I said.

We were in an unoccupied associate's office down the hall from Davis's. The blinds were pulled and the lights were off, but with the door shut the room was stifling. The trash can was littered with coffee cups and soft drink cans.

Standing, Connor opened the door and had a whispered conversation with one of the patrolmen. When he returned to his chair, there was a second notepad in his hand. He flipped slowly through a couple of the pages, looking over the scratchy handwriting. When he found something that interested him, he scanned it silently, his lips moving as he read. His breaths were audible in the still room.

Finally looking up, he said, "I see there are some other cartons missing containing liquor, memorabilia."

I nodded. "That's not unusual in a big move."

Connor seemed to drop that subject. "Let's talk for a minute about some of the people around here. Do you know of anyone who had quarreled with Ms. Hamilton?"

"I had."

He examined the notes again. "She yelled at you about that missing carton. A couple of your movers were involved in that, I understand. And your office administrator."

I confirmed that there had been an argument, and that Freddie, Billy, and ultimately Sam had been involved.

Connor nodded thoughtfully and asked, "How bad an argument was it?"

I didn't know how to answer that. As arguments went around Nutley, it really hadn't been all that special. A little nastier than many, sure, but it had stopped a long way short of death threats.

"A boss-employee-type argument. Kate said nasty things to us, and we mostly sat there."

"Do you recall what she said?"

"Not exactly, no. She suggested that I was inept at my job."

"She called you a nitwit?"

Connor looked almost unhappy when he read that from the pad, like he didn't want to hurt my feelings. He needn't have concerned himself. What I felt was anger, not hurt. That had to have come from Freddie Ferguson. My boss was trying to make me look guilty.

"That's not quite right. Kate called something I said 'a nitwit answer.' "

"How did you feel about that, Miss Indermill? Would you like to talk about it?"

His question, put that way, took me back a number years. I once worked in a Montessori preschool. Our method of conflict resolution among our rambunctious four-year-olds involved questions exactly like Connor's. "How did you feel, Joshua, when Christopher hit you on the head? Would you like to talk about it?'' Nine times out of ten, little Joshua didn't want to talk about it. He wanted to kick Christopher in the behind. I felt exactly the same.

"Nobody likes being spoken to that way, Detective Connor," I said. "I don't suppose Freddie Ferguson liked being called a drunk by Kate, did he?"

I didn't experience any guilt when Connor shook his head and started jotting on his own pad. As I waited for him to finish, the sound of his breaths filled the little room. They weren't just audible; occasionally they came in gasps and his chest heaved.

"Are you okay?" I asked after an episode of this.

He looked up from the pad. "A touch of indigestion. Let's talk about Billy Finkelstein. What did Miss Hamilton say about him."

"Kate suggested Billy Finkelstein was a fool," I told Connor. "Or something like that."

"What about Sam Finkelstein?"

I ran my fingers through my hair. My scalp was starting to feel parboiled. "Sam didn't show up until things were almost over. He told Kate not to talk to his son that way. But he didn't lose his temper with her. He just told her that she should speak to him about moving problems."

"And after you, Ferguson, and Sam, and Billy Finkelstein left Miss Hamilton's office, what did you all talk about."

I ran the scene through my memory. "We didn't leave together. Billy went first, and Freddie a few minutes later. Sam and I left last. Kate asked us to go. She seemed exhausted." I paused, trying to remember what had happened then. "Sam and I talked for a second. He said he was going to get some sleep."

"Sam Finkelstein didn't say that somebody should put Miss Hamilton 'out of her misery'?"

My head spun. I'd forgotten. Sam and I had been alone in the hall when he'd said that. It hadn't been a threat. It had been a statement based on anger and fatigue. But where had Connor learned about it? This couldn't have come from

Freddie, unless my boss had been hiding in another closet. I tried to replay the moment. We'd been standing near Jonathan's office. Andy's, too. Sam hadn't shouted, but he hadn't whispered, either. Either Jonathan or Andy could have overheard him.

I felt woozy, unable to get my thoughts in order. "Sam did say that, but he didn't mean it, you know."

A sly smile flashed across the detective's face, making me wonder if he already knew that I was involved with Sam. Connor's eyes scanned the second notepad again. "Apparently that kind of thing runs in the Finkelstein family. Billy Finkelstein told a couple of people he wanted to 'punch her lights out.' Did you hear about that?"

I nodded, feeling awful.

"Miss Indermill," Connor said thoughtfully, "what do you suppose the chances are that the Finkelstein kid took the cartons containing the valuables?"

"No chance at all," I responded. "Where did you get that idea?"

Ignoring my question, Connor shifted his weight in the chair. He wasn't overweight, and even if he had been, he hardly touched the chair's arm. The chair was one of the new ones, though. The arm collapsed, and Connor almost went with it. Righting himself, he stared at the thing.

"I think some of them are defective. The arms fall off."

"They don't make them like they used to," Connor responded.

I thought this was Connor's idea of humor until I saw how sadly he was looking at that chair arm. He was serious.

"That will be it for now, Miss Indermill. Are you going to be around?"

"Sure." I was almost out the door when he said, "I understand you asked for Tony LaMarca when you contacted the precinct. You're a friend of Tony's?"

"Yes. And of Tony's wife." In fact, I'd been invited to a barbecue at their house the following Sunday.

"Oh, yeah?" Connor actually smiled. "Nice gal. Haven't seen her in a long time. What's her name? Terry. That's it. Terry. I was at one of their kids' confirmations."

It *had* been a long time. Tony's youngest kid was seventeen. "I'm a friend of Tony's second wife, Amanda."

"Oh."

Connor's smile faded so fast I hardly believed it had been there at all.

A blow to the back of the head had killed Kate Hamilton. The wound was narrow and long, an indentation of about three inches. Traces of green felt were embedded in it. The police thought it had probably been made by the marble base of Davis's missing scales of justice. This statue, which hadn't been found, was apparently about a foot tall, and heavy. Judging from the relatively small amount of blood present on the curtain panels and carpet, Kate's death had been almost instantaneous.

No useful fingerprints were found in the office. Any prints that might have been on the coat closet had been smudged by the Pagano man's efforts.

The condition of the contents of Kate's stomach indicated that she had died Friday night, sometime between nine and eleven o'clock. She'd had the turkey turnover—"shoe leather," according to Harriet—and the Caesar salad—"disgusting"—from Nutley's cafeteria. What a last meal! The food hadn't killed Kate, though. Other people had dined at Chez Nutley and lived to talk about it.

The police were able to pin down the time Kate had eaten almost to the minute because a number of people in the cafeteria had heard her scolding the cook afterward. "Garbage," she had called his first culinary creation for Nutley. "Not fit for the trash can!"

Her parting blast as she stormed from the cafeteria had been aimed at the cashier, a pretty young woman who began her job at Nutley with a sweet disposition.

"Tell your chef that he should market his chocolate surprise as a hockey puck. He'll make a fortune," she had shouted. "And you can also tell him it will be a cold day in hell before I eat here again!"

10

KATE WAS CREMATED ON THURSDAY, without ceremony. A memorial service for her was held on Friday morning at a Catholic church in Greenwich Village. I shared a cab from the office with Rhonda, Harriet, and Margaret. Isn't that something? The four of us, together in an enclosed space. We were on our best behavior. Not a potshot was fired, not a snide remark uttered.

Harriet was being especially kind to Margaret. Margaret, in turn, was being nice to me. She complimented me on my dark gray dress. I'm sure it looked a lot better to her than my slinky red satin robe. Rhonda was doing her part in the behavior department, too. Her voice, and her hemline, were sufficiently subdued. She'd even done something more or less modest with her hair. Why, I'd be willing to bet that during our cab ride even our thoughts were pure. Mine were. Needless to say, that was a situation that wouldn't last, but I did enjoy my short-lived saintliness.

Our ride began typically. The cabbie—Omar, according to the ID card on the glove compartment—was a short man with an indescribable, and almost incomprehensible, accent. He had barely pulled into Park Avenue traffic before he let his New York City cabbie fury loose in a fit of fist shaking, name calling and horn blowing. All this was directed at two hulking men in a vehicle easily twice the cab's size, but that didn't stop little Omar. He was ready to mix it up, right in the middle of Park Avenue. There was much shouting back and forth about licenses and nitwits and fools. When it was over, Omar glanced at us through the rearview mirror, and at Rhonda, who was in the passenger seat next to him. His look was expectant, hopeful even, as if he thought we might praise him.

Nitwit. Fool. Those had been some of Kate's words. She'd used one of them on me. She may have used them on the others, too. Probably had. Omar got nothing but cool silence from the virtuous load in his cab. It bothered him.

"Going to have lunch in the Village?" he asked after a few blocks of this. "My cousin has a place . . ."

Oh, sure. With our drab outfits and drabber faces, we looked like a jolly group out for lunch.

"We're going to a funeral," Harriet prissily informed him. After that, Omar just drove.

We got to the church a little early. It was an old stone one on a corner lot. Unlike most things in Manhattan, it had a wide green lawn, which was shaded from the midday sun by big oak trees. An ornate wrought-iron fence separated the lawn from the sidewalk. On one side of the church there was a portico supported by stone pillars. Thick, shoulder-high bushes edged it. An altogether pretty place.

The first person we met up with was Andy, who was pacing the sidewalk. Relief showed on his face when he spotted us. He was on his best behavior, too. He opened the door for us and thrust some money at Omar. That added to the flurry of confusion inside the cab. Rhonda had started rummaging through her purse and managed to drop coins and bills all over the front seat. Harriet was pushing a handful of bills over the seat back, and Margaret was grappling with the clasp on her bag and saying, "Please let me get it." I had pulled a ten out of my wallet and was doing my part to make a jumble of things. My, we were nice.

It took a few minutes to get that all straightened out. Finally we were on the sidewalk.

"I didn't want to walk in there alone," Andy said to us. "It feels . . . strange."

Margaret nodded. "Friends are a comfort at times like these."

Friends. This from a woman who, three days before, had barely spoken to any of us. This was truly amazing.

A wide staircase led to the church's double doors. The five of us had just started up them when a small black car pulled over to the curb. It sported a thick layer of dust, a blaring radio, and a muffler that needed help. A plastic bag served as one of the back windows, and the trunk was secured with a knotted rope. Billy was driving. Our group stopped on the steps.

Rhonda's lips pursed. Andy's jaw dropped. Harriet's eyebrows rose.

Margaret spoke for all of them when she said, "He doesn't belong here."

"Surely he's not planning . . . ," began Rhonda.

We all knew that the police had questioned Billy at length twice. We all knew that, initially, he'd had no alibi for most of two hours the previous Friday night. And we all knew that Hillary, after a day of silence, had come through with Billy's alibi. She claimed that between nine and eleven the previous Friday evening, she and Billy were together for all but the ten minutes she was at the party. They had spent their time together, claimed Hillary, "making out," first in the front seat of a Finkelstein Brothers moving van, and later in an empty office on the twentieth floor, a bombshell revelation which did nothing for her reputation, or for her father's disposition.

My companions on the church steps surely suspected that Hillary was lying about the amount of time she'd spent with Billy. I didn't just suspect it; I was convinced. At the party, Hillary had looked at her watch and said to me, "I haven't seen Billy in a while. Have you?" "A while" is a lot more than the few minutes she now claimed they'd spent apart. Needless to say, if Hillary was Billy's alibi, then Billy was Hillary's, but no one seemed particularly concerned about where the girl had been during that hour and fifty minutes.

We all stared as Hillary got out of the passenger door of the dirty black car. Would Billy dare join her? The car burped and belched its way down the street. Benevolence returned to our quintet.

In the spirit of the occasion, Hillary had worn black. But then, she generally did. I had noticed, though, that Hillary's outfits were becoming more "downtown." Less linen, more funk. Today, her black cotton sweater reached to her thighs. Beneath the sweater she wore black tights. Scuffed black combat boots completed the outfit. Her earrings were silver shoulder dusters, tarnished black. Only her nose ornament was "uptown"—a tiny pearl.

She joined us on the steps, and we all talked in soft, gentle voices for a few minutes. No one mentioned Billy.

I'm not sure what I expected to see when I walked into the church, but it wasn't a crowd. Somehow I hadn't thought about Kate as having many people who cared about her. During the short time I'd known Kate, a good deal of my time had been expended trying either to appease her or to avoid her. To me, the woman had been a horror, my own personal hair shirt. The more I kept out of her way, the better. It hadn't occurred to me that other people might not feel the same.

The front pews were full, and this was a pretty big church. Stragglers dotted the back pews. We found places for ourselves near the center.

The crowd was predominantly women. Were they all friends of Kate's? I wondered. Probably not. A woman like that—a successful career woman—would belong to a lot of professional groups. Her clients would be there, too. Did she have a large family? As the rows around me filled, I thought about how little I actually knew about the dead woman.

While we waited for the priest, I glanced around at the crowd. Cornelia was a couple of rows in front of us, sitting beside one of the men from Maintenance. Jonathan was in front of them. He had almost an entire row to himself, which says it all about his personality. The firm's partners had gravitated to the front rows. My boss, Freddie, the useless but political animal, had slipped in among them.

Just before the service started, Bertram Davis walked in.

He had survived the staff mutiny, the police grillings, and the press roastings. His future chairmanship may have been up in the air, but so was his chin. You've got to give it to these corner-office types: they know how to keep up appearances. Davis was with a tall, well-cared-for woman. About fifty, I guessed, but a very good fifty.

"Your mom?" I whispered to Hillary.

She nodded.

Mrs. Davis was wearing a dark Chanel-style suit. Style? It was probably the real thing. Her simple haircut had probably cost a hundred dollars. Her gold earrings caught the light streaming through one of the windows. Needless to say, Mrs. Davis did not wear a nose ring.

Poor Hillary. Now I knew what she was up against. Recalling my own mother's closet full of polyester pantsuits, I felt an almost aching nostalgia. She must have a dozen of them, mostly in pastels. They don't come from Saks. "Attention shoppers, in aisle six . . ." is a refrain that really gets my mother's blood racing.

Mrs. Davis glanced back at her daughter and acknowledged the girl with a nod. Hillary started fingering her nose pearl nervously. Understandable.

I looked past the girl. Standing at one side, near the entrance to a little chapel off the church's nave, was a police officer who was working with Sergeant Connor. More of them were probably spread among us, keeping their eyes open. I didn't see Connor, but that didn't mean he wasn't there.

A hush fell over the gathering as the priest stepped to the pulpit. He began talking, but he didn't deliver a sermon. He didn't talk to us about getting our souls saved before it was too late or anything like that. Instead, he talked about Kate. It sounded as if she was an old and dear friend, which she may have been. I wasn't surprised when my eyes started to sting. Until that time, I hadn't cried at all over Kate's death. That strikes me as odd, now that I think about it, because I cry easily. My tears often have nothing to do with my real feelings. I cry in movies I don't like and during speeches by politicians I'd never vote for. Why hadn't I cried over Kate? Maybe I hadn't taken the time. Maybe my life was so hectic that I had pushed the tears aside. Well, they'd been dammed up for four days, and nothing could stop them now. They gushed, then and there. Margaret glanced at me and nodded slightly. At last I had her approval. Frankly, I felt like a hypocrite. I'd been so unconcerned about crying over Kate that I hadn't even brought a tissue. Hillary, dry-eyed beside me, shoved one into my hand.

When I was more or less composed, I dug through my purse for my glasses. They're slightly tinted, and with them sitting on my nose I might not look so ravaged.

The priest was talking about Kate's legal career now. I was surprised to hear him say that Kate had done a lot of pro-bono work. I hadn't expected that of her. Pro-bono is work done without charge, "for the good."

As he spoke, the faint smell of cigarette smoke drifted past me. Who would smoke in a church? I had taken my hat off. Almost unconsciously, I fanned myself with its brim. Something—a movement—made me glance toward the chapel at the side.

It was him! The Stalker! His eyes swept over me before he turned away. He moved deeper into the little chapel, out of my sight.

My heart started thudding. It couldn't have been him. I was seeing things. I'd been so virtuous all morning that I was having a religious experience. I'd had a vision, intensified by my crying jag. But I *had* seen him. That fuzzy blond hair and lean frame. And a cigarette. Always a cigarette.

Half-standing, I glanced around the church, desperate to catch the policeman's eye. Margaret must have thought I was becoming hysterical. She put her hand on my arm and pulled me back down. I turned in the pew. The police officer had moved to the door of the church and was looking outside into the street. There seemed to be a commotion out there. People were shouting and horns were blowing.

Not only was the priest keeping his message sweet, but he was keeping it short, too. He was talking about eternal rest now. His voice was raised, not so much in fervor as out of necessity, the commotion outside having become louder. Car horns blared, and the congregation strained to hear the priest. I couldn't bring myself to shout and disrupt what was left of the service. Getting up, I began pushing past the other people in my pew. As I stumbled over Hillary's boots, she whispered, "Are you all right?" I shoved by, not answering.

In the chapel, the smell of cigarette smoke lingered but the man had disappeared. I glanced out into the church again, frantic. Where had the policeman gone?

There was a door at the chapel's side, beyond the altar. I pushed the bar that opened it and found myself facing the shaded portico. Was someone on the other side of the hedge? The leaves swayed, but I couldn't be sure they weren't moving in the slight breeze. Stepping outside, I let the door close behind me.

The path led me to the lawn. I didn't spot the man right away. A crowd had gathered around two cars that had collided across the street. Smoke was pouring from the hood of one of them. As I trotted up the sidewalk and through the gate, the howl of a fire engine split the air.

I spotted the man at the corner. It was the Stalker, I was almost sure of it. Not thirty feet away, on the church steps, a policeman stood. I shouted to him, but a fire engine roared through the intersection, drowning out my voice. The policeman went back into the church.

The Stalker was across the street by then, moving quickly toward Broadway. Traffic was backed up terribly. I skirted around gridlocked cars to get to the other side of the street. The Stalker had rounded the next corner. When I got to Broadway, I looked both ways. I was afraid that I'd lost him until I spotted the steps leading to a subway entrance in the middle of the block. There was nowhere else he could have gone.

As I ran down the subway steps, a train was pulling into the station. If it was his train, he'd be gone by the time I got to the platform. I took the steps two at a time, shoving

past people on them. There were tokens in my wallet, and
I rummaged for one as I ran.

A southbound train, going downtown and into Brooklyn,
was pulling out. The platform on that side was empty. On
the northbound platform, passengers waited, reading papers, peering up the track. I scanned their faces. Nothing.
And then I spotted someone at the far end, resting against
the other side of a big iron support. Only a leg—blue-gray
trousers—and a bit of a white T-shirt showed. Dropping
my token into the slot, I passed through the turnstile and
began walking toward that end of the platform.

When I got within twenty feet or so of the pillar, I tucked
my hair back behind my ears and pushed my hat down hard
over my head. There had been no hint of recognition when
his eyes passed over me in the church, but if this was the
Stalker, I didn't want to take a chance.

The man behind the pillar moved to peer up the track.
Recognizing the hair, I stopped dead. After a moment I
took a couple more steps, until I was within ten feet of him.
Then I stayed against the wall and tried to adopt that bored,
impatient expression you see on most subway riders' faces.
He really *was* impatient. He kept looking up the track, shifting from one foot to the other. Once he scared me by turning my way, but he only wanted to check the clock at the
platform's center.

A train's lights shone from way down the track. The
Stalker moved a couple of feet away from the platform's
edge, nearer to me. A local train, bound for the Upper East
Side, pulled into the station.

I got into the same car as the Stalker, but by a different
door. It was the middle of the day, not a heavy commute
time, and the car was only half-full. He sat down in one of
those isolated double seats at the end of the car. I took a
seat on the other side, toward the center. I tried not to look
at him, but my eyes kept shifting in his direction. There
was nothing for me to read, nothing to pretend to study.
Tension was building in my neck, and I rolled my shoulders, trying to relax.

We stopped at the busy Fourteenth Street station. A couple of people got off, and three dark-haired women carrying big pink shopping bags and herding a small army of cranky children got on. They all chattered excitedly in Spanish. The man stared at them for a moment, then closed his eyes. That gave me a chance to study him.

I guessed his age was about thirty. He wasn't a bad-looking man, but I found his features coarse. The bridge of his nose was flat and wide, his eyelids were heavy. His hair, as I've said, was light, and his eyebrows and lashes were so pale they were almost invisible. My muscle-crazed mind-set may have influenced my perception of his build, but the chest and shoulders under that white T-shirt looked puny to me. On his upper right arm he had a tatoo. I'm not a fan of tatoos even when they're done well, and this one was crude and ugly. A red heart pierced by a black arrow. A word, perhaps a name, was in script under it, but I couldn't make it out.

At Forty-second Street, the Spanish women and their children left the train. Two pretty girls of about sixteen got on and sat directly across from the Stalker. His eyes opened, almost as if he had radar, and he stared at them frankly until I could tell they were growing uncomfortable. At the next stop, those girls left the train. The man shut his eyes again.

Where was I going with this lunatic? I live on the West Side of Manhattan. I've worked on the East Side often enough, but above Eighty-sixth Street the East Side is pretty much a mystery to me. What if he was going to the Bronx? Did this train go to the Bronx?

I was worrying about all this when the conductor announced, "Seventy-seventh Street," and the train slowed.

The man's eyes opened suddenly, and he stared straight at me. I quickly glanced away. He hadn't recognized me in the church, and now I was wearing a hat. If he saw enough of me, though, something was going to click in his memory. Don't be paranoid, Bonnie. You're nothing to him. I focused on the tacky medical-office advertisements above the train's windows—bunion removal, liposuction, hair transplants, hemorrhoidectomys. One way or another, you can have the body you want.

Standing, the Stalker moved to the door. He was holding an unlit cigarette in his hand, twiddling it between his fingers. When the door opened, I walked out behind him. The word tattooed on his arm was *Ronni*.

I followed him out of the station, up the steps, and into daylight. The August sun was high overhead now. Lunchtime. People were filing into the neighborhood cafés. It's an affluent, stylish neighborhood, but I didn't have time to so much as glance in a store window. We walked west fast, the Stalker half a block ahead, not waiting for lights, crossing Park and Madison. He had managed to light the cigarette without slowing. When he crossed Fifth Avenue, he turned north along Central Park.

He was moving so quickly I could hardly keep up. My shoes were for funerals and interviews, not for tailing nervous skinny psychopaths. My dress was made of a material that bears no relationship to any product of nature. It clung to my damp skin like plastic wrap.

I followed him across a wide plaza, past a fountain, and to the stairs that lead to the Metropolitan Museum. This lunatic, stalking Kate, making obscene calls and sending her obscene drawings, an art lover? Then again, those obscene drawings had been pretty good.

Up the stairs we went. You try that at a fast trot in August in tight heels! He was across the museum's big central hall in a flash and passed the guard with a wave of his hand.

Thinking it was a free day, I tried doing the same thing.

"Hold it, miss," the guard said.

I pointed, almost too out of breath to talk. "That man. There. Who is he? I owe him some change."

The guard looked over his shoulder. "Him? He works here. A guard, like me. One of the second-floor galleries. Oriental Art, I think. Or Near Eastern. You'll have to pay your contribution before I can let you in." He nodded toward the ticket desk. There were at least a dozen people waiting.

Grumbling and panting, I hobbled to the end of the line.

Five minutes later I had my green museum-contributor pin on my lapel. After picking up a museum map, I took the long flight of stairs to the second floor. I didn't want to waste time looking for an elevator.

The guard had thought that the man I was looking for worked in Oriental Art. Well, the Orient is a big place. For that matter, the museum's a big place. On the second floor, a wide balcony circles the Great Hall below. Galleries, and a gift shop, branch out from this balcony. I followed the walkway first, pretending to examine the Oriental vases and dishes in the cases lining the walls.

I'm embarrassed to admit this, but when it comes to museums, I have the attention span of a gnat. For me, the perfect visit to the Met is maximum thirty minutes in one small gallery, followed by about twice that time in the café with a cup of coffee and lots of people to look at. And now, as distracted and anxious as I was, the Oriental vases and pottery in the glass cases were a blur.

At each gallery door I glanced quickly around. There were guards—several of them moving slowly in their blue-gray uniforms—but not the one I wanted. The problem was, each gallery leads to another, and another and another. When I had walked the balcony's full circle with no luck, I knew I'd have to search many of them.

Bypassing the huge European and American collections, I began in the galleries filled with Near Eastern Art. No normal museum-goer would ever hurry from one room to another the way I did. I didn't even pretend to look at the art on display. A tour group of about a dozen people, led by a woman guide, blocked the entrance to one side gallery.

These early Greek artifacts are decorative, yes, but they were also functional. The works you see in this room all have to do with the theme of death. On your right, from the tomb . . .

Greek! I was in the wrong place. A guard walked past on the other side of the group. It was a white man, but I didn't get a look at his face until I threaded my way through the crowd. No. The guard was about fifty.

"Where can I find Oriental Art?" I asked him.

He directed me to the other side of the balcony, adding laconically, "You can slow down. It's not going anywhere."

Near the gift shop I studied my map and got my bearings. To the right of the balcony I would find Ancient China, the Japanese galleries, and the Chinese Garden Court.

Following the map, I eventually came to a passage where the museum's lights were low. From somewhere nearby came the sound of water falling. Passing through a round gate, I found myself alone in the Chinese Garden. What a lovely, cool place it is. There is a cascading fountain. Orchids sprout from between rough stones, and delicate plants bloom behind windows lit by what seems to be the gold light of the sun. A roofed walkway contributes to the feeling that you are outside. It's all illusion, but sometimes illusion is enough.

This was such a wonderful spot that I paused to catch my breath. The hairpins securing my hat had loosened. Pulling off the hat, I sat on a stone bench. My troubles, which at that moment were greater than I realized, seemed to disappear. I could have spent hours there. Days, even. If there's a public place in Manhattan I can imagine living in, that Chinese Garden is it.

My fear came out of nowhere, the way the fear in a bad dream emerges. Maybe it had something to do with the unusually meditative state of mind the garden produced in me, but in a skin-tingling way, I suddenly knew that someone was watching me. Forcing myself to look up from the cascading water, I saw the Stalker.

He stood blocking the entrance of the garden. The light there was brighter, and I could see that his eyes were pinned on me. I slowly got to my feet. His eyes followed me as I moved along the walkway toward him.

He doesn't know you, I told myself. He had seen me several times, but there was no reason for him to focus on me. I was no more to him than the girls on the train had been. He just wanted to stare, to make me uncomfortable.

I walked slowly, pretending to admire plants in one of the lighted windows. When I was within six feet of him, I looked at him again.

He was still watching me, and there was something in his eyes. Some hint of recognition, of knowing. My heart was pounding. The entrance gate was wide enough for two people, but he stood in its center, as if ready to stop me. I took a few more steps.

"Excuse me." I tried getting past him, but he moved directly into my path.

"You have something for me?" he asked.

I had forgotten about my lie to the other guard. Panic must have shown on my face, because he smiled then, a slight, cruel smile.

The circular entrance at the other end of the garden is called the Moongate. The Chinese characters you will see above the Moongate mean: 'In Search of Quietude.'

The guide's voice rose above the sound of the flowing water.

And what you see here is a fine wardrobe from sixteenth-century China. Constructed of rosewood, this piece, and its mate on the opposite side of the room, have brass fittings . . .

Another entrance at the far end of the garden had been hidden from my view by plants. Turning, I hurried away from the Stalker and out of the garden. I stayed with the tour group until it made its way into the more crowded Japanese gallery. Twice I looked behind me. Twice I caught him staring. No. Caught isn't the right word. He wanted me to know he was staring. The second time, he was smiling.

As soon as I left the Met, I found a phone and called Connor.

Saturday morning I met Connor at the precinct. He had me stand behind a one-way viewing screen and watch six men who were lined up in front of a dingy white wall. They were all tall, relatively thin caucasians. Hair colors ranged from pale blond to light brown. I had no difficulty pointing out the man I thought was the Stalker.

"Who is he?" I asked Connor afterward.

"Name's Munch. Leonard Munch. Lives in the East Village. Over the last few years, several women have brought harassment charges against him."

"Leonard Munch?" What a name. Sounded like a guy with thick glasses bent over some ledger sheets. "Well," I told Connor, "I'm sure he's the man I followed from Kate's funeral."

"The same man you saw on the twenty-ninth floor?"

There was the hitch. I couldn't really give a positive yes to that. "I think so."

Connor looked so unhappy at that pronouncement that I added, "I mean, I'm almost positive." I was positive, but on the twenty-ninth floor, even though I'd been wearing my glasses, the air had been thick with dust and I'd been a long way from the man. In court, my "positive" could be shattered by even an incompetent defense attorney.

As Connor showed me out of the room, he took a deep, rasping breath. "Almost positive. I wish that was good enough."

I wished it was good enough, too. Since Kate's murder, my relationship with Sam had been strained. It wasn't at the breaking point, but there was tension. I was friendly with at least one of the cops, and as long a Billy was a suspect, the police were, for Sam, the enemy.

"We've checked out the people in the office who had problems with Miss Hamilton," Connor told me. "The chef, the cashier, one of the maintenance guys. They all have solid alibis."

Connor said that the blow to Kate's head hadn't taken

an extraordinary amount of strength. "Your ninety-eight-pound weakling could have done that to Miss Hamilton's skull."

This was none of my business, and I didn't know why Connor was confiding in me until he added, "I'm still looking at that Finkelstein kid. Billy. You know him better than I do. Let me ask you this: can you see Billy Finkelstein being inclined to send dirty drawings and make dirty phone calls?"

"Of course not," I said. "Besides, the fight in Kate's office happened *after* the tickler file with the drawings in it was put in the carton, not before."

Connor thought about this for a second. "Could be like this: first came the fight; second came Billy or maybe his father finding the missing carton; and third came the kid taking the file out of the carton, putting those dirty pictures in it, and leaving it where it would be found."

I shook my head. "Possibly, but Billy knew that Davis had gotten Kate's corner office. Why would he direct an obscene call there? Besides, something was bothering Kate before the fight. She'd wanted to talk to Nutley's head of Security but never got the chance."

Connor shrugged. "Miss Hamilton could have wanted to talk to Security about something else, but you've got a point about the obscene call. The kid's alibi bothers me, though. It sounds like something he and his girlfriend cooked up."

It sounded the same way to me, but I still didn't believe Billy had killed Kate. Or maybe, because of my relationship with Sam, I didn't want to believe it.

After leaving the precinct, I walked to the office. The building had beefed up security until there seemed to be as many guards as there were employees. I passed three of them on my way to the elevators. Quite a change from my first visit there.

The upper floors were finally settling down from the move, but Nutley's lower floors, where the move was incomplete, were still hopping. Kate's murder was spoken about in hushed tones, but most of the people on the lower floors hadn't known Kate as well as the people in Litigation. There wasn't the same sense of horror.

There was, however, the same chaos. Every floor had its own version of Davis, its own Kate Hamilton. The head of one department looked like a warthog. Whether he acted like one I can't say, but my guess is that even a warthog couldn't be that much of a pig. Another partner threatened to hound me on my deathbed if I didn't find his antique movie posters. I didn't, and he spent a lot of that afternoon jumping at me from doorways shouting, "Well?"

In a way I didn't mind this. A new inventory of lost cartons, scratched desks, and broken chair arms took my mind off Kate Hamilton and Leonard Munch. I was getting pretty good at the corporate move business. I recognized all the contractors and knew what they did. My stack of punch lists was monumental and growing, but I was chipping away at it. I remembered many of the verbal complaints and had tried to do something about some of them. And only a handful of people were really mad at me anymore. At a big law firm, that's probably about as good as it gets.

That afternoon, when I finally got to sit at my desk, I looked at the cheat sheet Lorraine had left and realized that I'd memorized it. It was retired to my top drawer.

My top drawer, *my* nice roller-tipped pens, *my* nice wood desk. None were really mine, but they were mine for a while. I had earned them, and I was growing possessive about them. This was my ten-by-twelve room and my . . . stuff. Should I get a nameplate for my door? I was only going to be there a couple more weeks, but the idea was appealing. When you're a temporary office worker, nothing is yours. Nothing has your name on it. Nothing is ordered especially for you.

That was when I first found myself wondering if I'd found a niche. Not at Nutley—it would be half a century, most likely, before the monster moved again—but in corporate relocation. Could I become that big-money consultant I'd tortured myself with during my second day on the job.

I leaned back in my chair. It was one of the nice ones, with the pneumatic lift and the arms that stayed on. Temps get lopsided secretarial chairs; consultants get cushy high-backed chairs. My eyes traveled to my windows, which faced north. There was no sunset view to admire and no moonrise to get silly over. There were two windows, though. A window office in a Park Avenue building.

Not bad, Bonnie Jean Indermill.

I was gazing into space, smiling to myself, when Harriet tapped on the door. Her eyes were like saucers.

"What are you doing here on a Saturday?" I asked. "Haven't you finished unpacking?"

She nodded. "I'm doing overtime for Andy, but I had to run down here and congratulate you."

"What did I do?"

"You caught the Stalker, Bonnie. You amaze me."

Caught wasn't exactly the word I would have used, but what the heck. I don't get congratulated often.

"Where did you hear that?"

"Cornelia. Sergeant Connor called a while ago to ask her some questions about the security system here. Cornelia told Margaret, and Margaret told me. And I've been tell-ing"—Harriet flipped up her hands—"everyone."

For some reason, one of my father's sayings ran through my mind. My father doesn't have a lot to say, but he carries around a headful of old expressions. Most of them are so corny they make me cringe. This one was no exception.

"Loose lips sink ships," I said.

"Well, Bonnie," Harriet responded after a second, "peo-ple can't be expected not to talk about it. It will probably be in the newspaper tomorrow morning."

"You're right." I smiled to reassure her. I hadn't liked it the week before when Harriet was annoyed with me. "His name's Leonard Munch. He has a reputation for ha-rassing women. I hope he doesn't find out that I've done him wrong," I added.

Harriet shook her head in wonder. "You're so brave. When you ran out of the church yesterday, none of us knew what was going on. Rhonda and Hillary thought you were having an emotional breakdown. Andy said maybe you'd had a religious experience.'' The memory of that made her smile. ''I think he was joking.''

''I think he was, too. Why did Margaret think I ran out of the church?''

''Margaret?'' Harriet had the good manners to blush. ''Margaret said you probably spotted an available man.''

No doubt about it, Margaret had my number.

''I'd better get back,'' Harriet said. ''Andy's waiting for me. Oh, by the way, he's organizing a softball game for Tuesday after work. Litigators against contractors. Can you go?''

''Probably.''

''Good. Maybe you can get to know Andy better. I'm sure you'd like each other.''

''I'm not interested.''

She shrugged that off. ''He'd ask you out if you encouraged him. You two would make such a cute couple. You like the beach. Andy *always* takes a beach-house share in the summer. And he's just bought a co-op near Gramercy Park. He said it's small, but I'm sure it's very chic. You'd love that neighborhood . . .''

Visions of me pushing a baby carriage in Gramercy Park must have been dancing through Harriet's head. ''See you later, Harriet,'' I said firmly.

11

SUNDAY MORNING'S PAPERS ALL HAD A short piece about Kate's stalker. They gave his name but had very little about his background. Once again a witness was alluded to, but my name wasn't mentioned. That was fine with me. Less than three hours after he was picked up, Leonard Munch was on the loose again.

On one side of the LaMarca's backyard, a neighboring house cast shade. On the other, a stunted tree helped a little. The unshaded center of the yard, however, felt like the Sahara. The sun beat steadily on the dry, yellowing grass. I shaded my eyes with my hand. It was almost 6 P.M. This was the hottest summer in recent memory.

"I expect you want me to tell you about Leonard Munch," Tony said.

He expected right, but I gave him a disingenuous answer.

"If you really want to."

"If I don't, will you drop it?"

This was one of those conversations where we both knew the answers before we asked the questions.

"No," I said.

Tony gestured with his hand: stand back. His other hand, the one holding the can of charcoal lighter fluid, was thrust out at the red portable barbecue grill. Blue-white flames flew from the coals. My already warm skin was clobbered by a blast of heat. For a second it looked as if the grill might be in business, but when the flames died, there sat those coals like chunks of black ice.

All over New York City the heat wave continued, everywhere but in Tony and Amanda's top-of-the-line portable charcoal barbecue grill.

He wiped the sweat off his forehead with the back of his free hand and said sarcastically, "Man, I really love doing this shit."

There were five or six couples, in various stages of heat stroke and hunger, around the yard. There were also a few cops—both men and women—without dates. Somebody's elderly mother—I never did figure out whose—and about a hundred children under ten years old made up the rest of the guest list. I'm stretching the truth here. There couldn't have been more than eight or ten children. It just seemed that way.

We'd all been invited for four o'clock. I suppose that at one time the backyard had been geared for children, with the things it takes to keep them happy, but Tony's children are grown now and, in any event, live with his ex-wife. That evening, the children had no interest in the vegetable garden Amanda tends so carefully, nor in Tony's rosebushes. A young mother comforted a wailing infant. Two small children, a boy of about four and his younger sister, fought over a half-deflated basketball. It wasn't much of a fight. He was twice her size. What the little girl lacked in strength, though, she made up for in noise. What vocal chords! Every three or four minutes, the children's mother yelled at them: "You stop picking on her, Ronnie." Ronnie's father occasionally entered the fray. He called the boy the more mature "Ronald," but I promise you, that didn't make the kid any sweeter. "Ronald," he would bellow, "you leave her alone!"

I'd invited Sam, but with his son a prime suspect, he didn't feel like paying social calls on the police. How would he feel if he found out I'd once had an affair with the detective? As far as Sam knew, I'd met Tony through Amanda, Tony's wife. If and when I got into a confessional mood, I'd confess, but to that point the mood hadn't struck.

Speaking of Amanda, she was on the back porch doing battle with her new ice-cream maker. Every few minutes she looked around the yard nervously and peeled her damp hair from her neck.

I've told you about Amanda before. We met when we worked for a firm that devised tax shelters, or scams, depending on your point of view. Amanda's a real beauty, tall and slender, with black hair that reaches to center of her back. Since getting married, though, she's changed. Tony didn't marry her for her homemaking abilities, I promise you that, but for some reason Amanda's trying to be a good fifties sitcom wife.

Tony stared at the coals, dejected. "It's this damned humidity." His gaze rose from the uncooperative coals and settled, I could have sworn, on the big central air-conditioning unit humming away at the far side of the house. The house's windows were all shut tight and the curtains drawn. I knew, having spent much time in that house, that the temperature in there was about sixty-eight degrees. I also knew that on the other side of the ruffled, lace-edged kitchen curtains, there was a fully loaded kitchen—big microwave, gas grill, the works—much of it new, all of it tuned up and ready to hum at the push of a button.

All the other guests had managed to find shade for themselves. I was alone with Tony, in the beating sun, because I wanted to find out more about Leonard Munch. I didn't want to spend time watching Tony smolder over coals that were cooler than he was.

"We could move it all inside," I suggested. "The kids would be happier parked in front of the television. It's too hot out here anyway. Nobody's going to care if the hamburgers are cooked on the stove."

Tony's gaze shifted to the porch. "She will care," he said slowly.

He was right. Amanda would care.

I don't understand it. I had seen it happening even before they got married, but I'd thought it was a phase she was going through, like thumb sucking or platform shoes or something. I hadn't really believed Amanda's mania for housewifery would go on this long. This woman, who formerly had thought of meal planning as something you do with the yellow pages and a telephone, who could barely eat without a waiter hovering by her shoulder, was now held in the tight grip of home industry. She had turned herself into a slave.

Amanda had always had some tendencies in that direction, but when we first met, she'd been a slave of love. She'd been a lot more fun then, I can tell you that. Now she's a slave to Julia Child and Martha Stewart. These days her idea of a good time is a morning at Home Depot, followed by an afternoon in the pots-and-pans department at Macy's. I can hardly be with her without feeling guilty about the mildewed grout around my bathtub tiles.

"Son of a gun," Tony said.

The coals glowed. He shut the lid on the grill slowly, so that no sudden gust would extinguish them.

The little boy, Ronnie, had appeared at Tony's side. "When can we have dinner? I'm hungry."

Tony looked at me. "What do you think? Fifteen minutes?"

"What?"

"Before I can put the hamburgers on? It's been a while since I've done this kind of thing."

For all I knew about it, he could have put the burgers on right then. But for my purposes, fifteen minutes was about right. Over on the far side of the yard—far from Ronnie, Ronnie's sister, and the crying baby—were two empty lawn chairs, partly shaded by the neighbor's house. I nodded at Tony. "Fifteen minutes sounds good. Why don't we go sit down."

He gave me a hard look. Tony has nice wide brown eyes, but they can look real mean sometimes.

"I know you pretty well, Bonnie. You want to get me over there and grill me about Munch."

"Never. I want to talk about your roses."

He picked up the beer he'd been drinking and took a swallow. "Right. You get ten minutes."

That would be enough. Taking his arm, I led him toward the lawn chairs. Ronnie tried to follow but I stopped him with a glare. "You'll eat in half an hour."

Tony grinned. "You have a nice touch with kids, Bonnie. I like that."

Leonard Munch was twenty-seven, younger than I'd thought. Tony told me that the police had nothing on Munch until he was in his first year at City College in Manhattan. Leonard had been a mediocre student who planned to major in architecture. After receiving a failing grade from an English teacher, he had dropped out of school. The English teacher, a single woman with an unlisted home number, had, within a week, begun getting obscene phone calls at the office. Ordinarily this is considered a crank crime, and it ends with the victim getting her number changed. However, these calls were particularly threatening. A trace was put on the teacher's office phone. It led the police to Munch's parents' home.

At the time, Munch had been living with his mother and father in Riverdale. His father, a New York State assemblyman, somehow got his son's case dropped. Leonard had promised the court that it wouldn't happen again. And it hadn't. Not to the English teacher.

Over the next few years, two other incidents involving Munch were reported to the police. In the first one, he had stalked a young Puerto Rican postal clerk who refused to go out with him, watching her openly from a park bench across from a post office in Washington Heights. One afternoon, when the young woman left work, she found an obscene note stuck to her car window with what the police lab determined was semen. This time Munch's father paid a hefty fine and Leonard got a suspended sentence.

"How old was the teacher?" I asked, remembering the two girls on the subway.

"Youngish," he responded, "but the third victim wasn't. She was an older woman. Sixty-three. It happened a few years after the postal clerk. Munch had moved out of his parents' home by then," Tony explained. "He was working as a security guard in a building downtown, taking a couple of courses at the Art Students League. He got into trouble again, this time in the neighborhood where he lived."

"Where was that?"

"On East Sixth Street between First and Second. He had a cheap apartment in a tenement building."

"Where the Indian restaurants are," I said. Most people in New York City know that block well. You can probably buy any illegal substance you want on any corner, but that's not the reason for its current fame. The south side of East Sixth Street has become famous in recent years for the row of East Indian restaurants stretching almost its entire length. On weekend nights many of them have lines out the door.

Tony nodded. "Our boy had some gripe with his super, this older woman. Next thing you know, the super's getting hang-up calls at two A.M."

"Different ages," I said, "but always women."

"Yeah. Munch somehow got into a vacant apartment over the super's, plugged up the bathtub drain, and started a flood. It went through her ceiling, of course. Caused a lot of damage. The super knew he did it, but she couldn't prove it. Couldn't even get Munch evicted. The building's owner finally gave him a cash payoff to move out."

"He moved back in with his parents?"

"Nah. By that time Munch had himself a fiancée. A New Jersey girl, like you."

"A fiancée? I hope you're kidding."

Tony glanced across the yard at his wife. Whatever was going on with the ice-cream maker had caused Amanda to grip her lower lip between her teeth. One of her arms was waving, whether at us or just in general frustration I couldn't tell. As Tony watched her, a long sigh escaped from his lips.

"No, I'm not kidding," he said. "There's someone for everyone."

He was still staring at Amanda. Something's wrong here, I said to myself.

"Munch and his fiancée got married and had a kid," Tony continued.

"And lived happily ever after in New Jersey?"

"Not quite. I'm not sure where they lived, but she divorced him last year. She had a restraining order against him for a while, I understand."

"Do you know why?"

"No. I imagine he was giving her some of the same treatment he's given other women. Connor hasn't been able to talk to her, though. She's on her honeymoon. Hawaii," Tony added. "She just married a guy who owns a foreign-car dealership in New Jersey. Bergen County. She doesn't get back until Wednesday."

Tony didn't think Munch was still harassing his ex-wife. "The Bergen County Police haven't had any complaints."

So Munch had shifted his attention to Kate Hamilton. "And why Kate?" I asked. "What was Munch's interest in her?"

Tony shook his head. "He's not admitting he had an interest in Kate Hamilton."

"He's lying."

"Of course he's lying," said Tony, "but we can't beat the truth out of him. Unfortunately."

"Tony!" Amanda called from the porch. "I need some help."

He looked away from her and stared across the yard. And then, with no warning, he changed the subject and said something awful.

"Bonnie? Do you ever think that maybe you and I made a mistake when we broke up?"

What in the world was Tony thinking? He continued staring into the distance, which was just as well. His question flustered me, and I'm sure it showed.

When Tony and I broke up, it wasn't "we" that did it. It was "he." He did it. There! I admit it. The truth is, though, if he hadn't done it to me, I would have done it to him. That is reality; whatever was going on now in Tony's head was fiction.

"A mistake? No. I mean, if you're talking about . . . us. No. You know what I mean. That is, you and Amanda have a great marriage, and, you know . . ." I was not at my most articulate, but Tony didn't notice.

"Sure, Bonnie," he said, "except that I can't talk to her anymore. You and I always have something to talk about, even if its a creep like Munch. If you want to know, Bonnie, Amanda and I haven't even . . ."

Unbelievable! He was on the verge of telling me about their sex life. "I don't want to know," I said quickly.

"Tony!" Amanda called again.

I was tense as a guitar string. "I think my ten minutes are over anyway."

Tony smiled sheepishly. "Forget about this, okay? I'm feeling sorry for myself. But let's get back to business for a second. Amanda tells me you're seeing Billy Finkelstein's father."

I nodded.

"You know Connor's still interested in Billy? He thinks the kid's alibi won't hold."

"I know. But if they can prove Munch—"

Tony interrupted. "There's the problem. Munch has an alibi for last Friday night, too. It's not perfect, but it's a lot better than the Finkelstein kid's. And as far as violent crime, I'd say Munch is probably less inclined toward it. He's never done anything physical to anyone. Once the police come down on him, he moves on to another woman."

"What about that graffiti? *Kill.* Does that sound like something a nonviolent guy would write?"

"Graffiti? If I took all the graffiti in New York seriously, I would have been out of here years ago."

"I wish he was still locked up," I said.

"We can't keep a guy in jail for going to a funeral," Tony responded. "Munch claims he's never been near Nutley's office."

"Bull! I saw him a couple times."

"Prove it. Munch claims he didn't even know the deceased."

"Then why was he at her funeral?"

"He says he ducked into the church to get out of the heat."

"That's ridiculous," I said. "What's Munch's alibi for Friday night?"

"A big singles gathering at a church on Fifty-third and Lexington Avenue. It attracts several hundred people. He's been going most Fridays for the last few months. A couple women remember talking to him. The action starts at eight, lets out at eleven. At least three people remember Munch being there around nine-fifteen. He left when they closed up the church."

"That church is a five-minute walk from Nutley," I told Tony. "He had time to kill Kate and still be there by nine-fifteen. Or maybe he killed Kate after he left the church. The time of death can't be pinned down to the minute. For that matter, Munch could have slipped away from the group long enough to run over——"

Tony interrupted. "And get to the twenty-eighth floor of a building, bash a woman on the head, stuff her in a closet, and get back to the church without working up a sweat and with no visible blood on his clothes, before anybody missed him. That's what you're going to suggest, isn't it."

"Yes."

"You ever heard that saying 'clutching at straws'? That's what you're doing. There's this much of a chance"—Tony held his thumb and forefinger up; light hardly showed between them—"that Munch could have killed her before the singles thing, or while it was going on. Afterward, there's no chance at all."

"How do you know?"

"Because one of the women he met at the group left with him, went to his apartment, and spent the night."

"That's scary."

Tony had started to get up, but he sank back into his chair. "I agree. Munch is scary. But Billy Finkelstein is scary, too."

I shook my head. "I like Billy. He's a sweet kid."

"You like Billy because you like his father. I don't know the father, but the kid's been in trouble before." Giving me one of his long, hard looks, Tony said, "I wouldn't want you to get hurt in any way, Bonnie. I want you to promise me something. Two things.''

"Okay.''

"One, you will absolutely keep out of this and let Connor handle it. Okay?''

I nodded.

"Two, you will keep some distance—I'm talking emotionally and physically—between yourself and the Finkelstein kid.''

I couldn't promise that. "You actually think Billy could have killed Kate Hamilton?''

Standing, Tony walked away without answering, which was an answer in itself.

For the next hour and a half I forced myself to be sociable, but my heart wasn't in it. As for eating, forget it. One bite into my hamburger, done on the outside, oozing red in the middle, was the end of dinner for me. I shoved the thing into a trash bag when I thought no one was looking.

"You threw out your food. Don't you know about starving children? I'm going to tell Amanda.''

Ronnie. I moved toward the precocious brat, but he darted around a hydrangea bush.

"Bonnie!''

That was Amanda. She had overheard and looked hurt.

"You didn't like your burger?''

"It's not the food,'' I assured her. "It's me. I've got to go home.''

"So early? You haven't even had your ice cream.'' Motioning me aside, she said, in a softer voice, "We haven't had a chance to talk at all. I need to talk to you.''

Not her, too! What was going on? Was it their sex life? Another man? Another woman?

"What do you want to talk about?''

She squinted, confused. There was good reason for this. Amanda and I talk about anything and everything, all the time.

I hadn't been paying much attention to the way Amanda looked. She almost always looks terrific. I used to get jealous. Now it's part of the scenery. Amanda has her good points, I have mine. Sometimes, being just a little on the plus side of ordinary isn't that bad. People don't expect so much from you.

For the first time ever, I noticed that Amanda looked tired. There were faint lines at the corners of her eyes. Her lipstick had worn off, and without it, she seemed older and drawn.

"I wanted to talk about"—she shrugged—"things. With Tony."

This was going to be terrible. Right then I couldn't face it. "I'm sorry. I have to do my laundry tonight." In Amanda's housewife mode, laundry was something she would relate to. I looked around for Tony, but he had disappeared into the house. "Tell Tony good night for me, okay?"

"Sure. But if you wait a while, someone will drive you. You don't want to take the subway this late."

This from a woman who, in her single life, had lived on a block in Manhattan where twelve-year-olds carried Uzis. It was seven-thirty. The sky was still bright. I edged toward the gate.

"I'll be fine, Amanda. You want to have lunch this week, or dinner?"

"I'm not sure." We walked together toward the front of the house. "Did Tony tell you what happened?"

"No," I said, "but he seems kind of down."

What Tony seemed kind of was discontented, but I didn't want to bring that up.

Amanda glanced over her shoulder. There was no one around. "He failed the police department test for captain," she said miserably. "He's mad about everything. He's thinking of quitting the force."

"What would he do?"

"He said he wants to move to a desert island and stare at his belly button all day." Tears formed in her eyes. "I don't think he wants to take me."

It is a long subway ride from Queens to Washington Heights. The last twenty minutes of the journey is on my beloved A train. I make fun of it, I'm cynical about it, but when all is said, the subway gets me around fast and safely, cool in the summer and warm in the winter. Sure there's the occasional screamer, but these days in New York City, they're everywhere.

I got home at about nine, tired and feeling kind of down. I could hear Moses on the other side of the door before I put my key in the lock. He knows footsteps. He knows when he hasn't eaten, too. As soon as I opened the door he was all over me, circling my ankles, meowing, stretching full-length on his back in front of me. All these actions can mean different things at different times, but combined, they mean, "Feed me fast."

He's a fussy guy. A connoisseur. I try to cater to him. I have few illusions about our relationship. I'm mad about Moses. Replacing him would be hard, maybe impossible. Moses thinks I'm okay, too. I'm reliable, I can lug a bag home from the grocery store and handle a can opener. But if I were to disappear, he'd be out looking for love anyplace he could find it, pretty quick.

I opened his food cabinet—the one next to the refrigerator—and his ears perked forward. His eyes followed my hand as I rummaged through the little cans and found one that sounded good.

" 'Pacific salmon dinner, for cats seven and older.' How does that grab you?"

It grabbed him. He rubbed against my legs. By the time I got out the can opener, he had started making those funny speaking noises.

"Looks good," I said, scooping the stuff into his dish.

Tell you the truth, it didn't look half-bad. Better than the hamburger I'd tried to eat a few hours earlier. I examined the label and said to him, "Have to remember this one in case things get really tough around here." He had his head in his bowl and didn't respond.

I had told Sam I'd call when I got home, but I didn't feel ready to talk to him. He was certain to ask if Tony had said anything about Billy, and I wasn't sure how I'd answer. In any event, Sam wasn't expecting my call for about an hour.

Maybe after a warm bath . . .

I had been soaking for about a quarter hour when the phone rang. The warm water felt wonderful, but when I heard that ring, I leaped from the tub. Suddenly I wanted to hear Sam's voice, no matter what we talked about. Snatching a towel from the rack, I ran into my bedroom, threw myself across the bed and grabbed the phone.

"Hello?"

A man, his voice low, began speaking.

I'm not a child, or an innocent. I know all the words. Over the years, I've gotten a few obscene phone calls. In fits of temper, I've even used some of those same words myself. But I've never used them, or heard them used, the way I heard them that night—threatening, anatomical, sexual. I was so stunned that I couldn't let go of the receiver. Not until he said he could see me.

"I'm watching you right now. I see your hair, your—"

Terrified suddenly, I slammed the phone down.

I was nude except for the towel. Gathering my bedspread, I pulled it around my shoulders. I had no idea where he was, but even if he had been in my neighborhood he couldn't have seen into my bedroom. My blinds were down, my lights dim. The phone rang again. I started to tremble. No, I said to myself. Don't get scared. That's what he wants. When you stand up to him, he stops. That's his pattern. He moves on to another woman.

A second ring. I picked the phone up on the third one, my speech ready.

"Leonard Munch, I know it's you. I'm unplugging my phone—"

"Bonnie? It's Sam. What's going on?"

I didn't know whether to laugh or cry. I did a little of both.

Sam was there in an hour, offering a bottle of bad red wine and good company. He didn't mention Billy.

Once I calmed down, the two of us had the same immediate question: how had Munch found me?

Harriet and some of the others at Nutley knew that I'd identified the Stalker, but surely none of them would have called Munch and told him my name. One of the morning papers had identified the witness as a temp supervising Nutley's move, but I hadn't been named.

So, simply by reading the papers, Munch would have known what I did for a living, but that's all he would have known. My name didn't appear on any building directory, stationery, "From the desk of" pads, or anything else. I wasn't even on the phone list.

If this had happened on a weekday, Munch might have called the firm and, using some guise, gotten my name. But on weekends the switchboard was closed. Somehow, though, between the time I'd identified him to the police on Saturday morning and Sunday night, Munch had managed to discover my name. After that my phone number was no problem. It's in the book.

"What about the reporters?" Sam suggested. "They have sources. One of them could have found out about you from the police."

"And then called Munch with it? Why would a reporter do that?"

Sam grimaced. "For a story. They're heartless. One of them drives by my house a couple times a day. He hopes to catch my kid out in the yard stomping some old woman to death."

"Kate wasn't so old," I said. "She was forty-five."

Sam lay back on my bed with a groan. "I'm forty-five. Do I seem as old as she did?"

"Never."

"Who was her boyfriend, anyway?"

"Her boyfriend?"

"The guy in the dirty pictures. Or do you think Munch used his imagination."

The forgotten man. I hadn't really forgotten him. Once you've seen drawings like those, you don't forget. A man with white friar's hair and a big ring on his third finger. "No," I said. "The man's real. Otherwise Kate wouldn't have been trying to keep the drawings quiet. No one seems to know who he is. Probably some married, superrespectable type."

"Whoever he is, he was messing around with one pain-in-the-butt woman. He was either crazy or desperate."

"Maybe not," I said. I remembered the way the priest at her memorial service had talked about her pro-bono work. There seemed to be a lot more to Kate Hamilton than I had realized.

We lay there so quietly I thought Sam was dozing. My mind drifted away from Kate. I was surprised when Sam rose on his elbow and smiled down at me.

"You're looking pretty relaxed, for a woman who's getting calls from Munch."

"I was thinking about something else. What would you think of me trying to pass myself off as a move consultant?"

"You *are* a move consultant. I'll give you a reference anytime you want. I can probably get you some work."

Sam may have had a few rough edges, but what a cupcake!

Without moving his body, he reached toward the bedside table to turn off the lamp. Suddenly the phone rang again. I gasped, frightened. Sam looked at me for a second, then picked up the receiver.

"Hey, fucker," he said into the mouthpiece. "You ever call here again, and I'm going to come get you and kick your pervert ass all over New York City. Got it?"

He lay quietly for a moment, then whispered under his breath: "Jesus!" Finally he handed me the phone.

"It's your mother."

That night I had a terrible dream. Munch wasn't in it, at least I didn't think so at first. It was Ronnie, the little boy from the barbecue, who disturbed my sleep. In my dream I was starving. I quaked from hunger. Ronnie guarded the entrance of a dining room. Through the open door I saw tables loaded with broiled lobsters, fruit, cheese, corn on the cob dripping butter. Ronnie had grown enormous, a grotesque giant child. Whenever I tried to get through the door, he bounded in front of me shouting, "You shouldn't waste. Think about the starving children." Ronnie's mother entered the dream before I woke. I was crying the kid's name, trying to get him to give me some food. She shook a finger at my face and told me, ''We must call him Ronald. He's a big boy now.''

Waking, I sat up abruptly. Sam stirred at my side, then settled down again. Munch's tatoo swam through my mind. There was something important floating just out of my reach. Shutting my eyes tight, I forced it to the surface.

Ronald becomes Ronnie. Veronica becomes Ronni. If what Harriet had told me was correct, Kate had had a temporary secretary named Veronica. Munch had a red heart on his arm, pierced by a black arrow, with *Ronni* in ugly, looping letters.

12

As I remember it, I started out on Monday with a lot of good intentions. I intended to keep my promise to Tony and stay out of it. I intended to tell Connor that Munch was now interested in me, then let the police deal with it. I also intended to tell Connor that a temp named Veronica, who had worked for Kate Hamilton, might be the connection between Kate and Munch. Twice that morning I left phone messages for the detective. Both times, there was confusion at the precinct about when Connor would be in. By noon, he still hadn't returned my calls. I had the phone in my hand, getting ready to try him a third time.

My father has another saying. He's almost retired it since my brother and I left home, but when we were teenagers, he used it continually. It seems we always intended to call when we were going to be late. Sometimes, though, we didn't get around to it. "The road to hell is paved with good intentions," my father would remind us.

It was as if a demon took hold of my fingers and made me punch in Harriet Peterson's extension.

"You want to have lunch?" I asked. "I'll treat."

Harriet squared her shoulders and lifted her chin.

"Her last name was Price. Veronica Price. She was a perfect darling, too. I can't imagine her being married to that terrible Munch creature."

"Maybe she wasn't. I'd like to find out, though."

"You shouldn't get involved, Bonnie," she said testily. "It's the police's job."

Harriet was cranky. It wasn't my snoopy questions. It was the food I'd bought her. Long ago I discovered that one of the many routes to Harriet's tongue was via her stomach. Unfortunately, I'd chosen the wrong place for lunch. Nutley's cafeteria. Why? Because the price was right.

It looked terrific—two walls of windows, eight-foot-tall ficus trees in clay pots, lots of space between tables. The tables were light wood with tile tops, and the chairs were upholstered. The modern oil paintings along one interior wall were ugly enough to remind you that you were at work, but they were wallpaperlike. After the initial visual shock, they tended to fade from view.

The ficus tree that separated Harriet and me from the table nearest ours shimmered under the air-conditioning vent in the ceiling. The air-conditioning problem was a thing of the past.

Now the problem was the food. It wasn't my problem, though, and I intended to complain just like everyone else. If the chef had handed out punch lists, his In box would have looked like mine.

Harriet, being an optimist, had chosen the inappropriately named fettuccine with red clam sauce. She dragged her fork across her plate, lacerating the pasta.

"You show me one clam in this!" she said, piqued.

"I didn't make it. Complain to Freddie. He's office support services." I was having problems of my own with my Niçoise salad. The tuna bore an unsettling resemblance to the stuff in the can I'd opened for Moses the night before.

"Freddie's never around. I'll give the cashier a piece of my mind when we leave."

That poor cashier. She was getting hell from everybody. "She doesn't do the cooking. Now, about Veronica . . ."

Harriet shoved the pasta aside and started on her salad. "Iceberg lettuce," she grumbled, spearing a leaf. "You'd think they'd have something more elegant. A sprig of arugula, maybe?''

Arugula. The greenery of the moment. I remember when romaine was the last word in lettuce.

"Tell me about Veronica."

Harriet chewed her iceberg and looked thoughtful. "Well, she was a darling. Although, I must say, Margaret is being much nicer since . . .''

She thought better of what she was about to say. I glanced through the leaves of the ficus tree. Davis and another senior partner were at the next table with Jonathan and Andy. I don't know what Davis was saying, but he was making angry gestures at the loin of pork on his plate. Jonathan, who like me had gotten the cat food, was understandably sympathetic. Andy was polishing off what looked like a turkey sandwich. He happened to turn his head my way and, seeing me, smiled through the greenery.

"How's your lunch?"

"Not so good."

Davis swiveled in his chair and flashed me a sneer that I'm surprised didn't wilt the ficus leaves. We hadn't spoken since the scene in his office.

"Are you the person I complain to about this food?"

I shook my head. "Freddie Ferguson." And lots of luck finding him, Bert.

Harriet had leaned across the table so that she could whisper to me.

"He doesn't have a girlfriend."

"Yeah, but he's got a lousy disposition and a wife."

She shook her head so hard her yellow curls bounced. "Don't be ridiculous. I'm talking about Andy. And he's older than we thought. If things don't work out with that moving man, maybe you and Andy could get together. That moving man's not for you, Bonnie. How would you like to be stepmother to a murderer."

First my mother, then Tony, now Harriet. For one reason or another, I was continually defending my relationship with Sam. It was like being back in high school and dating a guy with long hair and a motorcycle.

"That moving man's name is Sam," I said, "and things are working out fine! And Billy's not a murderer!"

She drew back, prim as anything. "It was simply a thought, Bonnie. Andy likes you. I can tell."

I gave Andy a quick, corner-of-my-eye glance through the leaves. He seemed to be disagreeing with Jonathan, something I found easy to imagine.

"How old is he?"

"Thirty-five. He had an entirely different career before he went to law school. Something creative."

"Creative!" I sniffed. "I've had creative. These days I want brawn."

"Just the same . . ."

I hadn't paid for Harriet's nasty food so we could talk about my love life.

"How long did Veronica Price work for Kate?"

She had to think about this before answering. "It must have been a month. Margaret had gone to visit her family. She takes her four weeks there, every year. They live in Jamaica. The country," she added. "Not Jamaica, Queens."

"Fascinating. What about Veronica? Where did she live?"

Harriet shrugged. "Riverdale, I think. Yes. They were living with her husband's parents. She had a darling little girl. She showed me her picture."

"What was Veronica like?"

This question seemed to puzzle Harriet. "I told you. She was nice."

"I mean, was she happy? Anxious? Was her mind on her work?"

"It must have been. Kate didn't complain. And she would have."

That was for sure. I asked Harriet about Veronica's husband. "Did she talk about him?"

"Not much," Harriet responded. "But I think they were having problems."

"Where did you get that idea?"

"Oh, there were lots of little things. Once, I heard her on the phone with her mother. She said something like, 'I know he's impossible, but I'm trapped.' '' Harriet's brow crinkled. ''And there was something that happened one evening, too, but I can't be sure it had anything to do with her husband. Veronica and I had both worked overtime, and . . .'' Pushing her salad aside, Harriet eyed the infamous chocolate surprise I'd chosen for dessert. ''Can I have just a taste?''

''Help yourself, but keep talking.''

''Dreadful,'' Harriet pronounced the dessert after taking a minuscule bite. ''Anyway, Veronica and I had worked late. She was in Kate's office forever, taking dictation, I thought. The door was closed. A little later that night, though, I went to the ladies' room, and there Veronica was, washing her face.''

This wasn't quite the bombshell I'd expected. ''And?''

''Her eyes were all red, as if she'd been crying. I asked her if Kate was being awful to her, but Veronica surprised me. She said Kate was being wonderful.''

Wonderful? That was not a word I would have used when speaking about Kate.

''Do you know which temp agency Veronica was with?'' I asked, taking a bite of my chocolate surprise.

''Goodness, no.''

If Veronica Price was anything like me, she was registered with half a dozen agencies. Nutley's Accounting Department would have paid her agency and might still have a record of the name, but there was no way they were going to let me snoop through their files. When Connor showed up, though, he could.

Harriet had been watching me chew. ''Awful, isn't it?''

I agreed. ''A hockey puck, just like Kate said.''

As we left the cafeteria, we passed Davis. He was giving the beleaguered cashier a piece of his mind. I was glad to see that she was giving it right back to him.

I tried Connor again when I got back to my office. This time I got an unpleasant surprise.

''He's in the hospital. Chest pains,'' the woman on the other end of the line told me. ''He was admitted this morning. His doctor's not saying when they'll let him go.''

"Is he taking calls?"

"Not now. Maybe in a few days."

I asked the woman whom I should speak to about the Hamilton murder. She didn't know, but promised to have someone call me back.

So there I was, a blistering clue in my hand, and no detective to give it to. I could have called Tony, but our talk the day before had made me uncomfortable. Not our talk about Munch; Tony's always telling me to keep out of things. I seldom pay attention. It was his unexpected mention of "us" that bothered me.

One of the nice things about working for a big firm is the phone room. I called Nutley's, and five minutes later I had both a Bergen County, New Jersey, phone book and a Bronx one.

Bergen County is big and heavily populated. There were a number of Prices in the phone book. I could waste lots of time calling, asking for a Veronica who had temped at Nutley. And even if I was lucky enough to find her, she still might not be Leonard Munch's Ronni. The age was right, the child was right, and the marriage trouble was right, but the last name was wrong.

I put the Bergen County book aside and opened the Bronx book. Riverdale, whether it likes it or not, is part of the Bronx. I quickly located an L. Munch, Sr., with a Riverdale address. My fingers tickled at the buttons on my phone. Did I dare? Of course.

A woman answered on the third ring.

"I'm an employment counselor at Pro-Team Temps," I said. "I'm trying to reach Veronica Price about a job."

For a moment the line was so quiet that I thought maybe we'd been disconnected.

"Veronica left this number?" The woman sounded surprised at that idea.

I was surprised, too. Things had been so difficult for me over the past couple of weeks that I'd forgotten that sometimes things are easy.

"My file may be out of date," I said.

"It is. The last I heard, Veronica's living with her mother

in Hackensack. I don't have the number.''

"Do you know her mother's name?"

"It's Sandra. Sandra Price. On Mullen Place. I don't remember the exact address," she said hurriedly, "but it's something with zeros."

Well, well! As Freddie might have said if golf had been his thing, "a hole in one." With almost no effort, I'd found the line between Kate Hamilton and Leonard Munch. When I hung up, I smiled at the stack of punch lists festering in my In box. "Nothing to it," I said. If the punch lists could have answered, they would have said, "That's what you think, cookie."

In the Bergen County phone book, there was no Sandra or S. Price on Mullen Place. Checking information, I learned that the number was unlisted. That was understandable. If Leonard Munch was my ex-son-in-law, I'd have an unlisted number, too. Flipping to the Bergen County yellow pages, I looked at listings for foreign-car dealers. I should have asked Tony what kind of foreign cars Veronica's new husband sold. There were dozens of dealers, and none of them were named anything like Munch's Ex-wife's New Husband's Dealership. Not that I planned to call. That was a job for the police. But you never know.

Working on that principle, I stuffed the Bergen County phone book into my purple tote. Nutley's phone room wouldn't miss it for a while. Most likely by the time they needed it, they'd have forgotten who had taken it.

Hillary had been poking around at her desk. She stuck her head through my door. There was an open box, about the size of a shoe box, in her hands.

"These came for you."

"What are they?"

"Guess." She grinned.

The little plastic-wrapped things in the box were black metal, with holes in their centers and a small half window to slide across the hole. I'd seen these things before. My own desk had them. They fit in where there were holes for electric cords.

GROMMETS, the side of the box read.

"Finally," I said. "You want to make Jonathan's day?"

"No way."

The thin gold ring in her nose flashed as she shook her head. Staring at it, I asked Hillary if her father had adjusted yet. I certainly hadn't.

In response, she grinned and said, "He hates it."

Hard to believe, but E. Bertram Davis and I had something in common. Grabbing a handful of grommets, I headed for Jonathan's office.

No swamp of paper for that one. He was a minimalist, at least in his office-keeping style. He'd hung no art, just two diplomas. On his desk was one pen, capped and placed neatly to the side of a lined yellow pad. It looked as if he'd used a straightedge to arrange the files and books on his bookshelf. Only his In box indicated that a human being had been in the area. The sheet of memo paper on top was loosely folded.

"How anal," I said to myself, although I admit that if I'd liked Jonathan more, I might have thought, how pleasant and clean.

He wasn't around. I was going to leave the grommets in their wrappers on his desk, but I decided to be nice about this. I sat down in his chair and unwrapped two grommets. Fitting them into the little holes that had been so desperately awaiting their arrival was simple.

I had tossed the unused grommets on top of the memo in the In box. As I reached for them, I straightened the memo and my gaze fastened onto a word that had been typed across its top. *Confidential*. If that word hadn't been there, I wouldn't have given the thing a second look. But it was there, in capital letters and underlined, no less.

Stepping to the door, I peered into the corridor. Harriet and Margaret were both at their desks, both busy. Otherwise the hall was empty. Davis's door was closed. Through Andy's open door came the sound of his radio, jazz playing softly.

I opened the memo flat in the In box. It was from the Associate Evaluation Committee.

"As you know, your recent evaluation had been drafted

by Katherine Hamilton. The Evaluation Committee has learned that this evaluation was misplaced during the move. As a result, it is necessary that a new evaluation be prepared. Over the next several days, we will be meeting with other partners with whom you have worked. . . .'' The memo ended with a request for patience during this difficult period.

Refolding the memo, I put it neatly in the In box.

Connor had checked out a lot of Nutley's employees, and certainly all the ones known to have had problems with Kate. But what about the problems Connor didn't know about? No one knew what had been in Kate's evaluation of Jonathan. He'd looked grim that afternoon in the old building when he'd had an appointment with Kate. Not that he ever looked much happier, but maybe, when he'd knocked on Kate's door, he had an idea that something unpleasant was waiting for him.

Kate's evaluation process, Margaret had said, was in several steps. First there was an informal report that no one but Kate saw. After that came an interview with the associate. Finally, Kate had Margaret type a formal evaluation which was sent to the Evaluation Committee.

"Hillary," I said when I returned to my office, "I have paperwork to do. Please take phone messages."

After locking my door, I got a clean pad of yellow lined paper from my desk.

I'm a list maker. This isn't something I do on a regular basis, but when something—jobs, money, whatever—threatens to overwhelm me, which is more often than I like to admit, sitting down with a pad of paper and a pencil and doing some organizing makes me feel better. In moments of high stress I've been known to list my troubles, in descending order, to try to put them into perspective. I wanted to do the same with the suspects assembling in my mind—Munch, Billy, and now Jonathan.

I began listing them, their motives as I saw them, their previous encounters with Kate, and their opportunities. I also wrote down my gut feelings.

Munch was at the top of the list.

"Leonard Munch," I wrote. "Motive: connected to Kate by estranged wife Veronica Price. Did Kate help Veronica with divorce/restraining order?" I made a mental note to check on this. "Munch had been stalking Kate and wrote threatening graffiti, regardless of his claims of innocence." Under opportunity, I scrawled, "Has alibi for 9:15 on Friday night, but could have killed Kate and gotten to singles gathering by 9:15, or could have slipped away long enough to kill her."

My take on Munch was this: "I want him to be guilty. He's a disgusting human being. But his crimes don't seem to be those of someone who faces people physically. They're committed through the relative safety of phone wires and the mail."

"Billy Finkelstein. Motive: Kate insulted him. He made hotheaded threat against her. Has delinquent history." In my opportunity column, I wrote: "Has weak alibi. Probably has gotten Hillary to lie for him."

For me, this last part was much more damning than Billy's threat. If he wasn't with Hillary, where was he? Why wouldn't he say?

My take on it: "I like the kid. I'm dating his father. And car theft isn't murder."

"Jonathan Nash. Motive: Ambition. Evaluation prepared by Kate could have been negative, hurting his chance for partnership. Previous encounters with Kate: nothing out of the ordinary that I know of."

Opportunity was tricky. After thinking about it, I jotted down the following: "Jonathan might have known that Kate had her evaluations in her desk drawer. Since she wrote RIGHT DESK DRAWER on her carton, locating the carton wouldn't have been a big problem, but how would he have gotten his hands on it?"

"Jonathan often works with his office door closed. On the night of the move, assuming he could have stolen Kate's carton, he could have found, and destroyed, any negative evaluation. As for opportunity to kill Kate, he had plenty of that."

My take on Jonathan: I paused, my pen in the air, then

wrote, "Competitive, ambitious, and paranoid. A pain in the neck and a complainer. But I saw Kate's carton on the dolly in the old building. There were cartons on top of it. Snatching it there would have been impossible. In the new building, he would have had Margaret Brusk to deal with."

"Andy McGowan is in the same position," I wrote as an afterthought. "His evaluation was in the lost carton, too. His partnership's less of a sure thing than Jonathan's, and he might be desperate if he got a bad evaluation from Kate."

My take on Andy: "I like the guy, but that could just mean I've got lousy taste."

I put Bertram Davis on my list, but I didn't think he was in the running. Davis had carried on a vicious verbal war with Kate, but his entire life was a verbal war. He struck with his tongue, not his hands. Besides, though I hated to admit it, Davis's shock when Kate's body tumbled out of his closet had been as genuine as mine.

I also added Freddie Ferguson. Kate had insulted him in front of me. Of course, she'd insulted me in front of him, but I knew I hadn't killed her. About Freddie—"I can't imagine him taking the initiative," I wrote, "but he's sneaky, and he knows how to cover his backside."

At the bottom of the list I put Hillary Davis. Billy was her alibi. "Hillary doesn't strike me as vengeful or violent, but she was sure mad about the way Kate had talked to Billy," I wrote.

Rereading what I written, I again thought about that missing carton. Where had it gone? And how was it that Kate's tickler file, which I would have sworn she put in the carton, had ended up under Harriet's desk?

Harriet? I held my pen poised over my list. Was it possible that my friend, a respectable woman of a certain age and then some, was involved? No, it wasn't. I laid down the pen.

With the move winding up, the luxury of radio cabs ended. From what I understand, someone on Davis's beloved M-COM took a look at expenses and drew the line. Going home, I grappled for a handhold on a packed subway. It had been a while since I'd been on the train during rush hour. Back to reality.

My mailbox was crammed full. Riding the elevator to my apartment, I went through the mail. Mostly requests for money from causes I've never heard of. A few catalogs. My bank statement. And a cheap white envelope with my name and address typed. Postmark Manhattan. No return address.

I knew what it was. I was the lucky recipient of one of Munch's dirty sketches. The postmark indicated that it had been mailed on Sunday. Once again, Munch had gone to the GPO on Eighth Avenue. He was a regular customer there. I fed Moses and put in another call to the police. The person who answered—a man, this time—promised that someone would get back to me right away. I didn't believe him.

While I waited, I made myself a nice, cool white wine spritzer. With a slice of lime. I changed into a T-shirt and shorts, and spent some time trying to balance my checkbook. I'd been in a state of denial about it for a while, and it was a mess. As I plugged away at it, though, it felt as if an ax were hanging over my head, waiting to fall.

It's strange, knowing that an obscene drawing is waiting for your attention. My doors were double locked and there's a gate on my fire-escape window. I was still anxious. At the same time, though, I was curious. After a while, my curiosity grew stronger than my anxiety. Holding the envelope by one corner, I slid a nail file under the flap and used the file to force out the folded sheet of paper.

It was a drawing in the same neat, architectural style as the ones Kate had received. I might not have recognized myself in the sketch, except that I knew the nude woman with the reddish blond shoulder-length curls was me. The thin but stupendously endowed man I was involved with—and using the word involved to describe what we were doing is gilding the lily—was unrecognizable. His hair was a light brown scribble. We were shown on a pale pink surface. In the background was a window, and on the floor, a tan rug.

My bedroom quilt is burgundy. The Waldorf's was blue. To put it simply, my recent sex life hadn't involved any pink surfaces, or any thin men with light brown hair.

It was just your everyday, generic dirty picture.

At the edge of the drawing were these words: "Somebody doesn't like you."

Somebody? Why was this nut referring to himself in the third person?

The phone rang and I grabbed it, expecting the police. "Hello."

Near silence answered me. There were soft background noises, phone wire noises. I kept my voice as normal as I could.

"Hello?"

He whispered like he had the first time he called. This time, though, there were no sexual references.

"You got a special letter today, didn't you? I'm watching you all the time. Remember that, bitch."

He hung up before I did.

Connor's replacement, whoever that might be, was proving as elusive as my boss. I dialed Tony's home number and was relieved to get him. I told him about the call and about the drawing on the coffee table in front of me.

"You've already touched it?"

"Only by the edge. Listen, do you think you could put a tap on my phone?"

"I'll check into it," he said. "But they usually don't do that just for dirty calls."

"Even when the caller might be a murderer?"

Tony was silent for a second. When he spoke again, it sounded as if he was forcing out his words through locked jaws. "Forget about Munch, Bonnie! He has an alibi."

"Okay. What should I do about the drawing?"

"Handle it carefully," Tony said. "Put it, and the envelope, in another envelope and take it to work with you. When you get a chance, drop it off at the precinct."

"Whose name should I put on it? Who's taking over for Connor?"

Tony's voice exploded in my ear. "This week I've only

got three homicides, one of them a double, a serial rapist who mutilates his victims before he kills them, and a gay basher who's left three guys dead on the East Side Highway. I guess it's going to be me taking over for Connor, since I'm the guy with all the spare time.''

"I think you need a vacation," I said. "There's something you should know about Munch's—''

He made an angry noise into the phone. "What I need is a new job. What I don't need is you interfering with a police investigation. Keep pushing me, Bonnie, and I might let you spend some time behind bars!''

He hung up before I could tell him about the connection between Leonard Munch and Kate Hamilton.

Maybe the police already knew that Munch's ex-wife had worked briefly for Kate, but I didn't think so. Veronica wouldn't be back from Hawaii until Wednesday, and Munch, claiming he had never heard of Kate, certainly wouldn't have mentioned it.

I dropped the sketch off at the precinct the next morning, but before I did, I stopped in at Nutley and made a copy of it. I thought I was unobserved, but as I was folding the original back into its envelope there was a gasp from behind me.

"Another one?''

It was Harriet, looking properly shocked.

"Yes, another one. He's decided he doesn't like me now.''

"That's awful.'' She stretched, trying to look over my shoulder. "Can I see it?''

"No. I'm taking it to the precinct. It's evidence.''

"Then why are you copying it?''

Harriet's question was a good one. "For my scrapbook,'' I told her after thinking about it for a second.

13

MARGARET BRUSK STOOD IN MY OFFICE doorway, one fist full of envelopes, the other clenched at her side.

"I've never been so angry at this place. I should quit. You will not believe what they've done to me."

That wasn't true. My belief was that Nutley would do anything it could get away with to its staff.

"I've been reassigned," she said. "Another litigation partner. I told Personnel I was still busy with Ms. Hamilton's work, but they don't care. We're treated like chattel around here!"

It was early in the morning. I had nothing to do with Personnel. I was chattel, too. Why was she telling me this?

"I'm sorry to hear that," I said. "Are you still working for Jonathan as well?"

"Of course! You don't suppose they'd give me a break, do you? I've only worked like a dog for eight years."

They'd certainly never given me a break. I shook my head and tried to look sympathetic. With her next sentence, Margaret let me know why I was on the receiving end of her snit.

"I have no intention of taking Ms. Hamilton's personal belongings to her apartment—not when I'm working for two other attorneys," she said indignantly. "I packed everything. Four cartons and a stack of framed art. I told Ms. Hamilton's super that I would bring the cartons to her apartment, but now someone else can worry about getting them there.'' She slapped a set of keys onto my desk. ''And I certainly wouldn't trust those Finkelsteins. Any of them,'' she added pointedly.

What a fuss she was making. ''The firm's dispatcher will take care of the cartons,'' I told her.

Margaret drew herself up so straight she looked as if somebody had Krazy Glued her to my wall. ''You intend to let a strange messenger wander around Ms. Hamilton's apartment? I would never have done that. But''—a toss of her head—''it's out of my hands.''

I looked at the keys. ''Where is the apartment?''

''Eightieth and Fifth. It's one of the best neighborhoods. Close to the Metropolitan Museum.''

How convenient for Munch. If he felt like doing some stalking after work, he only had to cross the street and walk a block downtown.

Since Kate's murder, Billy had been assigned jobs that kept him out of Nutley's building. Sam's offer to let me ''borrow'' his son still stood, though. It might be interesting to see Billy's reaction to visiting Kate's apartment. I said to Margaret, half seriously, half to annoy her, ''Maybe I'll get Billy Finkelstein to deliver the boxes.''

Margaret huffed off, only to return within seconds to thrust her handful of envelopes at me.

''And I'm not going to take care of her personal bills, either. Now someone else can do it!''

''Did the police see these?''

''Ms. Hamilton's sister is working with the police. She stays in Ms. Hamilton's apartments some nights. The bills should be left for her.''

''Is her sister her ... ?'' Margaret was gone before I could say ''executor.''

I put the keys in my pocket, the bills in my handbag, and called Finkelstein Brothers control desk.

''Does Billy Finkelstein have some time to spare? I'm going to need help taking some cartons to East Eightieth Street.''

•   •   •

During the short ride uptown, Billy and I chatted about the softball game that Harriet had mentioned to me a couple days earlier. Andy had organized it: contractors—meaning anyone who worked at Nutley but wasn't on Nutley's payroll—against litigators. The game was that evening, and Billy planned to "kick some Nutley butt." There was no way I could bring up Kate's murder, and, in particular, his alibi.

When the station wagon we'd borrowed from Nutley's dispatcher pulled up in front of Kate's building, Billy, who was driving, whistled softly.

"Not bad!"

I'd called in advance, but the doorman, a suspicious, beady-eyed type if there ever was one, still gave both of us a once-over. I was in a short summer dress, and passed muster. This was one of the rare mornings when the fuzz Billy was trying to coerce into becoming a mustache had been trimmed. He'd even tucked his shirt into his pants. The little gold skull in his ear was an eye-opener, but at least it wasn't in his nose. He looked almost respectable. Not so respectable, though, that he was allowed to push the loaded handcart through the lobby. He was told to wait under the green awning that stretched from building to curb.

"I'll send your man up in the service elevator," the doorman told me as I followed him through the ornate little jewel of a lobby.

The elevator was paneled in mahogany. The real thing, not veneer. And no graffiti scratches. The brass control panel glowed under the soft lights. This was New York, though, and this was an old building. The elevator clanked and jerked its way to the seventh floor just like the one in my downscale apartment building.

The landing wasn't very big, but what it lacked in size it made up for in frills. Like the lobby downstairs, everything was either inlaid, gilded, papered, or mirrored. A small crystal chandelier hung from the ceiling. I thought about Kate: simple suits and plain hairdo, and her sexy shoes. What was I going to find in her apartment? A Zen-style retreat? A hedonist's lair?

There were five doors on the landing, three with apartment numbers, one that said STAIRS, and one unmarked. Opening that one, I found a hallway which contained the freight elevator and three other doors. These were unmarked, but must have been the apartments' service doors. Outside two of them were plastic bags. Even the rich generate trash. There was no sound coming from the freight elevator, so I had a few minutes before Billy would get there.

When I walked into Kate's apartment I wasn't really searching for anything. I knew of nothing to search for. The police already had been through the place, and Kate's sister had been going in and out of it for a week and spending some nights too. Just the same, I was glad to get a few minutes to snoop around.

Though the apartment certainly wasn't spare, it wasn't a rococo wonderland, either. The floors in the living room and the smallish dining room next to it were covered in a cream-colored carpet not unlike the one in Kate's office that she'd made such a fuss about. The wood furniture was light, and the upholstery on the chairs was pastel. A few watercolors hung on the walls. These rooms faced south, and, if you stood in the right place, you could see part of Central Park.

I liked the fact that the upholstered sofa and chairs looked soft and well used. I sat in the chair that faced a television set. What did Kate watch? "The Dating Game"? "Wheel of Fortune"? Public television and the evening news were more likely. Maybe an occasional movie of the week. I reached absently into a magazine rack at the chair's side. Kate wasn't a *Cosmo* girl, but *Vogue*, maybe? No. She seemed to read strictly business and news magazines. There were a couple of old issues of a Bergen County newspaper, but I couldn't imagine what connection they would have with Leonard Munch's ex-wife.

In a study off the living room, a cushioned chair faced a small, bare-topped desk. I thumbed through the bills Margaret had given me. There were several regulars: phone, electric, both a national and a department-store credit card bill. Who had Kate called in the days before she was killed? What had she bought? There was also an envelope from a well-known resort at the eastern end of Long Island. Had Kate spent time there? Alone? My fingers played along the envelope's flap.

It's not your business, Bonnie. Firmly, but with a stab of regret, I put the envelopes on the desk.

The rather old-fashioned kitchen was along the apartment's east side. A look through the plain white curtains showed me the wall of a neighboring building.

The remainder of the apartment consisted of two bedrooms, each with an adjoining bathroom. The smaller of these bedrooms, like the kitchen, faced east. In this room the bed was unmade. An open suitcase sat atop a chest of drawers. This must be where Kate's sister slept when she stayed over.

The heavy white curtains in the second bedroom were closed, and the room was dim. Walking to the *north-facing* window on one side of the bed, I pulled the curtains apart.

Across Fifth Avenue, less than a block uptown, I saw people moving up and down the museum's steps. Munch could have watched Kate's building from there, I realized, but he couldn't have seen inside. Turning away from the window, I studied the room. Daylight streamed into it, lighting the white-and-blue quilt on the bed. A brass lamp with a black shade was on the other side of the bed, on a willow night table. When I turned back the quilt, the thin blanket under it was white. It was possible there was a yellow blanket or sheet around, sure, but a bedside lamp isn't the kind of thing people change often.

The drawing Munch had sent me wasn't based on any reality. The unfamiliar man and I had romped on a strange pink surface. There had been no bedside table, no lamp, no hastily discarded clothing, no jewelry. The drawings Munch had sent Kate, though, had been so detailed: a window with yellow curtains, a yellow bedspread, a blue lamp, a red-and-white polo shirt lying on the floor.

Maybe it was the lover's apartment. Had the police

looked into this? Or did they care, since Munch had what they considered a decent alibi? They already knew Munch had been watching Kate, and that Kate had been worried about something. The drawings she'd gotten were the logical thing for Kate to have been worried about, but where Munch stood to study his subjects wasn't important, was it? Did even the identity of the man in the sketch matter to the police? Not if the police weren't interested in Munch, it didn't.

The doorbell rang, announcing that Billy and the cartons were there. I hurried from the room, pulling the door half-closed behind me, as I'd found it.

As soon as Billy had stacked the cartons in the living room, he pushed the handcart to the door.

"You're not curious?" I asked. "Don't you want to look around?"

He shook his head. "I just want to get out of here. This place gives me the creeps."

While I locked up, Billy maneuvered the cart toward the freight elevator. I was trying to think of a way, short of saying, "So, did you kill her?" to bring up the murder. As it turned out, Billy brought it up himself. When the elevator door opened, he shoved the cart onto it. I got in behind him and pushed the button for the ground floor. As we began clanking down, Billy slumped against the wall staring at his feet.

"Bonnie? Do you think I killed Kate Hamilton? Is that why you brought me here? Did you think if I saw her apartment I'd feel guilty and spill my guts?"

"Of course not. But I am concerned about your alibi," I added.

We jerked to a stop. When the door opened, we were nowhere near the lobby area. Billy pointed to a rear exit. "We go out here."

The door led to a driveway along the building's side. As we walked to the street, Billy shook his head. "The cops weren't real happy with my alibi, either. I'm sure glad you identified that Munch loony."

Billy didn't know it, but Munch, loony as he was, had the better alibi.

Our station wagon was parked a couple of feet in front of the driveway. We were already inside it, with the engine running, when a car pulled into the drive. The doorman hurried over to it, and his movement attracted my eye. A man had gotten out of a late-model Mercedes, leaving the engine running. He said a few words to the doorman, then crossed the sidewalk and disappeared into Kate's apartment building. Most of this time, his back was to me. I got only a glimpse of his face, but I saw enough.

He had a slight paunch, a monk's ring of white hair, and a big gold wedding band. None of these were really damning, but his shirt was. A polo shirt. Red and white stripes. He should have burned it.

"Don't pull out yet," I said. "He left his engine running."

Billy looked across the seat, puzzled. I adjusted the mirror outside the passenger window. As I did, the doorman, who had returned to his spot under the awning, glanced from me to the idling Mercedes and back at me.

"He thinks we're going to try to boost it," Billy said, adding, as an afterthought, "It's a real nice car. I know a couple guys in the Bronx who could strip . . . ."

I shook my head. "We're not going to try to boost it, Billy. Pretend something's wrong with our engine. I want to find out who the driver is."

"I thought you liked my dad," he said accusingly.

"I do. This isn't anything to do with me."

Mollified, Billy jumped from the wagon and lifted the hood. I stepped to the curb and joined him. The doorman looked on unhappily as we poked among the wires.

The man from the Mercedes was back, with company, a few minutes later. He was carrying two suitcases. This time I had a clear view.

As I said, my dress was short. As the man passed me, I glanced toward him. His gaze was moving up my legs. Stepping back onto the curb, I made brief eye contact. It wasn't hard.

His style was cramped by his companions—two young children and two women. The younger of the women, who appeared to be in her twenties, walked between the children, holding their hands. The older woman slid into the Mercedes's front passenger seat. There was a bustle about who was going to sit where. Both children wanted to sit with their grandparents. A minute or two passed before everyone was happily seated. By then I had figured out the relationships: a middle-aged couple, their daughter, and their two grandchildren.

I was back in the station wagon when the Mercedes finally pulled into the street. As it passed, I saw its MD license plates.

When the car had rounded the corner, I leaned from my window and said to the doorman, "I think I know that man. Isn't he a doctor?"

The doorman answered proudly. "That's Dr. Turnbull. One of the city's most famous cosmetic surgeons. You've probably read about him in *New York* magazine. They said he had 'magic fingers.' "

"Ah." And if those drawings in Kate's tickler file had a basis in reality, she probably would have agreed. "He and his wife live here?"

"Yes, but they spend most of the summer in the—" He stopped abruptly, tucked his chin into his chest, and fixed me with a wary look. The notion that I could be a thief casing his tenant charges must have hit him.

So the Turnbulls spent the summers "in" somewhere. Not "at," as in "at the Jersey shore"; or "on," as in "on Fire Island." There are two "ins" where Manhattan's prosperous types summer: in the Berkshires and in the Hamptons. The well-known inn Kate had gotten a letter from was located just beyond East Hampton. Now I could have kicked myself for not opening the letter.

During the ride to the office, I put together what seemed to me a logical sequence of events. Munch somehow had discovered that Kate was having an affair with a married neighbor. Furious because Kate had helped his wife with a restraining order against him, and perhaps with a divorce, he had followed Kate and her lover and sketched them in what they thought was a safe place.

Kate, receiving the sketches, was afraid the affair would be made public. She wanted to talk to Cornelia, but before she could, she was killed.

Why, though, had Munch killed her? Because his wife's remarriage pushed him over the edge? That was the best—and for that matter the only—answer I could come up with.

The actual moving of offices was ending. A week before, going to an office softball game in Central Park had seemed like an impossibility. Now, though, my work days had developed a rhythm I could deal with. At 5:30 that afternoon, when I locked my desk, turned off my light, and left for the park, I wasn't concerned about the In box full of trouble I was leaving behind. It was the trouble ahead that worried me.

Sam and I had made plans to meet at the playing field and go to his house in Huntington after the game. By that time I knew that Sam's wife had died of cancer after a long illness. According to Sam, their marriage had been "not perfect, but pretty good." To say that I was nervous about spending the night in the place where most of this pretty good marriage had happened was an understatement.

I ended up walking to the Park with Andy, which was nice. He diverted me, at least briefly, from my upcoming visit to Huntington.

I was crossing Fifty-second Street when he called out, "Bonnie. Wait up."

He was wearing shorts and sneakers and carrying a big duffel bag. Between the bag's handles he'd tucked a bat. He ran across the street, dodging a car to catch me.

"You're going to the game?"

"Sure. Can I carry something for you?"

He immediately tried to hand me the bag. Instead, I took the bat and propped it over my shoulder.

The game, as I've said, was contractors versus lawyers. There had been some grumbling among the staff about this. Elitism, Margaret had called it, though for the life of me I couldn't imagine Margaret sliding into home base.

Andy had fallen into step beside me. "Are you playing?"

"No. I'm not much of a softball player."

I could have played. I was a contractor. But the game had been talked up as a macho, crush-the-other-guy-into-the-dust thing, and I didn't want to be the contractors' downfall.

"If you're not good, you should play for them. Those Finkelsteins and Paganos are going to murder us puny Nutley types." He paused and shook his head. "*Murder*. That's an unfortunate word, all things considered."

We had stopped to wait for the light at Fifth. "Who are you going to cheer for?" Andy asked me.

He had to know that I was seeing Sam. Since that first night, when Sam and I had made a spectacle of ourselves in front of Margaret Brusk, we'd been discreet, but office affairs have a way of getting around. Even the guys in the mail room probably knew by now.

"I'll cheer for the contractors. I've got to be true to my own kind. Besides, they've worked hard."

"Nobody, but nobody, works harder than an associate at Nutley," Andy responded. "I would stack my hours up against one of your contractors any day of the week. And I'm not even one of the drudges. Think about Jonathan."

I didn't want to think about Jonathan. Andy, on the other hand, interested me. Not so much romantically, despite Harriet's urging, but as a person. How had someone with so much life in him ended up in a sweatshop like Nutley?

"Harriet tells me you used to do something else for a living. 'Creative,' she said."

He hooted so hard he almost dropped the duffel bag. " 'Creative!' Harriet has a nice way of putting things. During college I worked summers at the New Jersey Shore. After graduation I stayed on another summer and then spent the winter and spring in Florida doing the same thing."

"Lifeguard?"

"No. Nothing that clean-cut. I worked on the boardwalk, separating the tourists from their money. 'Step up, folks, and try your luck putting this oversized ball into this undersized basket.' ''

"You do that like a real pro," I said. "I've lost a few dollars to those guys. Did you ever feel guilty about it?"

"Guilty?" He grinned gleefully. "If guilt had been a big part of my psyche, I never would have become a lawyer. Anyhow, that's not all I did on the boardwalk. After a couple summers I tried my hand at something that required a little more skill."

"What was that?"

He hesitated. "Nothing I showed any talent for," he said finally, evading my question. "What about you? Harriet said you were an actress."

Even the loosest definition of the word *actress* wouldn't include some of the things I've done in the theater.

"An actress? Harriet said that?" Harriet hadn't just been pushing Andy to me. She had been pushing me to Andy.

"What she actually said was that you'd been 'onstage.' Why are you smiling? What did you do onstage, anyway?" Stopping abruptly, Andy turned to stare at me. The crowds on the sidewalk skirted around us, and one or two people glanced curiously. "Bonnie," he said seriously, "I've been working on a motion for summary judgment for Davis for nine straight hours. If what you did onstage was totally depraved, please tell me every detail. I am desperate for a thrill."

I started laughing. Depraved. Is dancing in a begonia outfit at a flower show depraved? Or tapping across a stage dressed as a tube of toothpaste? "I'm not sure *depraved* is the right word. *Ridiculous,* maybe."

He shook his head and started walking again. "That's too bad. I thought you were going to give me something to fantasize about for the next couple days. What did you do?"

He hadn't told me what he did on the boardwalk that was so "creative." I wasn't about to tell him about the begonia outfit.

"I was a hoofer. A gypsy. At the top of my career I got into the chorus line in a couple of Broadway shows. One of them lasted three months.''

"Hey, I'm impressed," he said. "Did you love it?"

"It was wonderful. It just wasn't secure. Not that temporary office work is any better."

Andy grinned. "The boardwalk was great for a while, too. Lots of sun, lots of beer, lots of girls." He gave me a quick look out of the corner of his eye. "A couple of them were even depraved. But it's not what you'd call a job with a future. It didn't pay much, either. So, I took the law school admission tests and applied to law school. I knew from my first day there that I was going to hate every minute of it, too."

"Then why did you stay with it?"

"Why? I had to do something for a living," Andy said, shrugging. "And I like finishing what I start. After going through the trouble of the admission process, it seemed crazy not to get the degree. Besides, much as I hate to admit it, I like the things money can buy."

We had stopped in front of a skyscraper at the corner of Fifth and Fifty-sixth. This one, with its shiny black facade and dark gray lobby, looked especially uninviting.

"So," Andy continued with a unusually sharp edge to his voice, "here I am, stacked up in a monster like this one, pushing paper sixty hours a week. A respected member of society." He had glanced across the street. "Speaking of which . . ."

We waited on the sidewalk for Jonathan. Once he had caught up with us, we walked past the fountain in front of the Plaza and then crossed Central Park South. Like Andy, Jonathan was carrying a duffel bag and was dressed casually in shorts and a T-shirt. There the resemblance ended. Maybe I was overly sensitive, but we hadn't walked two blocks before I was ready to push that particular respected member of society into an open manhole.

It started near the corner of Seventh Avenue, when Billy drove past in his funky black car. The window hadn't been fixed, and the plastic covering it flapped as the car rolled forward. The trunk was still fastened with rope.

Hillary waved at us from the passenger seat and called

out the window: "We're going to find parking near the field. See you there."

"Unbelievable," Jonathan said when the black car turned up Central Park West.

Andy smiled. "Unbelievable? Don't you wish you were Billy's age, with a rich girlfriend and a rock group?"

"Get serious," Jonathan said. "A girl with Hillary's background, poking a hole in her nose and going out with that . . ."

"That what?" I asked. Murderer? Moving man? Delinquent? Jew, maybe? Since I was going out with "that's" father, I wanted to know.

"Forget it," he said. "I got the grommets, by the way. And somebody finally fixed my chair arm. About time. Have you done anything about the things on my new punch list?"

"Jonathan," I said. "It may surprise you to learn that I haven't even looked at your new punch list."

"Actually," the smug bastard replied, "it doesn't surprise me in the least."

I didn't answer, but I made a mental note to steal back those grommets the first chance I got, and maybe loosen the arm on his chair again.

The temperature probably dropped fifteen degrees when we entered the Park at Seventh Avenue, but I was still inflamed about Jonathan's remarks. I wasn't sure Andy noticed, but he had. We got to the field, and Jonathan hurried to the bench where Davis and some other litigation partners had gathered.

"Try not to take Jonathan too seriously," Andy said. "He's been riding me since the day I got to Nutley. He'd been there all of two weeks. Senior man, from Harvard Law, no less. Knew everything."

"How do you stand him?"

After looking over his shoulder, Andy said softly: "Guerilla warfare. It's the only way to make it at Nutley. I've gotten good at it. Guess where Jonathan's first set of grommets went."

Andy went off to play softball, leaving me smiling. With

Andy around, there was hope for Nutley.

The bleachers in Central Park's Fleshcher Field rise about five rows. It's not Yankee Stadium, but it's fine. The bleachers are unshaded, but the sun was falling behind the trees. Dark clouds rolled across the sky, and it looked as if we might get some rain.

I scanned the bleachers. The litigators had clumped together on a couple of rows near the batter's cage. They had an ice chest filled with designer bottled water. The contractors were farther down on the bleachers. Their ice chest was filled with sodas and beer. Though she was a regular employee, Cornelia had somehow talked her way onto the contractor's team. She was dressed for warfare: a Finkelstein Boys tee with the sleeves cut off, worn blue-jean shorts, and running shoes that looked like they could take flight. I watched her narrow her eyes, coolly appraising the opposition—Davis, specifically. He was a Ralph Lauren vision in khaki twill, a well-dressed Park Avenue raja at play. When Sam crossed the field swinging two bats over his shoulder, Jonathan mumbled something that made Davis either smile or sneer. I said a quiet prayer: "Trample them, contractors."

Harriet and Margaret, loyal to the crown and the paycheck, were on the bleachers behind the litigators. Freddie's loyalties were divided. There was a beer in his hand, and it hadn't come out of a cooler of Evian water. He knew who signed the paychecks, though, and he had parked himself among the litigators. I joined my fellow contractor Rhonda, and Hillary, the rebel, on the contractor's side of the batter's cage. I knew who signed the checks, too, but my days at Nutley were numbered.

14

IT WAS THE TOP OF THE FIFTH. THE CONtractors were leading, eleven to five.

The sky was full of rolling black clouds. We'd heard the rumble of thunder in the distance. It looked as if the drought was going to end, right on Nutley's softball game. Even if it didn't rain, daylight was fading. It would soon be too dark to play.

One man was out and Jonathan was at bat. It's painful for me to admit this, but he was the best player on the Nutley team—a good pitcher and a strong hitter. He also displayed other previously unnoticed, interesting qualities. Rhonda had settled within reaching distance of the contractor's beer cooler. After going through a couple of cans, her tongue was even looser than usual.

"The way he looks in those shorts, Jonathan makes me wish I were twenty years younger."

I agreed. "He does look all right."

Hillary refused to give Jonathan even that. "He's a moron. Have you ever tried talking to him?"

"Who's talking about talking?" Rhonda cupped her hand over her eyes to block what was left of the sun, and looked across the infield to third base where Sam was playing. Giving me a sideways glance, she said, "He's taken, I suppose."

"Yup."

"Oh, well. Can't win 'em all."

A Pagano man—the same one who had opened Davis's closet door—was on the mound. He had the neck and shoulders of a bull. This was softball they were playing, but I wouldn't have wanted to be standing in front of the balls that Pagano man threw at Jonathan.

Cornelia was umpire for the contractors.

"Strike one," she called gleefully when the first ball streaked by Jonathan.

Davis, who was standing at the edge of the batter's cage, yelled, "It was a ball!" Cornelia yelled back, "Strike," and jabbed her finger at him. Freddie, loyal to the crown, jumped from the bleachers and joined in on Davis's side. As this was going on, Rhonda leaned in close to me and whispered, "What do you think of Freddie?"

"Freddie?" Could she possibly be weighing my boss's potential as a sex object? Her question seemed casual enough, but somehow I didn't think it was. I eyed her warily. "You mean to go out with?"

With a defensive lift of her chin, Rhonda said, "Good men are hard to find."

So this was a sensitive spot with Rhonda. Feeling guilty, I said, "Freddie's okay."

"I thought so, too, for a while. Two years, actually."

"You went out with Freddie for two years?"

She shushed me with a finger in front of her lips. "I'd just as soon the entire world didn't know about it. Though I do have Freddie to thank for the Davis job."

As soon as Rhonda had said that, frown lines creased her forehead. I couldn't tell whether the thought of Freddie or the Davis job had caused them. "Oh," I said.

"Anyhow," Rhonda continued, "it's all over between us."

"How come?" Personally, I could think of a hundred reasons why any sensible woman would dump Freddie.

Rhonda sighed. "I just got sick to death of the sight of that man stretched out on my sofa with a drink in one hand and my television remote control in the other. Last week I pitched such a hissy fit I'm surprised my neighbors didn't call the police."

Something clicked for me then. "Do you live near the office?"

She nodded. "Lately Freddie's spent so much time on my sofa it's got a permanent rut in it from his backside. I don't know how he's managed to get this move done."

"He hasn't managed to get this move done," I said.

Rhonda's eyes widened. "Do I detect a little anger in your voice?"

"A little." I didn't ask her whether Freddie had been drinking Chivas Regal, but that wouldn't have surprised me. "What a slimeball."

"Well, he was all right for a while," she huffed, defensive again.

Hillary broke in. "Why are you two whispering? Who's a slimeball, anyway?"

"There are more slimeballs in the world than you would believe," was Rhonda's response. She looked over at the Pagano man on the pitcher's mound. "What do you think of him? He's been sniffing around me. Kind of reminds me of my second husband." Smiling lasciviously, she asked, "Do you suppose Pagano means pagan in Italian?"

I grinned at her. "For your sake, I hope so."

The young can be awfully prim, can't they. Even the young with gold studs in their noses. Hillary groaned at our conversation. "You two are terrible for middle-aged ladies. My mother doesn't talk like that."

Rhonda and I shrieked in unison: "Middle-aged?"

"Aren't you both . . . ?" Hillary hesitated. "Well, if the average life expectancy is seventy-five, then when you get to be about thirty-five, you're middle-aged. Don't you think?"

"Hillary," I said, "in my family, the women live well into their nineties. Maybe in ten years I'll be approaching middle age."

Rhonda did even better than that. "In my family, the women live to be about a hundred and twenty."

Hillary rolled her eyes. "So you'll be middle-aged when you're sixty."

"Not if I have anything to say about it. I've already had

my eyes done. Next year . . .'' Her fingers tapped against the underside of her chin.

"I believe in aging gracefully," said Hillary.

Rhonda hooted. "Tell me that when you're forty-five."

"What about Kate Hamilton?" I asked. "Do you think she ever had plastic surgery?"

My two companions thought my question came out of nowhere, but their reactions were different. Laughing, Rhonda said, "I doubt it. Kate Hamilton was what aging gracefully looks like. Dowdy! I could never figure out where those 'Fuck me' sling-back shoes came from."

Hillary had been staring at me curiously. "It's so weird, your asking about Kate having cosmetic surgery."

"How come?"

"Well," she said, "it's no secret. Kate used to have a scar in front of her ear. She wore her hair to cover it. This past spring she had it removed."

"So she could pull her hair into that ugly French twist? It hardly seems worth the effort." That was Rhonda.

"Who was Kate's doctor?" I asked.

Hillary said she didn't know. I was pretty sure I did.

The Pagano man's second pitch was right inside. Jonathan swung this time. He connected hard and whopped the ball way into left field. On the litigator's side of the bleachers Harriet started screaming like crazy. Actually, almost all of us did. The battling factions were becoming less clearly defined as the game progressed. Even Margaret, who had spent most of the game looking as if she were attending an economics lecture, got to her feet as Billy, far in the outfield, made a desperate lunge. He missed and spent a few wild seconds stumbling over his own feet before he got a grip on the thing. By then Jonathan was safe on second. Davis sneered happily.

Andy was up next, and the minute I saw him swing the bat, I felt sorry for him. He was game, and strong enough, but he was no batter. He hit a couple of hard foul balls and struck out in no time.

Davis was about the only litigator, other than Jonathan, who was actually taking this competition seriously. Andy's performance at bat got Davis so worked up he turned the color of a tomato. Poor Andy had to walk past him to get off the field. Davis ignored him and went after the litigator's captain, a junior partner. Five minutes of valuable daylight were wasted while he harangued the guy. Davis finally left the field, but not before shouting at the captain: "Try to get a real slugger in there this time!"

Another associate was batting next. I suspect he would rather have been sweating out a brief in Nutley's library. As the poor guy picked up the bat and took a practice swing, Davis bellowed: "Bring Jonathan in!!"

He didn't add "or else," but it was there.

How did Andy feel about this? Embarrassed? Probably not. If I knew Andy, he was laughing up his sleeve. I looked around for him, but he had disappeared.

The best moment in the game, as far as I was concerned, came a few moments later. The batter hit a ground ball. Jonathan lit out like a shot for third base. Sam ran under the ball, scooped it up, and tagged Jonathan out before the litigator could slide his pompous ass into third. The contractors had won it.

Davis's mean little eyes burned into Cornelia. She was grinning ear to ear.

"Good game, Evelyn," she called to him from home plate.

Evelyn? The *E* stood for Evelyn? How had Cornelia ever discovered that?

Sitting beside me, Hillary whispered, "Oh no. He'll fire her."

That's what I thought, too. As Davis marched toward home plate, his lips twisted into something that made his usual sneer look friendly. Grin fading, Cornelia took a couple of steps back.

Rhonda muttered, "Oh, shit." Everyone else around was quiet as Davis glared at the security woman.

"You know," he said after a moment, "you would make a hell of a litigator."

I'm sure that, for Davis, there was nothing better he could say about a human being. He had paid Cornelia the

ultimate compliment. Her jaw dropped, and her eyes looked
as if they would pop from their sockets.

"Good game," Davis added.

All of us, even Margaret, cheered and surged onto the
field.

Our jubilation in the park was short-lived. Thunder rumbled, and lightning streaked across the darkening sky. Billy,
who had been collecting equipment, called to Hillary. "I've
got to fix the plastic in the car window."

Hillary was helping me gather empty cans and put them
in a bag. Always the terrific worker, she immediately
dropped a handful of cans. One of them rolled behind the
bleachers.

"Thanks a lot," I said to my secretary as she trotted
after Billy, but she either didn't hear or pretended she
didn't. Walking to the back of the bleachers, I stooped to
retrieve the can. I was crouched there, in the dimming light,
when a yellow spark caught my eye. It lasted no longer
than the blink of a camera shutter, and then it was gone.

A few feet behind the bleachers is a sidewalk. Past that
walk, there's a stretch of grass and trees. Finally, half-
hidden among the greenery, is a red brick building. Like
many structures in the park, it's old and ornate. The roof
overhangs the building by a couple of feet, making it a
shadowy place even on a sunny day. As I straightened, I
became aware of the hum of traffic from behind the building. In the excitement of the game I hadn't realized that
Sixty-fifth Street traverses the park not far from the fields.

I stared hard at the building. A second later there was
the soft red glow of a burning cigarette. Lightening flashed
again, and I made out the form of a man.

Munch! He was standing under the eaves. When he was
certain I had seen him, he raised the hand that held the
cigarette and waved it toward me. Just one flick of his wrist.

"You bastard," I said under my breath. Munch was
common knowledge around Nutley, but the fact that he was
stalking me wasn't. I didn't want to make a public announcement. Hurrying around the bleachers, I found Sam
putting bats into a duffel bag.

"I've been looking for you," he said. "Let's get out of here."

The bleachers were completely empty. A few drops of rain had splattered the dust of the field, causing players and fans to hurry away with their equipment and coolers.

"Munch is here," I told Sam. "In the trees behind the bleachers."

There was enough light so that I could see Sam's mouth take on a grim set. He dropped the bats, all but one of them, and peered into the trees. "I've had it with that lunatic. Where is he?"

I shook my head. "He was near that building, but I don't see him now. Maybe we ought to forget it."

Ignoring me, Sam walked into the trees holding the bat like a club. I dropped the bag of cans and ran after him. He was already at the side of the Sixty-fifth Street Transverse when I caught up with him.

"Let's go," I said. "We can't find Munch here and we don't want to be in the park after dark."

Sam shook his head. "The police haven't done anything about this creep, so I'm going to. You catch up to the others. I'll meet you at the corner of Sixty-fifth Street in fifteen minutes."

Central Park covers 840 acres. There are miles of roads and trails. There are open areas, sure, but there are also thick bushes, rocks to hide behind, and tunnels to run into. On top of that, Sam had seen Munch only in newspaper photos. He was fueled by anger, both at Billy's situation and at mine, but not by common sense. I refused to leave him, and we searched the lower part of the park for a quarter hour, until daylight was gone and we could hardly see our feet in front of us.

We never saw another sign of Munch that night. I was glad of that. I wanted Munch to leave me alone. I wanted him punished if he had killed Kate. But I didn't want Sam deciding how to punish him, and I definitely didn't want Sam doing the punishing. As we drove to Sam's house, Connor's words ran through my mind: "Your ninety-eight-pound weakling could have done that to Miss Hamilton's skull.'' Sam was no ninety-eight-pound weakling. He could have done it without breaking a sweat. Never for a moment had I thought that Sam might have killed Kate. I didn't want anything to happen to make me change my mind.

First Munch, then Sam's house. What a night! Munch was a spook, hiding in phone booths, slipping behind buildings, giggling his sadistic giggle. Sam's house didn't hide or giggle. It was just there, an albatross, a big fat white two-story bird casting a giant shadow.

We stayed ahead of the storm during the long drive on the Long Island Expressway. Partway through the trip, Sam started talking about his wife. I think he was as nervous as I was. Perhaps he thought that bringing the subject into the open would help, but it didn't help me.

''I had this tendency to get involved with Gentile cheerleader types,'' he told me. ''My parents didn't want any of that going on, so they sent me to a Jewish college upstate. Well, I managed to find the only Irish girl around. A pretty redhead. Eileen. She was working part-time in a fast-food place some of us less conventional types hung out in.

''Eileen was in her last year of high school. Within three months I'd knocked her up, pissed off both our families, and married her.''

The harsh lights of an oncoming truck lit Sam's face. He was silent until the road was dark again.

''She was showing by the time she graduated. The school mailed her diploma to her. Wouldn't let her attend the ceremony.''

So there was Eileen: Pretty, sexually appealing, multiplying fruitfully right from the get-go. A young martyr to two sets of parents and a school board. And thirty years later she'd died.

This was so depressing. Eileen's life sounded like the kind of four-hanky movie of the week that makes the cover of *TV Guide*. In comparison, mine was the kind of sitcom that gets panned by the critics and dropped after one show.

It was about half past nine when we reached Huntington. Sam drove through orderly streets, turned into a cul-de-sac, and pulled into a driveway. The moment I'd been dreading all day had arrived.

From the car, I could see that the house was two stories, painted white, with a small front porch, a two-car garage, and some decent-sized trees—in other words, it fit in perfectly with the neighboring houses. Not only with the neighboring houses, but with working-class suburbia as I know it. And I do know it. You could have picked up that house and plopped it down next to my parents' and I wouldn't have blinked.

That said, I would almost rather have spent the night searching through Central Park for Munch than in that house. The blue brocade world of the Waldorf had offered me fantasy. My own apartment—seedy neighborhood, noisy neighbors, and all—offered me security. This perfectly ordinary house offered both reality and insecurity.

When Sam pulled into the garage next to Billy's car, I had to force myself to get out of the car. It wasn't as if there had been a divorce, like Tony's, where there's animosity to begin with and it sticks around in the form of alimony and child care. A dead wife, regardless of what she was like alive, becomes sort of an angel, fluffy white wings and pure heart, floating over her household. Or haunting it, depending on your point of view.

Rock music greeted us when we opened the back door. At the stairs Sam shouted. "Hey, Billy. Turn it down a little. I've brought Bonnie home."

Home! The music dropped a decibel or two. "Hi, Bonnie," Billy called from somewhere above.

I made it through the kitchen okay. My own kitchen is so minimal that almost anybody else's looks good to me. The dining room and living room didn't give me serious trauma, either. There was lots of stuff—cushions, puffy curtains, groupings of photos. It reminded me of my brother and sister-in-law's house. Cleaner—most things are—but heavy on frills.

Sam was looking at me expectantly. He wanted me to like it. And don't misunderstand: I did like it. It wasn't "me," but when it comes to decorating, I don't know what "me" is. The few nanoseconds of my life I've devoted to decor have been ruled more by money, or lack of it, than taste. Given some time and some money, I could very well get into frills and ruffles, even lava lamps. Who can say?

I nodded. "Very nice."

"Eileen had good taste."

I nodded again. You can knock the divorced wife's curtains, but the dead wife's can't be touched. Walking to a window, Sam flipped on an air conditioner. Layers of white curtains billowed like an angel's wings.

I followed Sam up the stairs. I'll tell you, Eileen was floating over me when I walked down the hall, past the room music blared from, past a bathroom. By the time Sam pushed open the door at the end of the hall, Eileen had all but draped herself around me like a shroud.

"And this," Sam said needlessly, "is the master bedroom. My bedroom."

It was obvious that's what it was. A king-sized bed, yet.

The room was spotless, and I knew that he had cleaned it for me. "That sure is a big bed," was all I managed.

"It's two twins. Eileen was sick for a long time. It was more comfortable . . ."

He hesitated. I hadn't moved out of the doorway. It was as if my feet had sprouted roots there.

"Is this rough for you?" he asked.

"Very." Strangely enough, having said that I immediately felt better. "I feel more comfortable already, admitting that."

"It's hard for me, too, but . . . I live here. This is it, at least for now." He turned away from the room. "You want a drink? I could sure use one."

We were on our way downstairs when Billy opened his door and poked out his head. It seemed as if he tried to smile at me, but his smile didn't work.

"Do you have a second, Dad? I've got to talk to you."

"Come down and join us," Sam said.

Billy shook his head. "I'll talk to you later."

He slammed his door, setting loose a new worry in me: did Billy resent my being there?

Sam and I were in the kitchen when we heard the first clap of thunder nearby. He pulled aside one of the curtains.

"I've got to close up the toolshed. Fix us a drink. Liquor's over the refrigerator." He rushed out the door, and a gust of wind slammed it shut.

And there I was, alone in the angel's kitchen.

Ice. That was the first thing. The freezer wasn't the modern, self-defrosting, ice-making variety that Amanda so loves. I pried an ice tray from a glacier that made me feel more at home. Ice tray in hand, I reached for the hot water faucet. One step at a time. First you take on the refrigerator and the kitchen sink, next thing you know you've got your sneakers under the bed and your toothbrush in the bathroom.

The phone rang, startling me. It was mounted on the wall beside the refrigerator. Would Billy get it upstairs? Obviously not. It rang again, so I dropped the ice tray in the sink and grabbed the receiver. Munch, I thought. Did he know about Sam? Had he even followed me here?

"Hello?" I said cautiously.

"Bonnie?"

"Amanda?" Even Munch wouldn't have surprised me as much as my friend's voice did.

"Yes. I tried your apartment. Then I called information and got Sam's number."

A nervous tremor ran through me. "What's wrong? Has something happened?"

"It's awful. Is Billy Finkelstein at home?"

Through the window over the sink, I saw lightning split the sky. A second later, raindrops splattered against the glass. "Yes," I said. "Billy's in his room."

"You've got to get out, Bonnie. I'm scared to death for you. Go for a walk or something."

"A walk? It's starting to rain. What's wrong?"

"There's some new evidence. I don't know what it is, but if you can't get out, lock yourself in a room and stay there," she said breathlessly. "Tony questioned Billy's girlfriend again. She broke down, Bonnie. The alibi's a lie. Billy's a murderer. Tony got a search warrant. He's on his way out there right now. And don't ever tell Tony I warned you, okay?''

Sam burst into the kitchen. Rain had plastered his hair to his forehead. He glanced at the phone as I cradled the receiver. ''Who was that?''

I never had a chance to explain. Someone was pounding on the living room door. At the same time, two uniformed cops appeared at the door Sam had just come though.

''What's going on?'' Sam asked.

Five minutes later, we both knew. Bertram Davis's marble scales of justice were found in Billy's bedroom, with Billy. The statue was on his bed when he willingly opened his door for the police. As Tony and two other plainclothesmen escorted Billy down the stairs, the boy kept trying to explain what had happened.

''I found the scales in my car,'' he was saying. ''Under the spare tire. I never saw them before tonight. If I hadn't had a flat on my way home tonight, I never would have found them at all.''

Sam followed them into Manhattan. I spent the night in his house, sleeping fitfully on the sofa. The place didn't feel haunted anymore, at least not by an angel.

The following afternoon, Billy Finkelstein was taken to a holding cell, pending arraignment.

An anonymous caller had informed the police that Billy had the scales of justice. My statement—that I thought Leonard Munch had been at the softball field, and that he could have put the scales of justice in Billy's car—didn't sway the judge. I was the only one who had seen Munch, and I couldn't swear it had been him. A lot of people smoke. The judge did not allow bail.

Munch, as I might have guessed, had an alibi for Tuesday evening. Like his alibi for the night when Kate Hamilton was murdered, it wasn't quite solid. After clocking out of the Museum at 6:30 P.M., he'd gone downtown. A waitress in a coffee shop near his apartment building had served Munch dinner at approximately 7:00, and Munch's landlord had seen him going down the steps to his basement apartment shortly after 7:30. The landlord, who lived on the building's first floor, thought he had heard Munch's door open and close again. It was a steamy evening, though, and after having a beer, the landlord had dozed on and off in front of a fan. He wasn't sure about the time.

Billy's fingerprints had shown up all over the scales of justice. They were the only prints on them. Still, he stuck to his story that he'd never seen the statue before Tuesday night. He swore—to Tony, to the judge, to his father, to anybody who would listen—that when he'd cleaned his trunk the week before it hadn't been there. He said it had to have been planted there by someone who wanted him blamed for Kate Hamilton's murder.

Sam and I believed him. Before the game, Billy had parked on Central Park West at the exit nearest the softball fields. Anybody who knew what to look for could easily have found his car. Anybody capable of untying a knot, and with a minute to spare, could have put the scales of justice under Billy's spare tire.

When Sam and I last saw Billy, he was being led away by two burly guards. A police van waited to take him to the jail on Riker's Island.

Hillary quit her job at Nutley, but not in person, or even by telephone. She quit through her father. He probably wouldn't have bothered telling me if I hadn't run into him in the coffee room late that day.

"My daughter has resigned," he said as he poured milk from a carton into his coffee. "She won't be back."

"Oh. I wish I'd had a chance to say good-bye." Actually, I wished I'd had a chance to talk to her about Billy's now-defunct alibi.

Davis dropped a plastic stirrer into his cup. "That would hardly be appropriate, or helpful. I forbid it."

The emperor had spoken. *Forbid!* The word made me bristle. I should have kept my mouth shut and just called Hillary.

Davis had stooped to replace the milk in the refrigerator when something happened that I've never seen happen before. Without warning, the bottom of the carton collapsed. I jumped back quickly enough so that the splattering milk missed me. It did not miss Davis. He was cursing when I left the coffee room.

As I walked down the hall, I had to put my hand over my mouth to keep from laughing out loud. It wasn't much of a disaster when you look at the big picture. A dry cleaner and a shoe-shine man and Davis's milk problem was over. But heck! I've worked in offices long enough to know that you take your pleasures where you can get them.

15

THURSDAY MORNING I SLEPT LATE FOR a weekday. My clock radio woke me at 8:15. Moses was crouched beside me, staring into my eyes when I opened them. Once he felt sure I wasn't going to pull one of my well-known dirty tricks and shut them again, he jumped off the bed and trotted to the kitchen. I fooled him and stayed put for a couple more minutes.

The radio announcer said that during the night the heat wave had broken. Sitting, I parted my curtains. My bedroom looks out on my own fire escape and on the walls and fire escapes of neighboring buildings. It takes a lot of twisting to see the sky but I managed it. The yellow-hot sky had been replaced by a clear blue one. There were a couple of puffy white clouds high over the spires of a nearby church. I switched off my air conditioner. Walking into my living room, I opened the windows. A glorious breeze whipped through my nightgown.

My living-room windows look out at the Hudson River, and beyond that Bergen County, New Jersey. Looking through them, what I see depends on which way I turn my head. To the north, there are tall, tree-covered cliffs banking the Hudson. In the spring after a wet winter, there are waterfalls, and the leaves are a tender green. Autumn brings me a feast of red and gold. During the summer, I see signs of civilization in the boats docked at the little marina nestled against a cliff. In the winter, there *are* no signs of civilization.

That's looking north. If I look south from my living-room windows, it's a different story. There's the George Washington Bridge, two levels of it, eight lanes going each way, every one of them buzzing with traffic, far beyond the Hudson's cliffs is a vast, crowded suburb, a flatland of highways, shopping malls, apartment buildings, and houses. It's generally more upscale than the part of New Jersey I was raised in, but there are still those little pockets that remind me so much of my parents' home, or, God forbid, the ranch-style house where I dabbled in housewifery, that I experience a weird and unsettling dislocation, as if I've gone back in time.

I usually look north as I drink my coffee in my living room. The scene is so pastoral that, some mornings, I almost fool myself into believing that I'm in the country. This particular morning, self-delusion didn't work. There was too much on my mind.

At Nutley my In box waited, overflowing with punch lists. My telephone voice mail would, as usual, be gorged with complaints by the time I got to the office. All that seemed trivial, though. Kate Hamilton was dead, Billy Finkelstein was in jail, and Leonard Munch was free. That's what mattered.

I had no definite feeling about where to start, but I felt sure of one thing: Munch, that nasty, creeping degenerate, was at the heart of everything that had happened. So he had alibis. So what? People make mistakes with time. They forget to wind their watches. How could a waitress, busy with dinner customers, provide an alibi? And what about a landlord with a couple of beers in him? A couple? What if he'd drunk an entire six-pack? What if Munch's landlord had passed out dead drunk in front of his television at seven that night and didn't want to admit it to the police?

The police had been laying off Munch anyway. Now that they had Billy, they weren't going to waste a minute on Munch, much less on his ex-wife. Perhaps what Tony had said—that I was grabbing at straws—was true, but that's how my mind was working.

I found a map of Bergen County and studied it while I had a second cup of coffee. Hackensack, where Veronica Price's mother lived, is off Route 4. Mullen Place was easy enough to spot on the map. From what I could tell, it was only a couple of blocks long, and part of it ran along a park. Finding it on a map, though, wasn't the same thing as getting there. In northern New Jersey cars are not luxuries; they're necessities.

Craning my neck, I looked south out the window. Among the cars crossing the bridge, the occasional bus lumbered along. Would one of them get me somewhere near Mullen Place? Were there even cabs over there? Or would I end up hoofing it all over Bergen County?

Just do it! I finally said to myself. I probably had nothing to gain, but there wasn't much to lose, either. A few hours' pay, but Nutley had plumped up my bank account nicely.

I called Nutley at about nine o'clock. Thanks to Rhonda's hissy fit, Freddie was in his office.

It wasn't necessary for me to lie. They weren't about to pay me sick time no matter what kind of whopper I came up with. I was, after all, a temporary employee. A simple "I'll be in later" would have done it. Old habits die hard, though.

"Toothache," I told my boss. "I'll be in this afternoon, if I can get a dentist appointment this morning."

Freddie wasn't happy when he heard that. "What if you can't? What are we going to do about . . . ?"

Within seconds he had reeled off, with something nearing desperation in his voice, half a dozen problems. None of them were news to me, but Freddie was genuinely thrown by them.

What a peculiar situation. I had a boss who did nothing and knew nothing, and my secretary, who hadn't been any ball of fire to begin with, was gone. I was it, the big cheese in Nutley's relocation. I've been in jobs where I didn't know what was going on. I've also been in jobs where no one knew what was going on. But I don't think I've ever been in a job situation where I was the only one who knew what was going on.

"I'll handle the problems when I get in, Freddie," I said airily. "If I don't get in this afternoon, they'll wait until tomorrow." My boss's relief resonated through the phone wires.

Before catching one of the buses across the bridge, I called the Park Avenue office of Dr. Sidney Turnbull. A woman with a crisp English accent answered. Giving her my name, I asked for an appointment for a cosmetic surgery consultation. She offered me a half hour the following week.

"This is an emergency," I said. "Couldn't he fit me in? I'm pretty desperate."

"Oh, my. I suppose Dr. Turnbull can see you at five today. He can't spend long, though."

I assured the woman that my problem could be diagnosed in no time.

I caught one of the buses across the bridge. It took me to the remains of a bus shelter, where I then waited, alone, for a local bus to central Hackensack. I say "the remains," because the three-sided Plexiglas shelter had been plowed into by out-of-control automobiles to the point where it listed dangerously on its four steel supports. There was about a foot of clearance between the roof and the gray plastic bench where passengers were supposed to wait. I wouldn't have wanted to sit in there anyway, even if the shelter hadn't collapsed. It was a mess—the bench filthy, the concrete floor covered with the refuse from carryout restaurants. I stood on the narrow dirt patch at the side of the heavily traveled highway, hoping that some crazed driver wouldn't lost control and sideswipe me and what was left of the shelter.

It was almost 11 A.M., and the road was frantic with traffic. Though stores lined both sides of the highway, there were no sidewalks. New York is a walker's city. A window-shopper's mecca. How do people live without sidewalks? People did not walk between the stores on this highway. They drove. The few people walking went from one parking lot to the next.

As I waited, drivers occasionally glanced at me. I can't be sure, but there often seemed to be surprise in their expressions. What is a neatly dressed white woman doing waiting for a bus? they appeared to ask. My outfit—skirt, a striped shirt, loafers—was a little conservative for me, but if I was going to be knocking on strangers' doors, I'd rather be mistaken for a Jehovah's Witness than a potential thief. My purple tote added kind of a racy touch, but I could pretend it was full of religious tracts.

It felt like a century passed before the local bus arrived. There were half a dozen passengers besides myself on it. Two were black, and three were Hispanic. The one white man was bone thin and had red-rimmed eyes. His tennis shoes were worn and his pants cuffs ragged.

Once the bus turned off the highway, the scenery improved. A few blocks in and there were houses with lawns. No sidewalks, but hey, you can't have everything.

The ragged man got off first, across from a row of run-down apartments. Two stops later three other passengers filed off.

I stayed on for a few blocks more until the driver pulled over in front of a park. On the opposite side of the street, across a huge parking lot, was the back of a shopping mall. The remaining passengers left the bus as I studied my map. If I was right, Mullen Place was on the other side of the park.

The driver was staring at me. "This is the last stop."

I got up quickly. "Where do I get the return bus?"

"Other side, miss." He nodded toward a little sign posted across the street next to a public phone booth. "The bus runs every hour, until six o'clock."

If I wanted to make it to my cosmetic surgery consultation, I had to be back in Manhattan long before that last bus left. I followed a dirt path into the park, past a fenced playground where women sat on wood benches watching their children. You see a lot of women on benches watching children in Manhattan, but they're usually nannies. These women looked like mommies.

The houses on Mullen Place facing the park were small but well kept. The lawns were neat, the edges trimmed. And, wonder of wonders, there was a sidewalk, shaded by mature trees. When my feet were firmly planted on good old concrete, I felt almost at home.

Zeros. Munch's mother had thought that Sandra Price lived in a house with zeros in the address. One Hundred Mullen Place boasted a brass nameplate mounted between two spikes. The Ziwickis lived there. Continuing up the sidewalk, I looked at anything with even one zero. At 110 Mullen, a man mowing his lawn shook his head. No, he'd never heard of Sandra Price. At 120, a Pakistani family was unloading groceries from their car.

Two Hundred Mullen was at the corner of the second block. Like its neighbors, it was small and tidy. I didn't see a nameplate. As I walked up the flagstone path to the front door, I tried to think of what I was going to say to Sandra Price. Even if I found her, why would she give me her daughter's phone number? The simple truth, that my friend's son was in jail for a crime I was sure Munch had committed, might do it. It might not, though. These people had to be sick to death of Leonard Munch. The mention of his name might send them screaming away. I rang the buzzer at 200 Mullen, rehearsing my words. "I would like to speak to Veronica because . . ." After a few minutes of ringing, I knew I wasn't going to get to say them at this house.

As I turned away from the door, a mailman was pushing a handcart past the house. I called out to him: "Excuse me."

He was a black man, tall and slender and handsome. Removing his hat, he dragged a hand across his forehead. His skin shone with perspiration.

"Do you know if this is Sandra Price's house?"

"Yes. But she's gone."

"Gone?"

I must have sounded alarmed, because he drew back his head. "I don't mean gone forever. She put a one-week hold on her mail. People do that when they go on vacation."

"You don't happen to have a forwarding address for her daughter, do you?"

Shaking his head, he put the cap back on. "I don't sort the mail. I just deliver it."

As he pushed his cart down the block, I cursed under my breath. Damn! Here I was in the middle of God-knows-where, without Veronica's mother and without transportation.

The prospect of calling a zillion foreign-car dealers from a phone booth faced me. What did I say to these car dealers when they answered? "I'm interested in a Mitsubishi. By the way, did your boss just marry a woman named Veronica?"

Just married. Maybe I was going about this in the wrong way. Weddings, even second ones, can be major productions. And this wedding had involved a businessman, a sales type who might have to put on a show even if he didn't want to. It had, after all, involved a honeymoon in Hawaii. Sinking down on the vacationing Mrs. Price's steps, I dragged the phone book from my bag.

There could have been something about the wedding in the New Jersey papers. The listings for public libraries indicated that there were several in the area, but when I studied my map, I saw that none of them was within walking distance. I sat for a few moments, making a mental list of the things involved in a wedding and trying to think of ways I could use them to find Veronica: church or hall or private home, minister or rabbi or judge. A gown or a dress. Gifts.

Gifts. Would Veronica have signed up at the bridal registry at that Bloomingdale's over there in the mall? If she had, would Bloomingdale's tell me whom she had married? Probably not. As I gazed across the park, a local bus pulled up near the phone booth and then pulled away. The next one wouldn't be there for an hour.

I decided to try the neighbors first, and if that didn't work, I'd take a cab to a library.

My head was starting to hurt, probably a combination of

stress and the fact that I hadn't eaten breakfast. I shoved the phone book back into my tote.

At the house on the left, I got a cool response from a harried woman with a squirming, red-faced infant in her arms. "We just moved in," she told me. "I've barely spoken to anyone around here." As I walked away, the baby let out with a full-throated howl. At the second house, there was no one home.

"Ten minutes," a dispatcher told me when I called a cab from the booth near the bus stop, so I found a little shade for myself under a tree. The traffic in and out of the shopping-center parking lot was light. People drove as if they had a lot of time, with none of the horn blowing common to Manhattan traffic. After a minute or two I stopped paying attention to the cars and stood, lost in my thoughts. I wouldn't have noticed the white station wagon with the luggage rack on top if the driver hadn't blown his horn impatiently.

When I glanced at the wagon, I did a double take. Leonard Munch was at the wheel. He was wearing sunglasses, and a cap hid some of his distinctive hair, but it was definitely Munch. I quickly moved behind the tree but he didn't turn into the lot. He was in a hurry to get past the traffic that was turning. Farther up the street, he took a left. I lost sight of him for a minute, and then spotted the station wagon on the other side of the park. It slowed in front of 200 Mullen. Munch drove on after a few seconds and then repeated the route, circling the park again. The second time around, he stopped in front of the white bungalow and walked up the path.

My view was suddenly blocked by a bright yellow cab. I climbed in and the driver, a plump gray-haired man, looked at me expectantly.

"Do you see that white station wagon over there? I'd like to follow it if it stays in New Jersey. If it heads to Manhattan, I'm not interested."

He stared at Munch's car, then looked over the seat again. "You serious? Like in the movies?"

"I'm serious."

Munch was walking back toward his car. "Try not to let him see you," I said.

"Just like in the movies," the driver repeated as he pulled out. "You a cop?"

"No."

My driver kept one arm over the back of his seat and every few seconds glanced over his shoulder at me. He followed slowly, laconically, so far back that I was afraid we would lose Munch. As we passed the mall, he asked, "Husband problems?"

Munch certainly had been a problem husband, but not mine. I nodded. The driver shook his head sympathetically. I pointed ahead.

"Please watch the road. He's pulling onto Route Four, heading away from Manhattan."

"Don't worry. We won't lose him. I've been driving around here . . ."

As we made our way onto the highway and wove through the heavy traffic, I heard a long-winded recital of where this man had driven, whom he'd driven there, and how much they'd paid him.

"Newark Airport with three drunks in the back . . . Pregnant lady going into labor . . . Guy beat me out of my fare . . . Never pick up kids. That's my first rule . . ."

I kept my eyes glued to the white station wagon with the luggage rack on top. "You're going to lose him," I said a couple of times.

As I told you, much of Route 4 is lined with minimalls and restaurants and office buildings. And car dealerships.

"Gamblers . . . all the way to Atlantic City. Biggest tip . . ."

"There's a Toyota dealer up there," I said sharply enough to shut my driver up for a second.

"You want me to pull in?"

Munch passed without slowing. "No."

We followed Munch off Route 4 and onto another highway. There were no open spots between buildings here. It was an endless strip of stores, and an endless mass of drivers trying to get into and out of parking lots. We passed a couple of dealerships that sold American cars, and one that sold Jeeps.

"Paramus is one of the busiest shopping areas in the world," my driver told me. "One time I had this couple, looking for baby furniture, went to every . . ."

Ahead, through the maze of signs along the roadside, was one that read PARAMUS HONDA. Munch had pulled into the slow lane, so I told my driver to do the same. When Munch turned into a parking lot just beyond the Honda dealership, I said, "Stop."

"Here? I can't just stop here."

"Pull into this side of the Honda lot."

Munch had come to a full stop beside a store that sold pet supplies, but he wasn't shopping for cat food. He got out of the wagon, skirted a fence, and walked into the dealership's lot. I lost him among the rows of cars.

I paid the driver and assured him that he didn't need to wait for me. He looked disappointed. Had I provided him with fuel for another cabbing adventure story? "One time I picked up this lady following some guy. Said she wasn't a cop, but . . ."

The glass-fronted automobile showroom had glass doors at both sides. A number of people were inside, some at desks, some wandering around the cars on display. I was at one of the doors when, through the glass, Munch appeared on the other side of the building. He propped open the door with his foot and crouched. What's he doing? I wondered as his arm pitched forward in an underhanded toss. Something about the size of a paperback book skittered across the showroom floor, then flipped open. I looked back at the far door and saw Munch staring at me. An instant later he turned and fled into the rows of cars.

A volley of shots rang out from inside the showroom. There were shouts. A woman screamed, and a few people dove behind cars. I jumped out of the way as a mob of customers and salespeople raced toward the door where I stood. Otherwise I might have been trampled when they shoved through it.

●　　●　　●

"It's all right, folks," a salesman was saying a few minutes later. "Firecrackers. Some kid's idea of fun."

The shell-shocked folks took some persuading. Salespeople smiled, patted shoulders, offered coffee, comforted a crying child. Finally most of the customers and staff filed back through the door.

One woman on the staff, a youngish blond with a sunburned nose, remained outside. She wore a loose linen vest over a white shirt and was quite pretty, though very thin. A dark-haired man she'd been talking quietly with brushed her hair with his hand before he returned to the showroom.

The blond woman walked around the building to the door where Munch had been. I followed a dozen feet behind, pretending to examine the cars parked along the front of the showroom. Cupping her hand over her eyes, the woman gazed out over the lot.

"Excuse me," I said.

There were frown lines across her forehead when she turned. Thinking I was a customer, she forced a smile. "Are you interested in one of those?"

Those?

She indicated a sleek light green car beside me. I'd unconsciously rested my hand against the hood. The car was shaped like a bullet and looked as fast as one. I glanced at the sticker price. Good grief! Is that what cars cost these days? Sure I was interested in it. I have the same interest in owning that car that I have in owning a beach house. It would be nice, but . . .

"I'd like to test drive it. My name's Bonnie Indermill."

I hoped she would introduce herself, but she glanced into the showroom. The firecracker incident seemed to have sparked the action in there. Customers and salespeople chatted excitedly. "I'll see if I can find a salesman," she said. "It might be a few minutes."

I wasn't sure this was Veronica, but I had no intention of going for a useless test drive with a man I knew wasn't.

"Can't you do it? I'm in an awful hurry."

She chewed on her lower lip. "I usually work in the office. But why not," she said, smiling again. "I could use a break. We just got back from Hawaii yesterday. I'm suffering from culture shock.''

"Didn't have to worry about firecrackers in Hawaii, huh?"

"I didn't have to worry about a lot of things in Hawaii. My name's Veronica," she added. "You want a stick?"

I'd found Munch's ex-wife. That registered. But for one muddled moment I thought she was offering me an illegal drug, maybe something she'd brought back from Hawaii. My confusion must have shown.

"Stick shift. I can see you don't."

A few minutes later, I was behind the wheel.

Veronica had a well-oiled sales pitch. As I merged into heavy traffic, she talked about acceleration. When she noticed that I was out of practice as a driver and clearly nervous, she talked about safety. Both my hands gripped the wheel, hard. The air conditioner was blasting, but as cars streaked around me my hands on the wheel grew sweaty.

"What are you driving now?" she asked.

"Nothing. I took a bus and a cab."

I felt her eyes on me, appraising me. As I said, New Jersey is car country. Some boys in a convertible wheeled around us, blasting their horn. This was harrowing. I had zero interest in buying this car; I didn't want to be killed testing it.

"Would you mind if I tried a quieter road?"

"That's a good idea," Veronica responded. She directed me onto a tree-lined side street with almost no traffic. I relaxed immediately. "That's better. I guess you can tell I'm not used to driving."

She had started to say something about gas mileage when I pulled to the curb and unfastened the seat belt. My behavior was odd, I suppose, by test-driver standards. When I leaned over and grabbed my purple tote from the backseat, she was looking at me curiously. There were more graceful ways to bring up Leonard Munch, I suppose, but I was hungry and cranky and I wanted to get this over with. Digging out the copy I'd made of Munch's sketch, I handed it to Veronica.

As she examined it, the frown lines returned. I had the right woman.

"I see you've met my ex-husband," she finally said. She tilted the drawing and read, " 'Somebody doesn't like you.' That's a new one. Usually it's, 'I see everything you do.' "

Veronica dropped the sketch onto her lap. Her fingers scrambled nervously into her vest pocket. Pulling out a pack of cigarettes, she rolled down her window. "I hope you don't mind if I smoke. It's the one habit Leonard and I have in common," she added bitterly.

She hadn't known that her ex-husband was harassing Kate Hamilton until the day before. "When I found out about Kate's murder, and that the police wanted to question me, I figured something like that had been going on. I called this sergeant, Connor, right away," she said, "but he hasn't returned my call."

There was no point in explaining that Connor was no longer on the case. "The police might not call you back. They've arrested someone else for the murder. His name's Billy Finkelstein. He's a friend of mine."

"That's too bad." She puffed angrily on a filtered cigarette. "I'd like to see that creep locked up forever. How come he's treating you to some of his 'artwork'?"

I had identified Munch as Kate's stalker, I told her. She blew out a breath of smoke that billowed around her. "He is one miserable, disgusting thing."

"I think he's a murderer, too," I said. "I don't think Billy Finkelstein killed Kate."

I wanted to learn more about why Kate had ended up on Munch's hate list. When I asked about her few weeks as Kate's secretary, Veronica grimaced.

"It was when things were at their worst with Len. Rock bottom." Looking down, she seemed to study the cigarette burning in her fingers. "I hope you don't think I'm a total masochist. My relationship with Len started out okay. We met at a bar on the East Side. We only went out a couple weeks before he asked me to marry him."

Veronica told me that she was nearing thirty at the time.

She'd been feeling "not quite desperate, but . . . you know how it is."

I assured her that I did know.

"The thing is," she continued, "Len was just so . . . attentive. A couple times it was a little annoying, but hell! I was used to guys who promised they'd call and then they wouldn't. I didn't start thinking of the way Len treated me as harassment until after we got married." Glancing at me, Veronica added, "I was pregnant.

"Len was working in a print shop in lower Manhattan. I had a long-term temp job at a bank. He tried to meet me after work every day. If he couldn't, he'd call me right before I left my office." Turning slightly, she stared into the car's rearview mirror, then turned to me again. "You get used to watching your back when you're married to someone like Len. Anyway, we were living in Manhattan. The phone would be ringing as soon as I walked into my office. Len was fired, finally. Probably because he was spending so much time at work keeping track of me. After he was unemployed, things got unbearable, fast.

"Len went to work with me every morning. He'd walk me to the elevator of my office. He actually wanted to go to my desk with me. Can you believe that? The man I was working for was about half my height and weighed a ton. He had a wife and four kids and I was six months pregnant, but Len was still suspicious. He wanted to see for himself. I told him I'd divorce him if he tried to."

Veronica hesitated until a woman pushing a baby stroller had passed the car.

"One day, though, after work, my boss and I left at the same time. That's all there was to it—we walked out of the building together. But there was Len, waiting across the street from the building. He started yelling at us, that I was a slut and my boss had made me pregnant."

She'd been speaking so softly that her sudden, bitter laugh startled me. "That was the end of my job at the bank," she went on. "We were so strapped for money that we moved in with Len's parents for a couple months. The baby was born while we were there. When Len got another job, we got an apartment. His mother baby-sat and I went back to temping.''

Veronica pressed the cigarette into the ashtray on the dashboard and reached for another one. Her hand was trembling, and it took her a moment to touch the car's lighter to the cigarette.

"My first assignment was a one-month job with Kate Hamilton. She had a reputation for being difficult, and I was paid top dollar. Combat pay. I've got to tell you, I was a wreck. I had a ten-week-old baby and an insane husband. Len called me at work constantly. He'd started making these wild threats, things like if I ever tried to leave him, his parents wouldn't let me take the baby. I couldn't even go visit my mother without him calling her house a dozen times. It felt like I was trapped in hell.

"One day Kate asked me to work late. I hated working for her, but we needed the money. When I called Len and told him, he went nuts. He said the baby wouldn't be there when I got home. I didn't actually believe him—most of his threats were nothing but hot air—but he upset me. Then, as soon as I hung up, Kate called me into her office for dictation. It was terrible. I remember trying to concentrate on what she was saying, and I couldn't. My hands were shaking so hard that my pencil wouldn't stay on the steno pad. I started crying. Kate got up and shut her door. And then . . .''

Her eyes glistening, Veronica looked at me. "And then Kate saved my sanity. She got the whole story out of me, and then she said she could help, if I wanted her to. She knew about a place where I could go and hide with the baby until I got my life together. I couldn't believe it was happening. Here was this woman who had been such a bitch. Half an hour before she'd yelled at me about a typo.'' Veronica took a deep breath. "Anyway, Kate called someone. When she hung up, she helped me work out how I was going to get away from Len, with the baby.

"I made an appointment with a pediatrician while Len had to be at work. Kate picked me and the baby up there and drove us to a place where women with problems like mine, or even worse ones, could hide.''

She stretched and rested her head against the seat's high back. ''Kate told me to keep quiet about the shelter and how she'd arranged it for me. The fewer people who knew, the less chance there was of any of the husbands or boyfriends finding out about it. I didn't even tell my mother. My daughter and I stayed there for a couple weeks, until I felt strong enough to deal with a divorce.

''Len's parents found a lawyer for him. They threatened a child custody battle. By then I was prepared to go through anything to get rid of him. The resident manager at the safe house put me in touch with a divorce lawyer.''

Veronica seemed almost to have forgotten that I was there. Her eyelids were half-shut, and she talked almost as if she were alone.

''But, when it came time to go to court, Len dropped everything. Maybe he realized that with his past he'd never win. He really wasn't interested in our daughter, anyway,'' she added, shaking her head sadly. ''He didn't even send a birthday card.''

Who can say what motivates someone like Leonard Munch. ''About when were you divorced?'' I asked.

''This past May. I'd been working at the dealership for a couple months.'' For the first time since I'd stopped the car, she smiled. ''Ray—the guy I just married—invited me out to lunch on my second day there. I was such a wreck from dealing with Leonard that I almost didn't go.''

''How did Leonard find out that Kate had helped you?'' I asked.

''When it looked like the divorce was going to be a big deal, Kate made a statement on my behalf. It went in my file. Len's lawyer got a look at it, and I'm sure he told Len about it. And don't forget,'' she added, ''Len knew I was working for Kate when I ran away from him. He's totally paranoid. He would have suspected her anyway.'' Another, thinner smile played at her lips. ''You know, until this thing with the firecrackers, I'd been thinking I was rid of him.''

''You hadn't heard from him?''

''When my daughter and I left the safe house, we moved

in with my mother. There were hang-up calls in the middle of the night until we got an unlisted number, and once this spring Len followed me to work. He never did anything rotten until today, though. At least not that I know of. He left me alone most of the summer. The thing about Len is, if you ignore him, he usually stops. He only does these things if he thinks he's upsetting you.''

"This summer he had someone else to harass," I said. "Kate Hamilton."

The copy of Munch's sketch was still in Veronica's lap. Looking down at it, she said sadly, "And now that Kate's gone, he's got you."

I shrugged. "I'm probably not giving him what he wants. He can't see into my apartment and he doesn't know a thing about my personal life outside of where I work."

"This isn't your boyfriend in the drawing?"

"Not a chance."

Veronica crushed out her cigarette. "I thought he'd given up on me. Did you happen to notice what he was driving today?"

"A white station wagon."

Hearing that, she made an angry sound. "It's his mother's. You wouldn't believe how his parents protect him."

"I hope you don't have to go to the safe house again," I said.

"I better not. It's not there anymore."

"What?"

"I mean, it's been shut down. It was about five miles from here, in Teaneck. Before I got married I drove by. I wanted to show the woman who managed the place my ring. There was a realtor's FOR RENT sign on the lawn. That scared me," she added, shifting nervously in the seat. "After Len found out I'd been in a shelter, he said he was going to find it and blow it up."

And I'd thought my ex-husband was trouble! It's all relative, isn't it.

I asked Veronica for the name of the shelter's manager. If Leonard had done something awful that caused the shelter to close, it might not add weight to my theory that he had killed Kate, but it might make the police take a harder look at him.

"Her name was Jane," Veronica replied. "I never knew a last name."

"Do you recall who the realtor was?"

Veronica thought for a minute, then shook her head. Leaning across the seat, she looked at the clock on the driver's side of the dashboard. "We better get going. Maybe I should drive," she added. "You're not too good in traffic, and since you don't plan to buy a car anyway . . ."

"If I ever do buy a car, I'll buy it from you," I promised when we had changed seats.

"Thanks." Veronica turned the key in the ignition. "You know, in spite of everything, I doubt Len killed Kate Hamilton. He's too gutless to have faced a woman like Kate. You have no idea how scary she could be."

Actually I did, but for Billy Finkelstein's sake I hoped that Veronica was wrong.

16

THE MAIN PORT AUTHORITY BUS TERminal is only a couple of miles from Dr. Sidney Turnbull's East Side office, but the two might as well be on different planets. At 4:30 I was threading my way through a blitz of commuters, beggars, and a few types who looked as if they'd like to relieve me of my tacky purple tote and possibly my life. Fifteen minutes later I was standing in a sparkling sanctuary of chrome and leather, in front of a receptionist with an English accent and a face that looked as if it were encased in a transparent Latex girdle. No droops, no wrinkles. No animation, either, but perfection has a price.

"Bonnie Indermill. Oh, yes. We fit you in." She looked up from her calendar. "An emergency consultation, you said."

I hadn't had time even to comb my hair. Forget about makeup. Nothing in the receptionist's expression suggested that I didn't look like a candidate for emergency cosmetic surgery. I touched my hand to my nose expecting, secretly hoping for an argument. She nodded and said, simply, "I see."

She saw what? Feelings wounded, I took the form she gave me and carried it to the waiting room. There was a mirror against one wall. A glimpse revealed that my hair could have used some work, but I managed to slip into a chair without looking any closer at myself.

Three other women were waiting for Dr. Turnbull. Two were mother and daughter, I imagine. The girl, who looked about fifteen, had obviously been the recipient of Dr. Turnbull's magic fingers. Her nose was covered by a white bandage. Under her eyes were fading, yellowish bruises. As I filled in my form, a nurse called the two of them into an inner room. I was glad to see that the nurse, a stout black woman, had heavy jowls, an extra chin, and a crinkly smile.

After watching the mother and daughter walk from the waiting room, the third woman, who had been thumbing through a fashion magazine, glanced my way. She was an attractive brunette, perhaps a little older than I am, and definitely a lot better dressed. Her features were fine—if on the pert side—and I found myself speculating about why she was there.

"That girl's going to be so happy when that bandage comes off and she looks in the mirror," she said knowingly.

"Dr. Turnbull's supposed to be one of the best."

"He *is* the best," the woman responded, and she went back to the magazine. The subject of Dr. Turnbull's merits was closed.

In the blank on the form where it asked my profession, I wrote "dancer." Being in show business would lend some credibility to my need for emergency cosmetic surgery. Where the form asked for the name of the person who had referred me, I wrote, "Kate Hamilton." When I returned it to the receptionist, I watched carefully for a shudder of recognition, a quiver of shock. Her chin, her entire facade, remained as taut as the suspension in that car I'd driven a few hours before.

On my way back to my chair I took a surreptitious look at the other woman in the waiting room. She had pressed her finger against the skin near one of her eyes, as if she was trying to flatten the faint lines there. Was that it? Eye maintenance?

Before I could make it past that mirror again, my gaze locked onto my reflection. I didn't see much problem with my nose. What was with that receptionist? Did she see something I didn't? I wasn't wearing my glasses so I squinted. Creases, which I tend to ignore, fanned from the corners of my eyes.

In retrospect, and since I don't have the money or the inclination to get anything done about those creases, I've chosen to blame them on the mirror itself, or the lighting in Dr. Turnbull's waiting room. For all I know, the room was designed by the same sadists who design the dressing rooms where we try on bathing suits. At the time, though, I slumped into my chair, disheartened. If that attractive woman was worried about her few lines, I should have been hysterical.

I was the last patient Dr. Turnbull saw that afternoon. I never did get a look at the teenage girl without her bandages. Perhaps there was a second door for Dr. Turnbull's happy "afters."

When I finally met the doctor, it was in his brightly lit office. He greeted me from behind his desk with a warm smile and a handshake, and then sat down in his big leather chair. Along one wall there was an expensive-looking white leather sofa that I wouldn't have minded falling into, but the small hard chair across from the doctor seemed more appropriate.

At first Turnbull didn't recognize me as the woman whose car had broken down in front of his apartment building a couple of days before, but that afternoon he'd concentrated on my legs and not my face.

While the doctor studied the form I'd filled out, I studied him. The hair and the hands said fifty-five, the unlined face said ten years younger. He may have taken advantage of the profession he practiced, though he wasn't in his receptionist's class. Turnbull was good-looking in a way that, for me, bordered on being . . . too much. Too much good food had added a layer of padding. Too much sun—for a doctor, yet—had given him an unnaturally burnished complexion which was heightened by the bright white of his shirt. It was almost as if he were the victim of a surfeit of good living. That said, I knew that many women would find him attractive. Given a few more years, and a few more upheavals in my life, I might be among them. His eyes were an unusual light blue, his smile perfect, and his manner confident.

Turnbull glanced up at me when he'd finished studying one side of my form. There was no mistaking his shock when he flipped the page over and saw Kate's name. His shoulders stiffening, he asked, "You knew Kate Hamilton?"

"I worked at her law firm for a while."

He cleared his throat, said, "Um," and focused those baby blues on me. I expected he might have something more to say about Kate, but instead the doctor stood and circled the desk. When he raised his left hand to my face, I had a clear, close view of his wedding ring. It was wide and bright gold, with a narrow, paler rim. Munch had done a good job of sketching it.

"I see absolutely nothing wrong with your nose," Dr. Turnbull said. "It is ideal for your face which, I should add, is nicely proportioned."

Okay, I'm weak in the face of flattery. Even so, my reaction to this was absurd: Immediate, complete devotion. I'd been prepared to dislike Turnbull, but if his next words had been, "Follow me into hell," I would have stood and fallen into place behind him.

As he gently tested the skin on my neck, I perched on the edge of the chair, more nervous than I'd been behind the wheel of that car when I'd endangered myself, my passenger, and a good number of other drivers. That I had no intention of having my throat, or anything else, lifted, was irrelevant. I still wanted to hear this man, who I had just elevated to the status of a god, say, "You're beautiful. Why are you wasting my time and your money?"

"You're in show business," he said finally. "Many of my patients are. I understand your concerns. You're much too young for a complete lift, and it will be a few years before you have to worry about your throat, but"—he touched the skin next to my eye—"you might want to consider this area. It's not all that bad now," he continued, returning to the other side of his desk. "If you weren't onstage, I'd suggest you wait. In your case, though . . ."

The slippery bastard! Softening me up with my perfectly proportioned nose, then hitting me with my crinkled smile-lines. Being told I needed to brush up on my driving skills was nothing compared to hearing that the lines beside my eyes might end my stage career. This was completely il-logical of me—I don't have a stage career—but so what! I was being told I had the face of a has-been before I'd even *been*.

I had to get to the real reason for my visit. If I didn't, I'd end up laying out my MasterCard for an eye job. Taking a deep breath, I interrupted Dr. Turnbull.

"I'm not here about cosmetic surgery."

He braced his hands against the edge of his desk and said, "Then would you please tell me why you are here?"

In response, I dug through my tote for Munch's sketch and put it on the desk in front of him. He stared at it, clearly aghast.

"You, too," he said after a moment's silence.

"Me, too. I know Kate was getting them. What about you?"

Still staring at the drawing, the doctor shook his head. "No. Whoever was doing this seemed to have no interest in bothering me. Kate got it all: drawings, calls."

Then, without warning, Turnbull changed direction. "But who are you?" he asked, fixing me with a cautious gaze. "If you're with the police, why didn't you say so? And if you're not, why your interest in me? You have every reason to dislike the jerk who's doing this"—a nod at the sketch—"but because one of my patients got similar draw-ings and confided in me doesn't mean that this business has anything to do with me."

Unlike Veronica, who had run on jolts of nervous energy, the doctor was cool and deliberate. For a moment I was thrown, as I sometimes am when dealing with people who are supremely sure of themselves.

Veronica had been easy. She'd had nothing to hide, and possibly something to gain, by talking to me. There was the slim possibility that I'd come up with something that would get her miserable ex-husband out of her hair for a long time. Turnbull was another matter. If I was right, he had an affair to hide from his wife and family, and possibly from his adoring patients. He had nothing to gain by confiding in me. Munch had never bothered him.

"I'm closely involved with the police." A lie, sure, but not an outrageous one.

The doctor opened his mouth to say something. Before he could, I went on. "I saw the drawings Kate got." My eyes traveled to his wedding ring. "They were very—" I started to say "precise" but used the more loaded, "explicit."

He fidgeted uncomfortably, as if his big leather chair had just become too small.

"The artist did a good job with your ring," I continued, "and with that red-and-white polo shirt you still wear."

I thought that would convince him to talk to me, but he was even more cautious than I'd realized. Lowering his chin onto his hand, Turnbull stared at me hard. "Have I seen you before? Yes, I have. You were in front of my apartment building the other day. What is this? A shakedown? Are you connected to this"—he flicked his hand angrily at the sketch—"artist?"

"Hardly."

Turnbull studied the sketch as I explained how, and why, I'd found him. I gave him the same story I'd given Veronica, which was true as far as it went. Only Sam Finkelstein was omitted. "The police aren't particularly interested in Munch anymore," I told him. "I'm looking for something that will make them look at him again."

"And I should help you? You connived your way in here . . ."

This was the man I'd been ready to follow across smoldering lava and into the mouth of a volcano only minutes earlier? I could think of only one thing to do. A direct threat.

"If you won't talk to me about Kate, I'm going straight

to the Seventeenth Precinct and tell them everything I know about you.''

I tried to sound, and look, indignant, but if the doctor had said, ''So go,'' that probably would have been the end of it. I was a fraud. Nobody at the precinct was remotely interested in talking to me about Kate's murder.

Turnbull was still for a moment. When he picked up his phone and pushed a button, I grew even more anxious than I already was. If I was wrong about his affair with Kate, if it only existed in Munch's crazy imagination, Turnbull could call my bluff and report me to the police. And if Tony followed through on his threat, I could end up with the same stylish address as the kid I was trying to help.

''I'm going to be with this patient a while,'' Turnbull said. ''Hold my calls and let my wife know I'll be a little late.''

When he looked back at me, his expression was sheepish. ''There's an old Scottish saying: 'Confession is good for the soul.' ''

Turnbull didn't strike me as the confessing kind. In any event, the old Scotsman who said that probably didn't have me in mind as a confessor. But I needed all the help I could get, and if I got it from some old Scotsman, fine.

''For a long time, I found Kate an extremely difficult woman,'' Turnbull began. ''Our building is a co-op. I served a term on the board of directors, and Kate was a constant complainer. Frankly,'' he added, ''I was surprised when she consulted me as a doctor.

''There was a scar in front of her left ear. It wasn't long''—he demonstrated by holding his thumb and index finger about an inch apart—''but it was raised and jagged. It was near her hairline, and Kate had been wearing her hair in front of her ear to cover it. She told me she had been injured by broken glass in an auto accident years before.

''The scar couldn't be entirely eliminated, but I was able to make it much less visible by performing a cicatrisotomy. That is, recutting and reshaping it. When that had healed,

I injected a small amount of collagen. During these visits . . .''

Turnbull had been comfortable talking about Kate's scar, but he faltered when he started discussing Kate herself. He scratched the side of his nose, and his eyes wandered the office, stopping anywhere but on me. When he went on, he was staring at an invisible spot on the wall behind me. ''. . . Kate and I got to know each other better. I found her um . . .''

The second I heard that ''um,'' I knew that the scene Munch had captured was taken from life.

''. . . interesting,'' Turnbull finally said, his gaze returning to me. ''As you may have noticed, Kate seemed a bit severe, on the surface.''

Yes, I'd noticed. The woman had run over me like a steamroller. I nodded.

''Underneath, she was a caring person, and an intelligent one. My wife is bright, of course,'' he assured me. ''I don't mean to suggest that she isn't. But I found myself looking forward to Kate's visits. She could talk finance, foreign policy, anything.

''I remember the afternoon when the last bandage came off. Kate was thrilled with the results. I'll never forget her smile. She looked like an eight-year-old kid on Christmas morning. I realized, then, that I was sorry to see our relationship ending. It was Kate who suggested we go out for a drink to celebrate. We ended up . . .''

Once again he fumbled for words. ''I discovered that under her cool exterior, Kate was a passionate, seductive woman. We ended up coming back here after the office had closed . . .'' The leather sofa against the back wall drew his eyes.

I hate to say that it was the same old story, because when you know the people involved you know that the story is always different. But in its basics, it was the same old story. Kate Hamilton and Sidney Turnbull had begun an affair that afternoon.

The affair had lasted into the summer, though both of them had spoken about breaking it off. ''Kate wasn't interested in marriage," he said. "In any event, a divorce was out of the question for me. I'm devoted to my wife and family."

Not devoted enough to steer clear of that nifty sofa, but that wasn't any of my business. My business was Leonard Munch.

"How did Munch find out about you?" I asked Turnbull.

"He followed Kate. She'd had an obscene call about a week before she got the first drawing, but she'd thought it was a crank, a one-time thing. Until she got that sketch, she had no idea she was being watched.

"I have a place in the Hamptons. Kate was at a resort near Montauk for the weekend. One afternoon when my wife was at the beach, I drove over to see Kate. Her room faced out on the dunes." Turnbull looked away. "We didn't close the shades. It didn't seem necessary.

"A few days later I drove into the city. Kate was already home. I met her at a Mexican restaurant in Chelsea where we weren't likely to run into anybody we knew. When we'd talked on the phone earlier, she had sounded upset. She showed me the sketch, and I understood why. She'd gotten it in the mail that afternoon."

It had been the one with "I see you all the time" written on it. It had distressed him terribly, Turnbull told me. I can understand that. He had a life-style to protect. He had a self-image, too. We all do. How did Turnbull and Kate feel, I wondered, when they saw their secret passion—something they probably thought was pretty special—reduced to a dirty drawing?

Turnbull had been willing to go to the police right away, or so he now claimed. When he told me this, his eyes searched mine. He wanted me to believe him, I think.

"It was Kate's idea to avoid the police if possible," he went on. "She felt that if she was right about the Stalker's identity, our best reaction was no reaction. If he followed his usual pattern, he'd get bored with us. Over the next two weeks, she got two more sketches. By the time she showed me the third one, she wasn't so sure about this character giving up on us. She arranged . . ."

Three sketches? I'd seen only two—both of Kate and Turnbull in the room at the beach. Neither Tony nor Connor had mentioned a third one to me. I interrupted the doctor.

"I didn't realize there were three sketches."

"Oh, yes. The third one showed the two of us sitting in that Mexican restaurant."

"So it wasn't obscene," I said.

The memory of that drawing caused Turnbull's skin to redden under his tan. "Oh, he managed to make even that one obscene. The calls continued, too. But as I was saying, when that third drawing arrived, Kate arranged to talk to an acquaintance, a security woman who might have some ideas about how to handle this."

That would have been Cornelia. Unfortunately, Kate had been killed before they had a chance to talk.

"Was there anything more that Munch did?" I asked.

Eyes sharpening, he said, "More? Wasn't that enough? Filthy drawings, obscene phone calls?"

Enough. Sure it was enough. Enough to make him, and Kate, feel scared and embarrassed and foolish and a lot of other things. But it wasn't enough to reawaken police interest in Munch.

Suddenly I felt very drained. Part of it was physical—I'd been running around all day—but part of it was pure gloom. All my running around hadn't accomplished a thing. Tony was right: I didn't know what I was doing. The line I was pursuing went nowhere. The depressing notion that Billy really might be guilty passed through my mind.

"I know what Munch was doing was awful," I assured the doctor. "It's just that I was hoping for something more. I suppose Kate told you why Munch was harassing her?"

"Certainly," Turnbull responded. "He blamed Kate for his divorce. Apparently Kate got his wife into a shelter in New Jersey. Some organization that she did volunteer work for."

"Kate volunteered there?" Why hadn't Veronica mentioned that?

Turnbull's head was shaking. "I don't mean Kate worked there. Her volunteer work was legal. Pro bono. The shelter was one of her clients.''

Pro bono. For the good. A spark of excitement broke through my gloom. Whether the shelter paid or not didn't matter. It was one of Nutley's clients. It would have a client number, and it would have a file folder packed with information. The possibility that Munch had done something horrible to force the shelter's closing was slim, but I wasn't going to drop this until I was certain.

"Of course, Kate also had a personal interest in the place," he continued.

I was so eager to get to the office and find that file that what he had said almost slid past me.

"I wonder why?" I asked absently.

"It's easy to understand," he said in a matter-of-fact way. "That scar near her ear didn't come from an automobile accident. When Kate first consulted me, she lied about that. After she got to know me, she opened up."

I learned from Turnbull that while Kate was in law school, she had married one of her professors. "Her husband was such a heavy drinker that eventually he lost his job. They'd been fighting a lot, and finally he became physically abusive. It began with shoving, then slaps. Then, one night, he hit her with a glass hard enough to send her to the emergency room."

Yet another surprise in the life of Kate Hamilton. I shook my head, and Turnbull looked at me curiously.

"Kate wasn't very nice to me," I said as I pushed back the hard chair. "Actually, she was awful. Now, though, I feel kind of guilty about the way I judged her."

Realizing that I was leaving, Turnbull stood slowly. "Kate wasn't very nice to most people. She was definitely an . . . acquired taste.''

And did the taste linger for Turnbull? I wondered. It was impossible to say. I knew even less about him than I knew about Kate. When I left his office, though, the doctor was standing beside his desk, staring at the white leather sofa. From the angle where I stood, his unlined features seemed to have developed a pathetic droop.

I tried reaching Margaret Brusk from a phone booth on

the street. It was just after five-thirty, but there was no answer at her extension. Where would she have put Kate's list of files? In big law firms, files generally are stored in one central area and signed out like books in a library. File numbers are referred to continually, and most of the legal secretaries I've known keep their file lists on their desks in three-ring binders, handy for when their boss screams for information.

It was an easy twenty-block walk down Park Avenue to Nutley. It was an easier cab ride. Stepping to the curb, I put out my hand. I'd become a cab junkie. It was going to be a tough habit to break.

Despite her new slave-driving beast of a boss, Margaret had left on time. Harriet was still at her desk, staring at a marked-up document and typing rapidly. Andy paced nearby, keeping an anxious eye on her progress. Harriet's own beast, Davis, was in his office doing his best to live up to the label "mouthpiece."

"Harriet," I said.

She tilted her chin to let me know she was listening.

"Do you know where Margaret kept Kate Hamilton's list of file numbers?"

Harriet shook her head.

"That's right," Andy said to her. "Don't talk. Type."

"You're going to turn into a real Nutley type if you're not careful, Andy," she shot back. "I'll get this done much faster without you hanging over me. You're making me nervous."

"Nervous? You work for that"—Andy nodded toward Davis's door—"and I'm making you nervous?"

"Yes. I'll buzz you as soon as I've finished."

Grumbling under his breath, Andy walked into his office.

"Andy's not himself," Harriet told me. "The firm is announcing new partners on Monday."

"Do you think he's going to be one of them?"

"It looks that way. He deserves it. If I were you, Bonnie," she added softly, "I'd grab him."

"He's never indicated that he's interested in being grabbed," I whispered.

"We'll see," she said mysteriously. "That file list you're looking for is probably in Kate's office. Mr. Davis has been going through her work papers in his spare time. Oh, and you weren't in today, were you? Have you heard the news about Billy Finkelstein?"

"No." My heart thumped hard. Could there be any news about Billy that wouldn't be bad?

"He was let out this afternoon."

"On bail?"

"No," said Harriet. "He came up with another alibi. This one's apparently true."

If Harriet hadn't been so involved in her typing, I would have hugged her. What a woman! She had managed to put Andy in his place, fill me in on the hot news at Nutley, tell me where to find Kate Hamilton's client list, and make me want to shout with happiness for Billy. She'd done all this without letting her eyes stray from the draft document. Her fingers had scarcely paused in their keyboard tap dance.

"Harriet," I said, "you're the best."

My friend acknowledged this with, "Um-hmm."

"I'm going to ask for a file in your name," I said. "When you get it, put it in a drawer and hold it for me."

Fingers still tapping, she nodded.

I let myself into Kate's office with my passkey and left the door open a crack. Before I did anything else, I wanted to talk to Sam. When I dialed his home, he answered right away.

"Harriet told me the good news about Billy."

"Yeah. God, am I relieved, even if I do feel like a world-class jerk."

"What happened? And how did the . . . ?"

I wanted to ask about the new alibi, but Billy's voice broke through in the background. Sam said something to him and then spoke to me again.

"We've got to go, Bonnie. We've got a long drive. I'll tell you everything when we get home."

"Where are you going?"

"Camping. There's a lake in the Catskills where Billy and I used to go fishing when he was younger. We need to spend some time together. We'll be back Tuesday morning. I'll call you then. Bring you some trout if they're biting."

Had it occurred to Sam to tell me about this trip? Or was I supposed to spend the weekend worrying about where he had disappeared to while he was fishing in the Catskills? When we hung up, the emotional roller coaster I'd been riding was poised at the edge of a frightening dip. I forced myself to concentrate on finding the shelter's pro bono file.

The binder of Kate's clients lay open in the center of her desk. Near it was a computer printout which indicated the amount of time various attorneys had put in for various clients. Billable hours. From the pen marks on both the printout and in Kate's binder, it was clear that Davis was in the process of assigning her active cases to other attorneys.

Nutley's client-numbering system was typical of law firms—five digits beginning with 10000 and going to 99999 were assigned alphabetically. With this system, American Airlines has a low number and Zenith a high one. Various cases are tracked by three-digit extensions to these five numbers. However, pro-bono clients, since they aren't billed, are handled differently. It took me a couple of minutes of page turning before I discovered that at Nutley, pro-bono clients were numbered with three digits rather than five. Kate had been the partner in charge of two of these clients. One was a counseling center in East Harlem. The other was listed as simply "Teaneck House." The file number was 775. A quick look at the computer printout showed me that, in July, Kate had put in a quarter-hour for this client. No other attorney hours appeared.

I called the file room and gave a clerk the file number. He put me on hold, and was back a minute later.

"That file's not on the shelf."

"Oh. Can you tell me who has it?"

"No," he responded. "The record shows that the last person who had it was Kate Hamilton. She got it in July, before we moved. If she returned it, we never logged it in. Nobody's asked for it recently.''

"It's got to be somewhere," I said.

"Who is this?"

I suppose he wanted to find out how deferential he had to be. ''Bonnie Indermill.''

"Yeah, it's somewhere," he said, not very deferential at all. ''It will turn up. But with the move and all, who knows when.''

It will turn up. Those were familiar words. First Kate's carton of desk contents, and now Kate's pro-bono client's file.

''I'm calling for Harriet Peterson. When you find the file, will you please send it to her.''

''Sure,'' the clerk said. ''You might check with Jonathan Nash, though. He worked on another pro-bono thing for Miss Hamilton.''

As I hung up, there was a tap on the door. Andy was there, his head tilted quizzically.

''You're working for Harriet now?''

I didn't think Andy would care that I was digging through Nutley's files, but the fewer people who knew about this, the better.

''Harriet asked me to get her a file. Since you're keeping her so busy.''

He sat down across from me. ''The M-COM's meeting tonight to elect new partners. They'll be announced Monday.''

''So I hear. Are you nervous?''

''No, I'm not nervous.'' He held up a hand. ''This is shaking because I'm cold. Anyway, I was wondering if maybe you'd be available to do either some hand-holding or celebrating Monday night. I mean, I don't know what your relationship with Sam Finkelstein is, and maybe I'm out of line, but . . .''

I didn't know what my relationship was with Sam either. While I'd been tearing all over the place trying to find something, anything, to get his son out of jail, he'd been packing for a fishing trip.

"Gladly." As soon as I said that, I felt a hollow place in the pit of my stomach. Andy was fun, but I didn't want to lead him on. The damage was done, though.

"Great! We'll talk on Monday afternoon."

When I walked in my door that night, the red message light on my answering machine was blinking. "Hi, Sweetheart," I heard Sam say. "It's noon. I just got my kid out of jail. It turns out Billy was at an audition with Crisis when the Hamilton woman was killed. He was afraid to tell me. A dozen people saw him. Anyway, he and I are going fishing for the weekend. We need some quality time together." There was a pause. "I need some with you, too," I heard a moment later. "Let's talk about that Tuesday morning."

Moses was rubbing against my legs. Picking him up, I hugged him. "Isn't life something. One minute nobody loves me, the next minute my dance card is full."

Moses yawned in my face. Thanks to the vet down the street, his dance card never had a chance.

17

I SPENT FRIDAY CATCHING UP ON THE work that had piled up on Thursday. There was a paycheck to be earned, and I couldn't earn it chasing around after Leonard Munch. My one day of snooping had yielded very little. I knew more about Munch's marriage and had gotten a glimpse of a different side of Kate Hamilton. I knew about the pro-bono client and the missing file, which, when I left the office Friday afternoon, still hadn't turned up. But I didn't have any more proof of Munch's guilt than I'd had when I started grabbing at straws.

Tony wasn't returning my calls. After leaving two messages at the precinct and one with Amanda, I got the hint and stopped trying. Billy was in the clear; that was the important thing.

Friday evening I got home from Nutley late and tired. As I opened my mailbox, I tensed. If Munch had spotted me at the car dealership the previous day, and I was almost sure he had, he'd no doubt want to treat me to another one of his goodies. In my mailbox were two advertising circulars, a bill, and a letter from a politician telling me what a great guy he was. Nothing from Munch.

Maybe it's over for me, I thought as the elevator bumped up the shaft toward my sixth-floor apartment. Maybe he's decided I'm not worth the trouble. If Munch had had anything to do with the closing of the women's shelter, that was a shame. But what could I do? I was one person, with zero influence, even negative influence if Tony's response to my calls was any gauge.

The elevator door shuddered open and I stepped into the hall. My apartment is a corner one, about thirty feet from the elevator. As I started toward it my breath caught in my throat. Something wasn't right. The hall is dimly lit—my landlord has cornered the market on fifteen-watt light bulbs—but bright circular beams seemed to fall across my door. For a moment I wondered if this was the wrong landing, but a glance at a neighbor's door told me that I was in the right place.

It would take a very motivated burglar a lot of time to get through the armory of locks that guard my apartment, but at first I thought that had happened. "Moses," I cried, and ran for my door. A few feet from it I stopped.

No. It wasn't a break-in. It was graffiti. There on my door were sketches of humongous body parts. And I'm sure you know the parts I'm talking about. They'd been drawn with a fat gold felt-tip marker. I felt such a rush of fury that if Munch had been nearby, I would have had my hands around his throat.

I was vaguely aware of a door opening.

"Tsk, tsk. What kind of people do you associate with?"

Ethel and Eunice Codwallader jostled for position in their doorway across the hall from mine. One wore a black hairnet over pink sponge curlers. The other wore a plastic shower cap. Both wore flower-print housecoats, bedroom slippers, and identical prune faces that let me know exactly what they thought of me and my acquaintances. I've given up on trying to tell the sisters apart. Basically, they're the same person—cranky, complaining, censorious.

"The people I associate with didn't do this," I snapped. "Did you see who did?"

The sisters scooted back as if the devil had just spoken to them.

I suppose I've caused the Codwallader sisters a lot of grief over the years. My vices, by Manhattan standards, are the vices of a Milquetoast. Still, I have a date every now

and again, and one or two of them have even—gasp!—
spent the night. I have the occasional party. On rare occa-
sions, when the spirit moves me, I dust off my tap shoes
and try an old routine. In the hall, no less. The grimy marble floor makes a great sound.

"Certainly not!" one of the sisters said. "We do hope
you plan to remove it," said the other.

I shook my head. "No. I like it there. I'm going to leave
it."

The Codwallader's door slammed in my face.

I touched my finger to the gold ink. It was dry.

Even before feeding Moses, I tried Tony LaMarca at
home. By some fluke, he answered.

"Munch drew dirty graffiti on my door," I said, skipping
the pleasantries.

"Who?" he asked.

"Leonard Munch."

"What did he draw?"

"A—" How bizarre. It wasn't as if Tony and I were
strangers, but I found myself tongue-tied. I think it had
something to do with that conversation he'd asked me to
forget. I obviously hadn't forgotten it. What I finally said
was the euphemistic, "Organs."

"Organs?"

My facility for speech returned and I shouted several
descriptive words into the mouthpiece.

Tony got the idea. "Oh." After a second's quiet, he
added, softly, "You know, Bonnie, I love it when you talk
dirty to me."

I ignored that. "Tony, I have a lot of interesting things
to tell you about Munch. I found his wife—"

He broke in. "Hold it right there. I don't want to hear
another word about Leonard Munch. Our boy's father had
a talk with the police commissioner. If we don't leave his
little Leonard alone, we're going to be slapped with a law-
suit for harassment."

The notion of Munch suing anyone for harassment was
too ridiculous to consider. "What about the thing on my
door?"

"Did anyone see Munch do it?"

"Not that I know of."

"Then get your super to clean it up. I understand acetone is great for cleaning up graffiti. I've got to go now. Amanda's getting mad at both of us."

"Why?"

"Because while you and I are talking about 'organs,' her shellfish crepes are getting cold. Whatever you have to tell me will wait. And lay off Munch."

"Just one more thing," I said hurriedly. "Do you know about a third drawing Munch sent to Kate? It showed her in a restaurant with that same man."

"I don't know what you're talking about."

The phone went dead.

"Lay off Munch!" I grumbled to Moses. He had given up circling my feet and had fallen into his starving cat position. That's the one where he flops on his side and looks up longingly. Sometimes he makes pitiful sounds. The whole act would be more effective if he didn't have a big pot belly.

"That's it," I said to him. "I'm through with this nonsense." I meant it, too. I was done with fishing around for clues that nobody wanted. If I left Munch alone, sooner or later he'd leave me alone. And if he was a murderer, so what? Nobody else cared. Why should I? Billy was free, and I hadn't liked the dead woman anyway, regardless of how many secret lives she'd led.

My super, George, took care of the graffiti that evening. After triple locking my door, I slept fine. Munch didn't once disturb my sleep.

My mother has strict orders not to call me before 10 A.M. on weekends. When my phone rang at ten sharp Saturday morning, I knew who it was. I'd been awake for almost an hour. I was sitting in bed, drinking my second cup of coffee and thumbing through some of the million catalogs I get in the mail. When I heard Mom's voice, I tried to make her feel guilty by mumbling incoherently into the receiver. It didn't work.

"Good," she said. "You're already awake. I have to talk

to you about this Sam character.''

"His last name is not Character. It's Finkelstein.''

"That's the problem, Bonnie. You know Lydia, from next door. Her daughter married a Finkelstein. He's a doctor.''

"A podiatrist,'' I said hatefully.

"Lydia says it's the same thing. They live on Long Island. Where does Sam live?''

"Long Island.'' What on earth could this be leading to?

Moses hadn't gotten enough of the kind of breakfast he likes and was in a licking mode. What an operator.

"I was wondering if Lydia's son-in-law is related to Sam,'' my mother said.

"Why?''

"Because Lydia is always bragging about the doctor in her family. You can't imagine how she goes on about it. Sam being a mailman, I hate to think of how they might snub you if you ran into them at any Finkelstein family functions.''

The only Finkelstein family functions I knew of had been held in a police station.

I love my mother. When she's not worrying about me, she shows a lot of common sense. But this was ridiculous. I started giggling so hard I could barely talk. "Mom,'' I choked out, "I promise that if I'm ever snubbed at a Finkelstein family function by your neighbor Lydia, I won't let it bother me.''

That conversation got me started off in such a silly mood that, later that day, I put my Bloomingdale's credit card in my wallet and got on a midtown-bound bus.

It was after seven when I got home. I hadn't done anything too terrible with that credit card: a pair of shoes, a summer dress on sale. My mood was fine. I hadn't thought about Leonard Munch all afternoon, and when I put my key in the mailbox, I wasn't even nervous. Munch had made his ultimate effort the day before, I figured. He couldn't possibly surpass the artwork he'd done on my door.

When I saw the cheap envelope, with the typewritten

name and the postmark from the GPO, I groaned. What now? I lugged my purchases to my apartment. My door, my locks, my cat were all fine. When I had triple locked myself in, I slit the envelope.

Munch had surpassed himself after all.

It was another drawing done with colored pencils. This one, however, wasn't generic. It showed a couple—a light-haired woman in jeans, and a muscular, dark-haired man—embracing in a darkened room. It was a drawing of me and Sam, but in this drawing, Sam wasn't everyman; he was Sam. His shirt was striped, his arms were strong. We were lit by the gigantic moon shining through a window.

I was astounded! In my hand was the proof I'd been looking for. Munch had been in the office the night Kate was killed. Otherwise he wouldn't have been able to reproduce this scene. With this drawing, he was incriminating himself. There was no message at the edge of the paper this time, but he might as well have written "I was there" on it. It was that precise.

I carried the sketch into my kitchen and laid it on the counter under a light. Munch had worked hard on this one. There were spots on the paper where he'd erased and re-drawn.

Regardless of what Tony said, this was vital information. I picked up the phone and started to dial his number. Midway through it, I cradled the receiver.

Why was Munch doing this? It made no sense. His father had gotten the police to lay off him. So why do something guaranteed to bring him back to their attention? And if his purpose was to upset or frighten me, what was there in this picture that would do it? There were no exaggerated sexual 'organs,' no menacing words like "I see you all the time," or "Somebody doesn't like you." There wasn't even an effort at obscenity. The night Sam and I had embraced in Kate's office, Sam's hand had found its way under my T-shirt. In this drawing, Sam's hands rested chastely in the center of my back.

And, I asked myself suddenly, if Munch had known about Sam, why hadn't he depicted him more realistically in the earlier drawing? Why now?

The duplicate I'd made of the first drawing was still in my tote. Digging it out, I placed it alongside this new sketch. Though the copy was black and white, the similarities struck me right away. In both drawings, the pencils had been handled with the same quick, deft strokes. The human figures were the same size. My hair, in both drawings, was a curly scribble of yellow.

The longer I stared at the sketches, though, the more differences I saw. Or thought I saw. In the earlier sketch, the generic one, the perspectives were very good. There was the illusion of real space between the window and the bed. In the new sketch, the perspective was way off. There was no space between the moon shining through the window and the embracing couple. The moon could have been growing from the top of Sam's head. The desk, which should have been in the background, was on the same plane as the couple. I examined the figures in this new sketch closely, then looked at the first sketch and again at the new one. There were similarities, but there were slight differences, too. These new people were more robust, more animated than the figures in the early one.

The longer I looked at the two sketches, the more convinced I became that they were the work of two different artists.

Moses jumped on the counter. " 'Somebody doesn't like you,' " I read out loud. Moses made a pitiful sound. "Not you, tubby. Me." As I scooped food into Moses's dish, those words ran through my mind: *Somebody doesn't like you*.

On the sketches Kate had gotten, there had been personal pronouns: *I* and *me*. "I see everything you do." "You can't hide from me." But on my first sketch—the one I was sure was Munch's work—there had been the impersonal "Somebody." Why? It was bizarre. Unless . . . Munch hadn't been referring to himself at all. What if a third person was involved, a "somebody" who really didn't like me or want me snooping around?

I recalled the night when Munch had first contacted me,

and my curiosity, then, about how he'd discovered my identity. What if he'd had help? What if an unknown third person had called Munch and told him my name?

Ridiculous, Bonnie. Why would someone do that? Because this third person wanted Munch to harass me. Again, why? So that I would suspect Munch of killing Kate and use what influence I had to keep the police interested in Munch. But another why? What would this third person, if he or she existed, gain if Munch was arrested for Kate's murder?

The answer to that question was chilling: By sending me a drawing supposedly done by Munch, this third person was placing Munch at the murder scene. Munch, the tormentor, was being set up by the person who actually had killed Kate.

On Saturday nights the Metropolitan Museum is open until 8:45. If I took a cab, I'd be there before it closed. I wouldn't have wanted to confront Munch in his apartment, but what could he do to me in the museum?

The closing strains of Vivaldi's "Four Seasons" floated across the museum's Great Hall. By the time I paid my fee and got to the top of the long flight of steps, the quintet that entertains on the balcony on weekend evenings was leaving. The people who had gathered to listen to them were preparing to leave, too.

"We're closing in fifteen minutes," a guard told me as I started toward the Chinese Garden Court.

"I know. I'll be right back."

I hurried past the gift shop and through the galleries of ancient Chinese Art. Near the entrance to the Chinese Garden there was a guard, a tall black woman.

"I'm looking for Leonard Munch. Is he working tonight?"

The woman nodded. "He's around somewhere. Probably went for a smoke. The museum will start closing soon," she added.

I raced from room to room, one exhibit to the next. No Munch. Several times I had the creepy sensation that someone was watching me, but when I looked around, no one was there. I hurried back to the garden and found the same guard was on duty. Seeing me, she shook her head and shrugged. "Maybe Munch got off early."

When I got back to the balcony, a gate had been pulled across the door of the gift shop. The floor was almost deserted. I had started into another gallery when footsteps echoed behind me. "We're closing in five minutes," a guard warned. On cue, a loud bell jangled, its sound resonating through the museum.

I stopped and caught my breath. If Munch was still in the museum, he had to end up on Fifth Avenue regardless of what door he left by. My chances of finding him were better outside than they were in here. I followed a few other stragglers down the long flight of steps to the Great Hall.

The screams started when I had almost reached the museum's exit. The warning bell had just rung again, and at first the one voice, the eerie howl that filled the air, seemed to be echoing it. Spinning toward the sound, I caught sight of a flutter of blue-gray cloth hurtling through the air. There was only an instant before it crashed into the hard marble floor and lay still as a sack of old rags. And then a dozen shrieking voices rose and bounced off the hard walls of the huge space.

Two men in uniforms raced past me, followed by several people in street clothes. I stood stock-still. The screams quieted, but the silence that replaced them was as terrifying to me. Munch. It had something to do with Munch. I don't know why I had that feeling, but I was frozen to the spot by it.

I waited near the outside door for several minutes. A light rain had started falling, and the steps down to the street glistened. A Senegalese street vendor had set up for business at the museum door. "Umbrella umbrella umbrella," he chanted. As I stood there, two police cars pulled up outside the museum, sirens wailing. Seconds later an ambulance pulled onto the sidewalk and stopped alongside the fountain. The light on top of one of the police cars was turning, tinting everything in its path a ghostly pale blue.

Police and ambulance attendants pushed through the entrance and ran past me, leaving a damp trail on the marble floor. The guard who had blocked the entrance to the museum had disappeared, and museum employees and visitors hurried toward the fallen shape. A clerk at the coat check leaned across her counter. "What's happening?" she kept asking. No one answered.

I had to find out what was going on. I joined the crowd moving toward the thing on the floor. We were almost beneath the balcony railing when a couple in front of me stopped short. Pointing a long, red nail, the woman cried, "Oh, my God. It's a man. The poor guy must have lost his balance."

"Who is he?" someone asked.

"Looks like a guard."

I pushed past the couple. The body lay facedown on the hard marble floor. The legs and arms were splayed, the neck twisted unnaturally. When I saw the pale, frizzy hair, I grew faint.

A balding guard with a ponytail said softly, to no one in particular, "It must have been suicide." I glanced up, trying to see the rail at the edge of the balcony.

"He jumped," a woman said.

The ponytailed guard nodded. "Looks like a tall guy. He could have gotten over the railing easy."

"Police coming through."

Two men in damp suits shoved past us. One of them had a camera. As he snapped pictures, the other man joined the group kneeling over the body. An ambulance attendant shook his head. "He's gone." I looked away when they turned the corpse and didn't see the dead man's face. Seconds later the guard with the ponytail whispered, "Munch, I think."

The name reverberated through the crowd: Munch, Munch. The name couldn't have meant anything to most of them, but I could hardly force air into my lungs. I had to tell these policemen why I was there. I tried getting through the crowd around the body, but more uniformed officers had arrived. "Keep back," one of them barked at me. Before I could say anything the area was roped off and I was outside the rope. Still edging toward the body, I caught the eye of the ponytailed guard. All business now, he said, "Everyone who doesn't belong here has to leave."

"But . . ."

He was no longer looking at me. "All of you have to go. This isn't a party," he added unnecessarily.

Suddenly I was drenched in sweat. I needed air. Hurrying away from the body, I crossed the rotunda and ran out into the rain.

Leonard Munch's fate was sealed when he went off the balcony over the Great Hall. Once Tony got a look at the second sketch I'd received, it looked as if the fate of the investigation into Kate's murder would be sealed, too.

I turned it in at the precinct on Sunday morning. Tony wasn't there at the time, so I left him a note explaining when, and where, the scene in the sketch had taken place. He called me that evening, contrite.

"So," he said, dragging out the word.

"So?"

"So it looks like maybe you were right about Munch. He was at Nutley the night of the Hamilton murder. Which means I was wrong. Sorry."

I don't get many apologies from Tony. Gloating would have been fun, but I was too troubled by the way things were turning out. The differences in the two drawings I'd gotten were only a part of it.

Munch's suicide baffled me. Why had he done it? Guilt? The Leonard Munch I'd known—as far as I'd known him—had stood on a Manhattan street during broad daylight screaming insults at his pregnant wife and her boss. In the middle of the day, Munch had stuck a note to a windshield with semen. He had thrown firecrackers into a car showroom with dozens of people standing around. Sure, people change, but when had Munch changed to the point that he experienced guilt?

Trying to figure this out, I had made a list of the things

Munch had supposedly done that week, and my take on each of them:

"Tuesday night: hid the murder weapon in Billy's car. Possibly done by Munch, but he's never harassed men before.

Thursday morning: threw firecrackers at ex-wife's business. Definitely done by Munch.

Friday morning: mailed a drawing to me which tied him to the murder scene. The drawing's substance and style are both un-Munchlike.

Friday afternoon: drew giant sex organs on my door. Probably Munch.

Saturday night: committed suicide. Doesn't seem possible."

The way Munch had killed himself was giving me trouble, too. The balcony over the museum's Great Hall appeared to be about fifty feet up, and the marble floor under it was sure to make a mess of any jumper. The thing was, it wasn't absolutely guaranteed to kill them.

I wanted to talk to Tony about these things, but with the mood he was in, it was hard to know where to start. "Maybe you weren't wrong," I began hesitantly. "Has the medical examiner looked at Munch's wounds yet?"

The quiet on the other end of the line lasted a long time.

"Tony?"

"No, Bonnie," he snapped. "The medical examiner's office has been waiting to hear from you before they do anything."

"Stop it."

He responded angrily. "You stop it, Bonnie! This was none of your business even when your boyfriend's kid was in jail. It's definitely over for you now."

"But if you compare the sketches . . ."

"We'll have an expert look at them," he said sharply.

"We do that, you know. We're not totally incompetent. I've got to go. I'll be in touch."

On Sunday night, the local news announcer talked about the suicide of Leonard Munch, principal suspect in the murder of attorney Kate Hamilton.

And that appeared to be the end of it.

18

WHEN I WALKED IN MONDAY MORNING at 9 A.M., I was surprised to see Freddie behind his desk. I suspect he was surprised about that, too. He was staring at his still-packed cartons and looking stumped. Seeing me, he brightened.

"Have a second?" he asked.

"Sure."

He waved a hand at the cartons. "I'm not clear on the game plan here."

"What do you mean?"

"Unpacking. Isn't this a job for a second-string player?" Wrinkling his brow, he added, "We have a secretary, don't we?"

Was it possible that Freddie didn't know what had happened to our secretary? Yes, it was possible. It was possible that Freddie didn't even know who our secretary had been.

"Hillary Davis was our secretary, but she quit."

"Quit? That's too bad. I'll see if I can get a temp for this afternoon. This"—he flicked his fingers at the cartons—"will be very time-consuming."

So, what else did he have to do with his time, now that Rhonda's sofa was off-limits?

From the way Freddie was acting, you'd have thought there were a dozen cartons waiting to be unpacked. There were five of them, to be exact. I'd seen them before, but I hadn't paid attention to them. Looking at them now, I noticed something peculiar. They had been tagged twice. Under our green, twentieth-floor tags were red tags from another floor.

"Were these cartons originally intended for you?" I asked my boss.

"No. The Corporate Department put together too many cartons, so I took their extras and covered their tags with mine. Saved my energy."

If there was an energy bank around, Freddie's account surely had the largest balance. He ran his fingers across his scalp, creating havoc among the carefully arranged hairs. "I don't suppose you have time to help . . ."

Spotting trouble, I said hurriedly, "I better get to work."

"Oh, before you go, Bonnie, there's something . . ." He cleared his throat. "You may be aware that the M-COM met late Friday afternoon. Your name was mentioned."

There was only one reason my name would have been mentioned at an M-COM meeting, and it damned sure wasn't to vote on a partnership for me. I could feel my expression hardening as I waited for Freddie to go on. He noticed. He stood so abruptly you'd have thought a cattle prod had made contact with his rump. Prying open a carton, he mumbled, "The M-COM decided . . ." When his face was safely buried in the debris from his old office, Freddie dropped the bomb. ". . . that after tomorrow, we won't be needing your assistance."

"Tomorrow?"

"Well," his voice boomed from inside the carton, "the job was only for a few weeks."

I had known this was coming, but I'd put it out of my mind. Now there was no getting away from it. I tried, though.

"My In box is still full of punch lists." My voice had risen, and there was a whine in it that I hated.

Freddie started shifting files from the carton onto his desktop. It wasn't easy for him to do that without looking at me, but he somehow managed.

"Surely you'll be able to tackle most of those today and tomorrow, won't you? I hope so."

You can bet he hoped so. He had no more idea of what

was happening with the move than my cat did. Forcing myself to sound unruffled, I said, "I'll try."

Finally he peeked from the carton. "You've done a good job helping me carry the ball during the move. I don't suppose you'd want to be traded down to the minor leagues. From what you tell me, we'll have a secretarial spot . . ."

The horribleness of that prospect made me shudder. It had been okay for Hillary because she hadn't cared. It would not be okay for me. If I had to, I would go to another office and beat on a typewriter all day, but I wouldn't do it at Nutley, and I especially wouldn't do it for Freddie.

I shook my head. "The minor leagues don't interest me, Freddie."

I made it into my office, closed the door, and flopped into my chair in a blue funk. This was irrational, of course, but the working world is an irrational place. Why should I have to make sense?

The problem was, I'd let myself get attached to what I was doing. I like working alone, making my own decisions, even being responsible for my own mistakes. God knows, with Freddie as a boss, I'd worked alone. It wasn't only the job I'd gotten attached to, either. Tears burned my eyelids, and my vision blurred until my two-window office, my desk, my nice chair took on a pretty, impressionistic quality.

I was feeling sorry for myself and working up to a nice cry when my gaze moved away from all the good stuff I was losing and settled onto my In box. The miserable thing was crammed full. Complaints bulged from it, overflowed its sides. Bertram Davis must have submitted a dozen punch lists. Jonathan had a new one. And there was that awful partner who had lost his posters, and the Chivas Regal maniac.

Until then I'd handled the punch lists fairly—first-come, first-served. Now I had two days to get through a huge stack. And most of those lists had more than one problem on them. And I had no secretary to help me assign the jobs to the various contractors and maintenance people.

Scooting the In box to the center of my desk, I began

leafing through the lists. Here was one from Andy. "Top desk drawer sticks." Nice guy. He hadn't once nagged me about it.

I liked Andy. Pulling his list from the pile, I set it aside. A little farther down there was a list from Margaret. Margaret and I had gotten off to a rocky start, but we were okay now. I put her list with Andy's. There was a man from Accounting whose chair had fallen apart the first time he sat in it. He always greeted me with a smile. Into the short stack went his list.

And that's how I decided what I would do for the next two days. First came the lists of the people I knew and liked, second came the lists of the people I didn't know, and last came the lists for Jonathan, Bertram Davis, the autographed baseball lunatic, and anybody else I didn't like. Since I knew very few people, most lists went into the middle stack.

I had just about finished with this sorting an hour later. My priority stack was very short indeed. I should be able to get through that in a day and a half, I thought. I would start on the twentieth floor—my floor—with that nice man in Accounting, and work my way up. . . .

My phone rang. "Bonnie Indermill," I answered.

"Hello. This is Jane Lincoln. I understand you want to talk to me."

Jane Lincoln? She was calling from outside, and her voice was unfamiliar.

"I'm sorry, but I don't recall—"

"We have a mutual acquaintance," she said. "Veronica. She was married to Leonard Munch, that awful man who killed himself Saturday night. I ran into her this morning in a grocery store."

My God! This was Jane of the closed women's shelter, of the missing pro-bono file.

"Thank you for calling," I said, "but now that Munch is dead, I suppose that the subject is closed. I just hope that he didn't hurt anyone at the shelter."

"What do you mean?"

"Well, I understand the shelter is gone. Since Munch threatened to blow it up . . ."

"We haven't closed," Jane said. "We had to move. Leonard Munch didn't have a thing to do with that, though. It wasn't nearly as dramatic as being blown up."

I asked her what had happened, and she explained that it had been a legal matter. "A couple of our neighbors complained about having the shelter in a family neighborhood. You've heard the expression 'NIMBY?' It stands for 'Not in my backyard.' They convinced our landlord to start an eviction proceeding. Kate thought we could fight it. For some reason, though, the matter fell through the cracks at Nutley."

This was surprising. There were probably as many cracks at Nutley as there are in any other business, but it didn't seem like Kate Hamilton's style to let something she cared about fall through them. "You mean Kate didn't submit papers on time, or—?"

Jane interrupted me. "No, no. I doubt that the fault was Kate's, but in any event she couldn't have done a thing for us herself."

"Why not?"

"Kate wasn't a member of the New Jersey Bar," the other woman said. "When we spoke at the end of July, she said she was going to assign the matter to an associate. I tried to reach her a couple times after that, but she was always busy with one thing or another and I hated to pester her. I feel guilty saying this now, and I really did admire Kate, but dealing with her could be awfully difficult. So, anyway, the next thing I knew we were on the street and Kate was dead." A long sigh traveled through the phone line. "Difficult or not, the shelter lost a good friend when Kate was killed."

Had Kate mentioned which associate was going to handle the eviction matter? I asked Jane.

"No. When we opened about six years ago, a young woman associate helped us, but I understand she's no longer at Nutley."

When we hung up I had a hard time getting back to my

punch lists. A pro-bono client had fallen between the cracks. It's file was missing. And evaluations for Jonathan and Andy were missing. Jonathan was known to have done some pro-bono work for Kate. What about Andy?

Freddie opened my office door and walked in, never bothering to knock. "Here's my punch list. When you have a chance." Looking at the mountains of lists on my desk, he recoiled. "I didn't realize there were so many. Do you think you'll be able to get through all those in the next two days? Don't hesitate to play hardball with the contractors, if you have to."

I can't say that Freddie chased the ugly thoughts I'd been thinking out of my head, but he sure gave me something else to think about. The man was so obvious, and so useless, and such a user that his very presence in the room I had thought of as mine really got my back up.

"I'm prioritizing the lists right now," I said.

"Good idea," Freddie responded. "I've always said that before the big game, you've got to spend time getting your plays down cold."

My plays were down cold, all right. As soon as Freddie left, I played hardball with his list and put it on the bottom of the lowest priority stack. Then I began assigning the jobs in my high-priority stack to the responsible contractors.

There was, I soon discovered, something liberating about knowing it was my next-to-last day at Nutley. Occasionally I had to go look at a job before I knew which contractor to assign it to. Over the past weeks I'd dashed around like something demented when I'd had to do this. Now I wandered, relaxed, and spent time talking to people I liked. I took a long lunch and bought myself a pair of fake turquoise earrings from a street vendor. When I got back, I called Amanda and we talked for a long time about her marriage. "Tony's just in such an awful mood these days," she said. I put my new earrings in my ears and examined them in a compact mirror. Very pretty. "I noticed that Tony doesn't seem happy," I told my friend. We made plans to meet for dinner. After that, I called a couple of temp agencies and offered them my body.

I can't claim that the missing pro-bono file, and my conversation with Jane Lincoln, didn't enter my mind during that time. These things shadowed me all afternoon, but whenever I found myself dwelling on them, and on the fact that I would leave Nutley without ever knowing what really happened to Kate, I forced myself to think of the pile of trouble I was leaving Freddie, and was cheered.

"The M-COM has announced six new partners. My darling Andy made it!"

Harriet was beaming so, you'd have thought the M-COM had elected her to the partnership.

"Where is he? I'd like to congratulate him." I also wanted to firm up our plans for that evening.

"They've all gone to the chairman's office for a glass of champagne." As an afterthought, she said, "Jonathan made it, too."

"How nice." I looked at Andy's punch list. "Do you know anything about Andy's stuck drawer? Is it a lock problem, or a wood problem?"

"He hasn't said. Andy's not a complainer. Pretty earrings," she added.

"Thanks. I'm going to take a look at the drawer before I assign it to a contractor."

"Feel free."

I waded into Andy's mess of an office, sat in his chair, and gave his center desk drawer a yank. It put up a fight but I won. The drawer was a problem for the Pagano people.

As I wrestled with the drawer, trying to shut it again, a yellow-lined tablet that had been pushed to its back slid forward, catching my eye. Beneath a handwritten paragraph of legal blather, there was the funniest little caricature of Harriet. There were my friend's high cheekbones and the tight curls that circle her face. Her swooping eyebrows and peaked lips had been exaggerated until they would have done an early movie vamp proud. There was life in her face, too. You almost would have expected words to come from between those vamping lips. I was positively ticked by the thing.

But the perspective was wrong. The keyboard Harriet's fingers were poised over appeared to sprout from her wrists. The back of her chair grew from her shoulder.

In the lower right corner of the drawing, Andy had penciled his initials: "A M."

Fear started picking at me. Jonathan had gone to school in Massachusetts. There was no reason for him to be a member of the New Jersey Bar. But Andy had worked at the Jersey Shore. My fear grew quickly as the dreadful knowledge of what I was looking at grew. I'd found my secret caricaturist. I'd found an artist who could almost convey the life in a face, but who couldn't handle perspective.

Was it Andy I'd heard in the hall the night Sam and I had kissed in Kate's office? Was it Andy who had sent me the sketch of that scene? And was it Andy who had murdered Kate?

It was. That truth erupted in my head. Lighthearted Andy, the God of Parties, the guy who practiced guerilla warfare at Nutley, was a killer. My instinct told me that I was right. All my strength seemed to drain away. I had to get out of Andy's office. That was the first thing. Forcing the drawer, I slammed it shut.

There were things only Harriet could tell me, but as I left Andy's office, voices sounded from around the corner. Andy and the others were returning. I darted into the stairwell.

Cornelia was on her way out of the cafeteria. Seeing me, she touched a finger to her ear. "You lost an earring."

I felt my ears. Sure enough, one of my street jewels was gone. "Oh, well. Now I'll have one for my nose." As I unhooked the second earring I tried smiling. I felt too grim to fake it, though.

Cornelia looked at me uncertainly. "Are you okay? You don't look so good."

I couldn't tell her what was troubling me. "Freddie told me that tomorrow's my last day."

"Oh, that's a shame. You mean the move's all over? Still seems like a mess around here."

My job problem had become so insignificant to me that it was a struggle to talk about it. "Oh, there are lots of punch lists and complaints, but . . ." I shrugged.

"Maybe you should talk it over with Bert Davis."

That was such a ridiculous suggestion that I gaped at her and said, "What have you been smoking?"

"He's not such a bad guy when you get to know him," Cornelia went on happily. "Called me into his office this morning and gave me my gift, along with a nice thank-you card."

"I don't know what you're talking about."

"The M-COM gave me two tickets to———" She named one of the hottest musicals on Broadway.

"Why? It's a little early for Christmas."

"They're giving presents to employees who worked extra hard during the move. I was one of the people Bert Davis recommended."

I made a nasty noise. "Congratulations. Bert and his M-COM recommended me for the unemployment office."

"Talk to him," Cornelia repeated. "Ever since that softball game he's treated me all right. You've got to put him in his place. That's all."

My chances of putting Bertram Davis in his place were slim, but before Cornelia left, I told her I'd think about it.

The cafeteria was almost deserted. I went straight for a phone on the wall and called Harriet. When she answered, my first words were, "Don't say my name."

"What?"

"Is Andy around?"

"Yes. He's in his office. He just tried calling you, I think."

"Then don't say my name. You've got to answer some questions for me. And please keep your voice low."

"Is this a joke?" Harriet asked softly.

"Sort of. Andy used to work at the New Jersey Shore. Is he from New Jersey? Did he go to law school there?"

"Yes. Rutgers."

"And is he a member of the New Jersey Bar?"

Harriet responded like a proud parent. "New Jersey and New York. He's very bright."

Very, very bright, and very, very sneaky. "One morning last week you saw me copying a dirty sketch I'd gotten from Leonard Munch," I said. "Did you tell Andy about that?"

She didn't answer right away. When she did answer, she was defensive. "What if I did? It was common knowledge Munch did that sort of thing."

But it wasn't common knowledge that Munch had done it to me. "And did you tell Andy that the detective assigned to the case is a friend of mine?"

This time Harriet waited even longer before responding. I was afraid she would blurt out something Andy could overhear. With her voice lower, though, she whispered, "Andy's interested in you, romantically. I keep telling you that. It's normal to mention these things to him."

"How do you know Andy is interested in me?"

"He's always asking about you."

If my guess was correct, Andy's interest in me didn't have a thing to do with romance.

"You two have a date tonight, don't you?" Harriet asked.

"Yes. But don't mention this conversation to him."

She promised she wouldn't, and then said, louder, "Oh, I forgot to tell you: Margaret and I each got one-hundred-dollar gift certificates from Saks, and nice thank-you cards, because we worked so hard during the move. Mr. Davis gave me mine."

"Congratulations." There was a vicious bite in my voice, but I don't think Harriet noticed. When we'd hung up, I got myself a cup of coffee and carried it to a table by a window. It was about five o'clock. Far below on Park Avenue, people hurried toward Grand Central in the week-day migration to the trains that carried them away from midtown's commercial canyons. I stared down at the street vacantly and thought about how Andy had done what he'd done.

Guerilla warfare. He hadn't been kidding when he told me he was good at it. He was an expert.

I couldn't be certain about the details, but I imagined the whole thing starting with an oversight. Andy had let Kate's pro-bono client "fall through the cracks." After that initial carelessness, though, his movements had become purposeful and crafty.

Knowing that Kate's evaluation would mention his carelessness, and curious about what she would say, Andy had diverted the carton containing the evaluation to his office.

How? That was easy. The answer had been staring me in the face since the night Kate's carton disappeared. There had been an example of it that very morning in Freddie's office.

On the afternoon when the move began, Andy had helped Billy steady the cartons on the dolly. Billy had then left the dolly unattended outside Andy's office, giving Andy the opportunity to cover Kate's tags with his own. That evening, the carton had been delivered to Andy's new office.

I'd seen Andy that night, sitting among his torn-apart cartons. He'd torn one of them apart for good reason. It made it easy to smuggle the incriminating bits of Kate's carton—her handwritten RIGHT DESK DRAWER and the concealed tags—from the building.

Skip to the next night. In the process of looking for his evaluation, Andy had discovered Munch's obscene sketches. He'd killed Kate while the rest of us were at the party in the conference room, then planted two of the sketches where they would be found. The blame for Kate's murder was certain to fall on the artist, whoever that was.

Here was where my part began. Leonard Munch's name had been in the papers the day after I identified him, but the papers hadn't mentioned Munch's reputation for harassing women. I'd mentioned it, to Harriet. And my good friend had carried that information straight back to Andy.

Munch's words, "Somebody doesn't like you," made sense now. Andy had wanted to keep the police interested in Munch. Hoping Munch would start harassing me, he had called Munch, anonymously, and given him my name.

When it turned out that Munch's alibi was stronger than Billy's, Andy had shifted his attention to Billy.

I thought back to the night of the softball game. Andy, like a lot of other players, had carried a duffel bag. But if I was right, Andy had had more than mitts and softballs in his bag. He also carried the scales of justice he'd used to murder Kate. Andy had disappeared from the field early. I recalled looking around for him, wondering how he was tolerating Davis's insults. But Andy's mind hadn't been on Davis at all. He'd been hiding the murder weapon in Billy's car. After that, Andy had made another anonymous call, this one to the police.

The second sketch, the one I was now sure was Andy's work, had been sent to me after Billy's second alibi checked out. I didn't know if *desperate* was a word that could be applied to Andy, but with Billy absolutely in the clear, Andy surely must have worried. The investigation may have been sidetracked by Connor's illness, but the murder of a respectable attorney isn't the kind of thing that the police let slide forever.

And so Andy had turned his attention back to Munch. The sketch he sent me was an attempt to make me, and thus the police, think that Munch was in the building the night Kate was murdered.

Had Andy shoved Munch over the railing at the museum? Had he crept up behind him on that almost-deserted balcony? Had the closing bell been ringing, concealing his footsteps? It seemed reasonable, but I couldn't prove it.

For that matter, I couldn't prove anything. Kate's evaluation of Andy was long gone. The file for Kate's pro-bono client was probably long gone, too.

I finished my coffee. Proof. That was a problem. I didn't have it, and I couldn't get the police to listen to me. And another problem was, I had a date with a murderer.

"The M-COM gave me Yankee tickets. Great seats." Freddie held the thank-you card toward me. "Nice of them."

My "Congratulations" had acquired a savage snarl by

this time, but Freddie was as oblivious to that as he was to most other things.

The temporary secretary at the desk that had been Hillary's was Hillary's opposite: short, plump, gray haired, all business, and still there at almost six o'clock.

"Your phone hasn't stopped ringing," she said. "Mostly complaints. I would have handled some of them, but I don't know a thing about what's going on."

"You've got a lot of company." I took the fistful of phone message slips she handed me.

Seeing them, Freddie's jaw dropped. "I hope you're not down for the count on those."

"I'm working on them. In a pig's eye," I added under my breath as soon as he was gone.

I thumbed through the messages. Complaints, all afternoon. And Andy at 5:20. Andy again. "Are we still on for tonight?" he'd asked at 5:30. Tony LaMarca had called twice that afternoon. His second message read, "Return call ASAP." Interesting.

And, even more interesting, at 5:45 a clerk from the file room had left me this message: "Found the pro-bono file. It's on my desk."

I called the file room immediately. There was no answer. I spoke to the temp. "You took this message?"

She nodded. "They were leaving for the day. He said if you want to pick it up, they don't lock the door. Otherwise in the morning he'll send it to someone—I think the name was Peterson—like you asked."

Things had changed. There might not be anything pointing to Andy in the file, but I didn't want it going to Harriet. Not the way Andy was always nosing around her desk.

"I'm going down to the file room. I'll be back in ten minutes." As an afterthought, I added, "Don't tell anyone where I've gone."

There was still activity in the basement. In the long hall leading to the file room, I passed one of the security men who had been hired after Kate's murder. He nodded and walked into the duplicating center, where an operator stood over a big, churning copy machine.

Nutley's file room had been moved into the building's basement before I started. I'd been in there only once, when Kate's carton was first missed. I didn't know my way around it, but from what I remembered, there weren't many desks. I wouldn't have much trouble finding the file.

When I opened the door, the huge space was dark so I felt for the switches at the door's side. As the fluorescent bulbs flicked on, I saw row after row of tall steel shelves rising from the gray tile floor. The shelves were lined with files.

And each row of shelves hid a space big enough for a dozen murderers.

None of that, I told myself. Find the file and get out.

Along the room's front wall, half a dozen desks had been situated. The big, mahogany-colored accordion folders that hold numerous files were stacked on all of them. I didn't know the name of the clerk who'd called, so the nameplates on the desks wouldn't help. I had to search until I found what I wanted.

The room was so quiet that my own breathing seemed loud. I was at the second desk, moving files around, when suddenly I heard the distinctive sound of a chair rolling over the tile floor.

I spun and realized then that I had made a terrible, and perhaps deadly, mistake.

"Hi, Bonnie," Andy said. "I'm glad you're here. I was getting tired of sitting in the dark."

He had hidden behind one of the loaded steel shelves. Propelling with his legs, he rolled in his chair to the door. Noticing the accordion folder still in my hands, he shook his head.

"The file you're after disappeared long ago. That message you got from the file clerk was actually from me." He held up his hand. My lost earring dangled from his fingers. "I found this in my desk drawer. It was on top of a drawing I'd done. When Harriet said it belonged to you, I decided that we better have a talk. Sit down and relax."

He tossed the earring toward me. As it dropped on the

floor by my feet, my mind worked wildly. The duplicating center was too far away. Even if I screamed, the operator wouldn't hear me over the noise of his machine. I had an almost overpowering urge to run somewhere, anywhere, but Andy blocked the only door I knew of. Propping myself on the edge of a desk and clutching the folder in front of me like a shield, I tried to steady my breathing.

"I heard you calling for that pro-bono file the other day," he said. "I was hoping you'd just get the hell out of here tomorrow and that would be the end of it. But you couldn't resist picking at it a little more, could you?"

"I don't know what you're talking about, Andy." The bravado in my voice was so obviously false that a grin flashed over Andy's face.

"I think you do. I spotted you at the museum Saturday night, too. You were so busy looking for Leonard Munch that you didn't see me."

"You pushed him?"

Andy rolled his shoulders indifferently. "Munch was nothing. Less than nothing. A minus. The world is better off without him. Think of it as a humanitarian gesture on my part."

Though I'd suspected Andy of doing this, his easy admission shocked me. "But what about Kate?" I asked weakly.

"Kate?" He sat silently for a moment, and then nodded. "Okay, I'll tell you about Kate," he finally said. "Let me try to put it in a context you'll understand, Bonnie. You've been working hard around here for a couple of weeks. And now you've been let go. From what I hear, they didn't even give you the gift certificate or the dinner for two at the Four Seasons. You must feel awful."

Pausing, he watched me, perhaps waiting for my response. I didn't say anything. I did feel awful, but being fired was the least of it.

"So how do you think you'd feel if you'd worked like a coolie for eight years and you found out you weren't going to get the gift certificate or the night on the town or anything else but more work? One lousy slipup, for a client

that never paid a nickel, was going to cost me my partnership. That's what it amounted to. I was never a shoo-in like
Jonathan. Kate's evaluation was going to ruin me.''

A note of self-righteous anger had crept into Andy's
voice. I was icy cold, and my knees shook with fear. And
under my fear there was disgust, and a crushing disappointment. Andy had fooled me, and everyone else, so completely. And he'd tried to blame it on an innocent kid.

''I didn't start out to kill Kate,'' he continued. ''I hated
her guts after I read the evaluation she gave me, but I didn't
think there was a choice. I had to go along with it, play
the good loser, look for another job. And then I came across
those dirty drawings.'' The memory brought a smile to his
face. ''Our Kate, being naughty with a guy wearing a wedding ring. I wasn't sure what I was going to do with them,
but I figured they'd come in handy.''

He sank deeper in his chair, so that his legs sprawled
across the floor. The right arm on his chair moved, but he
didn't seem to notice.

''The night of the party—that was when I snapped. I'd
put in sixty billable hours that week, and moved offices. I
was relaxing for a few minutes, having a beer. And that ass
Davis suggested, in his unique and charming way, that I
get back to work. How do you think I felt?''

I didn't reply. I had to get away from him. There was a
wall on my right and a desk behind me. The rows of steel
shelves were to my left, less than a dozen feet away, but
if I ran into them I would end up playing tag with a murderer. That was a game I could very well lose.

''On my way to my room, I passed Davis's office,''
Andy said. ''Kate was at his window. Probably admiring
the view she thought she should have had. I was so furious
about the way I was being treated that I confronted her. I
offered her a deal. If she redid the evaluation, I'd give her
back the dirty pictures and forget I ever saw them. Well,
of course Kate had to be difficult. Worse than difficult. She
gave me a flat out no and said that she was going to do her
best to get me fired. Davis's ridiculous statue was next to

my hand, almost begging to be picked up. And so I did it. And you know what?''

I shook my head. Andy shrugged lazily, and his chair's arm wobbled again. I was suddenly aware of the accordion folder resting on my lap. It was so heavy, so filled with documents, that its weight dug into my thighs.

''When it was over, when I got her body wrapped up and stuffed in that closet and got back to my office, I was nervous, but I didn't feel one damned bit of guilt. It was like working the booths on the boardwalk. The tourists should have been smarter with their money; Kate should have been smarter with her life.''

He scooted his chair away from the door, toward me. When he was about eight feet away, he rested his hands on the chair's arms as if preparing to stand. My heart was racing. Shifting my weight forward, I tensed my legs.

''And now, Bonnie, the cops think Munch killed Kate, and he's not around to deny it.'' Andy considered me thoughtfully. ''My only problem is you. I'm hoping we can work out something. You don't have a job, and Harriet tells me you don't have much money . . .''

I'll probably never know what Andy was going to suggest. I lifted the folder like a club. Maybe he'd lifted Davis's scales of justice the same way. And then I sprang. Andy flinched and raised his arm. As I swung with all my strength, I said, ''That's for Billy.''

The accordion folder hit the left side of Andy's head, real hard. He toppled to the right. The chair arm gave and he went to the floor with it. I didn't stick around to see whether he was conscious or not.

IF I'D KNOWN THEN WHAT I KNOW NOW, I would have returned Tony's call before I went down to the file room. By then, an NYPD art expert had spotted the differences in the two drawings I'd gotten, and Tony was eager to talk to me. What can I say? Hindsight is great, but at the time, going to the file room seemed like a good idea.

A background check revealed some interesting things about Andy. He'd taken a couple of drawing courses in college. His grades in them had been mediocre. "Problems with perspective," one professor had noted. At the Jersey Shore, he'd eventually moved from the basketball booth to the booth that did caricatures. His boss there thought he remembered Andy, even after eleven years. "A friendly guy," he recalled. "Always joking around. Everybody liked Andy."

There were signals that I'd ignored, but then everybody had ignored them. Like the man said, everybody liked Andy. The fact that he'd happily cheated tourists at the Jersey Shore didn't make him a potential killer. Maybe, though, if Andy hadn't been quite as likable, I wouldn't have shrugged that off. When I asked Andy about the "creative" work he'd done at the shore, he had evaded the question. I think I know why, now. He was already wondering how to put his talent to use, so the fewer people who knew about it, the better. Munch's drawing of Kate and Sidney Turnbull in the Mexican restaurant showed up when the police searched Andy's apartment. I suspect that Andy used it as a style guide when he drew me and Sam.

Andy has pleaded not guilty. Apparently his lawyer is going to claim temporary insanity. More than two weeks passed, though, from the time Andy killed Kate Hamilton to the time he pushed Leonard Munch over the railing at the museum. You have to wonder how long the law allows temporary insanity to last.

Outside of the law, temporary insanity can last a long time. I drove Tony and Amanda to the airport this morning. They're loaning me their car while they're off to a Club Med in Mexico for a week. They were cranky with each other when I picked them up, but by the time they checked their luggage they were giggling and whispering. After passing through the metal detector, they seemed to become joined at the hand, hip, and shoulder, and I was definitely superfluous. That's when I waved good-bye.

My driving is improving, I think. It wasn't all that bad, but I'm getting more comfortable behind the wheel. I better get comfortable there. I spend half my time on the Long Island Expressway, going between my apartment and Sam's house.

Eileen's ghost still peeks from behind billowing curtains occasionally, but I'm learning to ignore it. Will it ever completely disappear? Sam has ordered new bedroom furniture, which may solve the problem. I sure hope so. Sam's the best.

He's really trying with Billy. We went to see Crisis the other night. They had second billing at a club in the East Village. They're not half-bad. What they lack in training, they make up for with enthusiasm. Hillary was there. She showed me her artwork for the group's first album, assuming there is one. She takes photographs in black and white after smearing something—Vaseline, blackberry jam—over her camera lens. The example she showed me was truly hideous. The kids in Crisis look like they've been fished out of an oil slick. I told her I liked it, but Sam rolled his eyes and groaned.

Harriet apologizes to me continually. Her darling Andy is now "that devil." We keep making noises about having lunch, but it hasn't happened yet. I'm sure it will.

I had a drink with Rhonda yesterday afternoon. Her Pagano man has already taken the leap from hot and heavy to slumped in front of her television. She mentioned Jonathan. He's not exactly flirting, she says, but now that he's a partner the knot in his tie isn't quite as tight as it was. He's a little young (about fifteen years by my calculations) but what the hell!

And so, all in all, things are good.

Oh, yes. I'm employed. Guess where. A week after I left Nutley, E. Bertram Davis himself called me on behalf of the M-COM. It seems that all those complaints on the punch lists weren't being handled. And so I said, "I'll be happy to come back, but I must have some stability. I'd like a twelve-week contract at the same salary"—I started to call him Evelyn, but why rub it in?—"Bert," I said.

And do you know what? Bert said yes, and the next morning when I walked into my nice two-window office, there was one of those Saks gift certificates on my desk. Cornelia was right. Bert's not such a bad guy. You've just got to put him in his place.